MR MIDSHIPMAN FURY

This is G.S. Beard's first novel in a series of John Fury stories. He lives in Lincolnshire. His second book *Lieutenant Fury* is published by Century.

Also available by G. S. Beard

Lieutenant Fury

MR
MIDSHIPMAN
FURY

G. S. BEARD

arrow books

Published in the United Kingdom by Arrow Books in 2007

5 7 9 10 8 6

First published in Great Britain in 2006 by
Century
Random House, 20 Vauxhall Bridge Road,
L:ondon SW1V 2SA

www.rbooks.co.uk

Addresses for companies within The Random House Group Limited
can be found at: www.randomhouse.co.uk/offices.htm

The Random House Group Limited Reg. No. 954009

A CIP catalogue record for this book
is available from the British Library

ISBN 9780099498681

The Random House Group Limited supports The Forest Stewardship
Council (FSC), the leading international forest certification organisation.
All our titles that are printed on Greenpeace approved FSC certified paper
carry the FSC logo. Our paper procurement policy can be found at:
www.rbooks.co.uk/environment

Typeset in Palatino by Palimpsest Book Production Limited
Grangemouth, Stirlingshire
Printed and bound in Great Britain by
CPI Cox & Wyman, Reading, RG1 8EX

*In dedication to the memory of
Ernest John and Isabella Pickford*

Prologue

September 1783, twenty leagues north-east of Martinique

The harsh blast of a whistle drowned the noise of wind and sea as HM brig *Wasp* thumped her bluff bow into yet another wave.

'Last man down shall get a flogging! By God, I'll have the skin off his back, you lubbers!'

The words were said in a mounting rage, the veins standing hard and clear against the speaker's throat and the spittle forming at the corners of his mouth as he gave vent to his fury. No speaking trumpet was needed for the voice to carry easily to the men aloft, standing on stirrups with bodies braced against the yards to negate the *Wasp*'s pitch and roll.

'Bastard!'

The highest topmen, standing against the topgallant yard eighty feet above the sea, cursed openly as they scrambled back in towards the mast in a panic, each man striving to avoid becoming the next victim of their captain's increasing insanity. They were watched keenly by the small knot of officers on deck, enjoying the sport as the men attempted to get down to the deck as quickly as they could.

Their tormentor, Lieutenant Charles Fury, stood looking upwards with a mirthless smile creasing his face. Nothing gave him more pleasure than to see men running in fear from his wrath, and the men aloft were certainly not disappointing him today. All were off the yards now except one. That man could see he was the last one and his panic was such that he could already almost feel the lash of the cat o' nine tails as it tore open his back in a bloody mess. There was only one way he could avoid that now, and that was by jumping from the yard on to the shrouds below, bypassing the man who was next in front of him and already beginning his hurried climb down. The officers on the deck, sycophants as they were, nevertheless gasped in horror as they watched the man jump from the yard. It seemed for a moment, one relieved moment, that he had managed to grasp the shrouds safely, but a lurch of the brig as she hit a wave was enough to wrench free his grip and send him tumbling to the deck, his arms and legs flailing grotesquely as he fell. The body hit the deck with a sickening thud near the lee scuppers and lay there, broken and bloody.

The deck was in utter silence now; even the men aloft who had been hurrying to gain the deck had stopped halfway down the shrouds and were merely staring in shock at the body. Those stares soon turned in mute hatred to Lieutenant Fury, who stood looking at the deck planking near the body which was now beginning to turn dark red as the man's blood seeped from his lifeless form. His brows came together in a frown.

'Clear that God-damned mess up. It's staining the deck.' Lieutenant Fury glared at his officers, who hurriedly moved away, shouting at the men on deck to get the task done.

The topmen resumed a slow descent to the deck, all still seething with shock and anger.

'You there!' Fury was shouting again and pointing to a

seaman just stepping off the weather main shrouds on to the bulwark. 'Stand where you are.'

The man froze, glancing round at his shipmates as if to find some support among them.

'Bosun!'

Fury's call was answered immediately by a short but stocky man with thick forearms who looked every inch the pugilist he once had been.

'Sir?'

'That man there,' Fury pointed to the now terrified seaman, 'he was the last man off the yard! Is that not so?' He spun round to his officers with a look of glee on his face as if for confirmation. The sailing master reluctantly provided it with a small nod.

'Indeed he was, sir, indeed he was.' The master knew very well what was coming and cursed himself for his weakness in standing by and doing nothing.

Fury swung back round to face the seaman in question, still rooted to the spot but visibly shaking.

'Bosun!' Fury rapped. 'Take him below under guard. He will face punishment in two hours for his tardiness. That should give him sufficient time to consider his fate.'

The seaman swung his head round left and right in near panic as if looking for a saviour, or perhaps momentarily considering a futile attempt at escape. Finding none, he managed to restrict himself to a verbal protest.

'But sir—'

'Silence!' Lieutenant Fury erupted, the spittle and the veins returning and the eyes opened wide as if in madness. 'How dare you speak without being spoken to? You see that?' This last question was addressed to his officers once more. 'Not

3

only is he lazy, he is also mutinous!' Fury himself was shaking now with his anger as he turned back to the helpless seaman. 'You will soon learn never to answer me back. If I have to flog you till your ribs show, you will learn! Bosun, take him below.'

The hopelessness of his situation quickly seemed to sink in and the seaman submitted meekly to the proddings of the bosun's cane as he trudged below. Fury's rage rapidly began to subside. It was replaced by the usual dull paranoia that hung over him every day like a cloud, as the surgeon supervised the removal of the body and men set to work on the deck with holystones to clean up the seeping blood.

The rest of the men standing around the deck began muttering, not quite loud enough for the officers to understand but just loud enough to let them know they were not happy. Lieutenant Fury was oblivious to this, however, as he turned to go below, quite satisfied that the crew was better trained after this lesson in discipline.

Two hours later he was back on deck, in full uniform and with the entire crew standing in a hollow square facing the capstan. Tilted and strapped against the capstan was an upturned hatch grating. The small detachment of marines on board the *Wasp* stood behind Lieutenant Fury with muskets at their sides, and a small awkward silence ensued before the bosun and his mate escorted the unlucky seaman through the ranks of surly men. His shirt was stripped from his back as he stood there and his wrists were strapped to the grating so that he was leaning forward against it, his bare back exposed to the waiting crew. The bosun's mate attempted to thrust a leather pad into his mouth to stop him biting off his tongue during the punishment, but the man swung his head wildly from side to side in refusal. His struggle prompted an angry stirring from the men, which soon grew to a strong murmur of dissent.

'Silence!' Fury roared. 'Silence or I shall have the marines open fire!'

The murmuring subsided reluctantly in the face of that threat.

'Let this man be a lesson to you all. Idleness is a disease and I will not have it spread among my ship. I had intended to be lenient to show you all I am a reasonable man, but his display of mutiny has made me reconsider my decision. He will receive fifty lashes.'

The murmurs erupted again at this last statement, prompting the marines to level their muskets at a signal from Fury. Fifty lashes was a huge punishment, tantamount to a death sentence. By Admiralty law a captain was only allowed to order a dozen lashes; anything more had to be sentenced by a court martial.

'Silence! I will not tell you again. Perhaps now you will learn to obey my orders.'

There was a cold silence, which allowed Fury to continue with the proceedings. He brushed aside a mop of brown hair from his forehead, wet with spray, and turned to the bosun.

'Bosun, you may begin the punishment, and lay 'em on.'

The bosun ran the strands of knotted rope through his fingers to separate them as he loosened his shoulders ready for the first blow. Swinging back high, he laid it on across the man's back, drawing a half-stifled scream and an involuntary convulsion. The cat was passed between the bosun and his mate after every ten lashes to ensure that the victim did not benefit too much from their tiredness. By thirty lashes the man was insensible, his back a mess of bloody, tangled flesh. More than once the bosun looked up to Lieutenant Fury for a signal that he was satisfied the man had had enough, but he received only an icy stare in return, and so the punishment continued until all fifty lashes had been applied, and a trace of white betrayed where a rib was showing through the man's flesh.

'Cut him down and take him below,' Fury ordered. 'And a tot of rum to every man!'

He smiled at the men as he went below, his previous threats seemingly forgotten. The murmuring between the men rose as he left, prompted not by the promise of extra rum, but by the madman who was tormenting them under the protection of Their Lordships at the Admiralty.

Dusk saw HM brig *Wasp* making four knots under topsails alone. The wind was light and darkness closed in quickly, the overhead clouds presaging rain squalls. Down below decks the men not on watch huddled round a single lantern hung from the deck beams just forward of the foremast. The swinging light cast flickering shadows over the grim faces gathered round it, huddled closely together so no one could overhear them. The constant slap and gurgle of water as the *Wasp*'s bow gently thrust aside each low wave, combined with the groaning and creaking as her timbers worked with the pitch and roll of the brig, were not enough to drown out the voice of a single man in the midst of the huddled group. He was one of *Wasp*'s bosun's mates, the most senior man present, and he had the attention of everyone, not least because what he was suggesting could have every man jack of them hanged from the nearest yardarm.

'Mutiny.'

That single whispered word sent a shiver of fear through every man present, but not one ventured to protest. The bosun's mate continued.

'Listen, lads . . . that was murder today. You know it and I know it.' He paused to glance around and let his words sink in. Still no one disagreed. 'He may not have cut his throat with a knife, but he was responsible just the same. Poor Johnny had a wife and kid.'

Johnny was the name of the man who had fallen from aloft in his desperate bid to avoid the promised punishment for being last to the deck. Murmurs of agreement arose from the group. The two men who had been stationed further aft to warn of the approach of any officers turned to look at the group, wondering what was being said.

'As for Billy, you all saw the state of his back. I hear the sawbones had to replace the skin over one of his ribs before he bandaged him up.'

Further murmurs greeted this news, more angry and voluble but thankfully drowned out by a sudden rain squall sweeping the deck above. The rain hammering on the deck planking rose to an alarmingly loud crescendo before dissipating remarkably quickly, leaving only the trickling of water as the rain found its way below decks via a thousand routes.

'So what do we do?'

The question came from an old hand who had served in the navy since he was a boy, and it was the question every single conspirator had been wanting to ask.

'Well –' The bosun's mate paused, as if uttering his next words meant there was no going back. 'We all know he's mad. He's getting worse every day and the officers won't do a damn thing. Some of 'em are nearly as bad! I for one don't intend to sit by and watch while he murders us one at a time.'

'So what do we do?' The question was repeated by another hand, his exasperation at their predicament all too evident.

'We take the ship!'

Silence reigned. Every man was shocked at the suggestion, and yet everyone had known exactly why they were having this discussion.

'There are seventy of us. Only thirteen marines, and half of them would side with us given half a chance. We can take the ship no problem, and then hand her over to the French. Martinique can't be very far to the south-east, and once we're there we'll be safe. The buggers'll never take Martinique!'

Still no one raised an objection. Another rain squall hit, this one lasting for a full five minutes before abating.

'And what do we do about the captain?' The voice came out of the stygian gloom once the rain had stopped.

'We throw him overboard, and the officers. It's the only way.'

Another unknown voice sounded from the shadows.

'Can't we just have one of the officers report him to the Admiralty once we get home?' The question was asked more to ease the guilt of what they were suggesting. To make some pretence that other options had been considered.

'Don't be daft, lad. The Admiralty won't take a blind bit of notice of us. Besides, the rate he's going, there'll be none of us left by that time.'

Again there was silence. The objections seemed to be exhausted now and most of the men were nodding resignedly as the lantern light cast its dancing glow around the group.

'Right then, this is how we'll do it . . .'

The men leaned further forward as the plan was formed. A plan which would send shock waves throughout the navy. A plan which would mean that no man who was signed on board HM brig *Wasp* would ever be able to return to England again, would ever again see his home or his family, and would hang as sure as night followed day if he was caught. A plan which would involve murder. But the men had been driven to it, driven to it through weeks of abuse, weeks of cruelty and overwhelming fear. Lieutenant Fury was mad, of that they were convinced. And soon they would gain vengeance for those weeks of fear, a terrible vengeance.

A thick mist had settled over the Atlantic where HM brig *Wasp* lay rolling over the long swell. The wind had dropped just before the pale disc of the sun had dipped below the western horizon, and with the darkness the mist had thickened, as if it wished to hide from the world the horrors which were to take place that night.

The watch on duty were huddled round the deck in the darkness as the sails hung limp in the damp air. Hands closed quietly over belaying pins as they waited for the word. It was decided. Not one man among the crew had raised a strong objection to their plans, and now it just remained to carry out the job.

Down below the men slipped quietly out of hammocks in the darkness. Further aft, snores and grunts could be heard from the marines as they slept. The men crouched low in a huddle, pulling out stashed weapons as the leader, the bosun's mate, gave the final instructions.

Fitch, the man selected for the first, most important task,

swallowed hard as he steeled himself for what lay ahead. He stood up as far as the low deck beams would allow him to and walked aft with apparent unconcern. He passed the marines in their hammocks, half expecting a grunted challenge, but they were dead to the world. They soon will be, the man thought grimly, as he passed them and continued beyond the officers' cabins each side of the brig, his heart thumping so hard it felt as if it would burst out of his chest.

His crewmates were creeping along in the darkness behind him, crouching low and with weapons ready as they approached the slumbering marines. He could see the marine stationed outside Lieutenant Fury's cabin from the dim light of a hanging lantern. It was doubtful whether the marine could see him yet, looking forward into the gloom as he was, but from the noise he was no doubt aware of someone's approach.

'Who's that?' The marine's nervousness was obvious as he snarled the challenge into the darkness. It seemed loud enough to wake the whole ship yet still no one behind him stirred.

'Fitch,' he replied clearly. 'Mr Webber sent me to rouse the captain. He thinks he heard gunfire over to starboard.' Webber was the officer currently on watch, and the sentence had been practised so much that it rolled off the tongue without hesitation.

He could sense the marine relax as the report was given, and so he stepped into the small circle of light cast by the lantern. Lieutenant Fury's paranoia was such that he insisted on having the door to his quarters locked during the night, with only him and the marine sentry on duty allowed a key. Fitch was well aware of this, and the corners of his mouth creased into a vicious grin as the marine turned to the cabin door with key in hand to rouse Lieutenant Fury. His nervousness and subsequent relief had blunted his judgement, so it did not occur to him that Webber would never have sent a common seaman to report to the captain. Fitch brought out the knife which he had concealed in his trousers, and waited for the sound of the key scraping in the lock.

The marine had begun to turn the handle of the door when Fitch's left arm came round his neck. The musket clattered to the deck as the marine instinctively brought up his hands to try and release the arm from his neck. His shout was cut off almost as soon as it had begun, to be replaced by a gasp as the knife was slashed across his throat. The gasp turned into a gargle as the knife blade was sawed viciously back and forth to slice through the windpipe and arteries. Warm blood was pumping uncontrollably over Fitch's arm as he held the marine upright. The body went limp and so Fitch lowered it carefully to the deck.

He became aware of dull thuds and cracks behind him as the rest of the crew went to work on the sleeping marines with belaying pins or knives. Another half-scream sounded as one of the marines awoke just before the belaying pin smashed into his skull again and again. The men were in a rage now, their former anxiety all disappeared now that the killing had begun and there was no going back.

Fitch picked up the fallen musket of the marine and turned to enter Fury's cabin. He swung back, startled, looking to his left as the sleepy master emerged from his cabin, rubbing his eyes to accustom them to the light of the lantern.

'What's all—'

His sentence was left unfinished as Fitch thrust the musket

forward and the bayonet ripped into his stomach. He gasped, looking down in astonishment as the blade was twisted and withdrawn, before he crumpled to the deck to rest in the widening pool of blood around the dead marine. He was still not dead but Fitch let him be – of all the officers of the *Wasp* the old master was the most likeable, and, if he hadn't surprised him, then he might have let him live. It was too late now.

Fitch opened the door of Fury's cabin and paused as his eyes became accustomed to the darkness once more. To his left he could see the captain's desk in the day section of the cabin. On his right was a bulkhead with a closed door in the middle. That was where Lieutenant Fury slung his cot. Fitch walked over, grasped the handle, gulped, and pushed inwards. The door swung open and Fitch stepped into the small cabin with his musket ready. Fury was standing with some difficulty on one leg as he struggled into his breeches.

'Who is that?' Fury demanded with a hint of terror in his voice. He reached for his sword and pulled it half out of its scabbard before the loud click of the musket being cocked checked him.

Fitch was only supposed to guard Lieutenant Fury, to save him for a different fate, but seeing his past tormentor helpless and terrified in front of him, his finger began instinctively to close over the trigger. A shuffling sounded behind him just as he was pulling the trigger. The musket was knocked aside a fraction before the flint sent a spark down to the powder in the pan. There was a momentary flash of light in the dark cabin as the musket was discharged, the ball embedding itself harmlessly in the brig's timbers.

Fury gave an involuntary scream before he realised he had

not been hit, and Fitch turned round to see the bosun's mate next to him.

'Don't kill him yet, Fitch, we want to 'ave a little fun with him first.'

Even in the dark, Fitch could see the man's face break into a wicked, toothless grin.

'Get him up on deck!'

The men gathered behind Fitch shuffled past and closed around Fury, clamping his arms to his side. He was bundled roughly out of the cabin and led up to the deck, the men wasting little opportunity in landing sly punches as he was led past. The stench of blood was thick below decks. They passed the littered bodies of the marines down below and the officers of the watch on the deck, and Fury began quietly to sob as the realisation of his predicament hit home. They stopped him near the capstan and stepped back, releasing their grip and allowing Fury gingerly to nurse the several bruises he had collected in the brief journey from his cabin.

'Please –' he stammered, desperately trying to talk his way out of trouble. 'I have a wife and two children to look after. Please, I beg you.'

The men were all gathered round him, looking on in disgust at their former commander, now half hysterical and sobbing like a child.

'Shut up!' shouted the bosun's mate, pushing his way through the crowd of men and striking Fury on the side of his face. He turned back to the men. 'Get that grating up and lash it to the capstan. We'll give the lieutenant here a taste of the cat.'

There was a cheer at that announcement, and a moment later a grating was strapped almost vertically to the capstan barrel. Fury was led over to it, writhing and struggling now like a madman, but held in a vice-like grip by a score of men. He was pushed, chest first, on to the grating. Rope was found and his hands and legs were tied to it. Several hands grabbed at his shirt and ripped it unceremoniously from his back. The tears rolling down Fury's cheeks and the occasional sobbed pleas only served to make the men loathe him even more.

The cat o' nine tails was found and the bosun's mate ordered the men to get into line.

'Now then, lads,' he shouted, 'you'll all get one strike apiece. One, mark you – we don't want to finish him off too early. We've a little more in store for him.'

The men were grinning in the darkness, anticipation welling up within them at the chance to strike at this man who had made their lives a living hell during the past few months. The first man stepped forward, fingering the cat lovingly. He braced his feet on the deck, raised his arm back and swung as though he could put all those months of torment into one strike.

Fury screamed as the rope flayed into his back. He twitched his arms and legs and writhed in an effort to get free of the rope, but he was held fast. One by one the men stepped forward to deliver a strike, each one putting all his strength behind the blow. Fury's screams drifted across the empty ocean until at last they turned into nothing more than sobs as his sanity broke.

The sky was beginning to lighten slightly as the last man, the fifty-ninth in line, laid his blow on Fury's torn back. The flesh was hanging down in strips and the seat of his breeches was a dark stain of blood.

They cut him down afterwards, and a bucket of sea water was tossed over him to bring him back to some semblance of consciousness. Fury screamed again as the salt water hit him, but the sea water did the job, bringing him back sobbing into the real world, albeit reluctantly. The crew's vengeance was not yet sated, and they wanted him to be conscious of his pain until the very end.

The bosun's mate knelt down so that his face was only inches from Fury's.

'Have you learnt your lesson, Mr Fury?'

Fury nodded eagerly as he sobbed, a surge of hope springing within him that they might yet let him live. That hope vanished abruptly.

'I don't think so.' The bosun's mate spat contemptuously into his face and stood back to his feet. 'Reeve a whip from the main yardarm, lads! We're going to have a morning hanging!'

The men cheered once again and the front of Fury's breeches, which still bore some resemblance to whiteness, slowly discoloured as his bladder gave way in his terror.

By the time the rope was in place the sun was beginning to peer over the eastern horizon, slowly burning through the mist which still lingered from the previous night. The wind was returning with the dawn, causing the damp sails to flap restlessly as they hung from the yards. Fury's hands were tied behind his back and he was dragged over to where the rope dangled down to the deck. Eager hands fastened it around his neck and tried to get him to stand, but he would not, or could not. Each time they let him go he crumpled to the deck in a sobbing heap.

'Leave him be!' the bosun's mate shouted. 'Clap on to the falls there and take up the slack.'

There was a mini-stampede as the men fought to find a place on the rope which would run Fury up to the yardarm. A couple of steps back to take up the slack saw Fury pulled to his feet, gasping as the rope tightened around his neck.

'Do you have any final words?'

Fury stood there with the tears rolling down his cheeks but said nothing apart from a half-choked 'Please'.

'All right lads, run away with it.'

The men ran forward eagerly and Fury was raised quickly off his feet, surging upwards with his legs kicking until he was dangling just below the yardarm. His body twitched horribly for almost two minutes before the spasms subsided and he dangled there, the last vestiges of life strangled out of him. His eyes still wide open, they stared lifeless out over the brightening Atlantic as HM brig *Wasp* wore round and headed for Martinique.

Chapter One

May 1792

It was turning out to be a rare day, a very rare day indeed. The sun shone down from a cloudless blue sky with such brilliance that the reflections thrown up from the wave tops made it difficult to keep one's eyes open. Indeed, many of the men scattered about the deck of His Britannic Majesty's frigate *Amazon* as she thrashed her way southward had an almost permanent squint now due to the brightness. It was not this, however, that accounted for the rarity of this particular day, as the weather in those climes hardly varied from one month to the next. Nor was it the fact that the daily ritual of the noon sight on board had just shown their position to be latitude zero degrees, fifty-six minutes south – the frigate having passed the invisible line of the equator a short time earlier. The rarity was in fact due to the unaccountable joviality of one of those men on deck, the Honourable Henry Farquhar, soon to be Governor of Bombay, who was standing by the larboard mizzen channels on the quarterdeck clasping tightly on to the shrouds to keep his footing on the sloping, heaving deck.

It was nearly two months now since the *Amazon* had left Portsmouth on a crisp early spring morning, slowly making her way through the maze of shipping anchored in Spithead before wearing south on their journey. Day by day during that period, as the climate had gradually warmed, Farquhar had been possibly the worst passenger Captain Barber had ever had the misfortune to carry. Farquhar himself was ashamed to admit that he had been suffering from acute homesickness, and he had allowed it to cloud his behaviour towards the *Amazon*'s officers. On several occasions the captain had invited him to dine with those of his officers whom he could spare from the duties of running the ship, and each time Farquhar had sat aloof at the table, joining in the surrounding conversation only with reluctance and with a certain air of condescension. He now had the firm impression that the officers of the *Amazon* made a special effort to avoid his company, and he could not in all honesty blame them. Now, with the memories of home slipping to the back of his mind more and more each day, he could feel his spirits lifting. He needed intelligent company once again, and the realisation of it prompted him to reflect on his treatment of the *Amazon*'s officers with keen regret.

He made a mental promise to rectify the situation as soon as possible. An invitation to the captain and his officers to dine with him should do the trick, he decided, using some of the stores he had purchased for the voyage. Especially considering the cost of those stores.

Shifting his portly frame and with hands still clasping tightly onto anything solid, he looked around for sign of the captain to make his invitation. His gaze rested forward with interest to where a group of seamen had brought up a large tub on to the fo'c'sle and were now in the process of filling it with sea water using the wash deck pump, the clank-clank of the handles as the men pumped carrying aft on the wind. The tub nearly full, the men gratefully ceased pumping and the cascade of water reduced to a trickle.

His curiosity aroused, Farquhar edged forward along the bulwark to get a better view, making sure to keep a tight hold of the hammock nettings as he went. Even after two months at sea he found it almost impossible to keep his balance unaided on the constantly moving deck.

By the time the men forward had secured the wash deck pump, Farquhar had almost reached the point where the quarterdeck joined the gangway leading forward. Three of the seamen on the fo'c'sle were now making their way aft along the starboard gangway to the quarterdeck, moving as effortlessly as if they were on land. Each man – barefoot and deeply tanned – respectfully knuckled his forehead as they stopped in front of the captain just forward of the main capstan.

'If you please, sir,' began the man at the front, evidently the leader, 'may we ask if you have ever before been in these parts of Neptune's dominions?'

He was carrying what looked to Farquhar like a makeshift trident, and had a net hanging from his other hand.

'I most certainly have,' replied Captain Barber with a slight smile, betraying not a hint of surprise at the strange question addressed to him on his own quarterdeck.

The seaman knuckled his forehead once again and turned to the first lieutenant, Mr Douglas, standing next to Captain Barber, and put to him exactly the same question. Lieutenant Douglas gave him the same answer as his captain, and Farquhar listened intently and with increasing curiosity as the remaining two lieutenants of the *Amazon*, Mr Scott and

Mr Carlisle, were asked the same question in turn, each one answering in the affirmative.

The three seamen then moved on to the two midshipmen who were present on the quarterdeck, both little more than boys, and asked them each in turn. The first boy's response was out of earshot of Farquhar, but evidently the three seamen were satisfied at the reply, each moving off with a knuckle of the forehead to the next young gentleman, standing by the quarterdeck rail overlooking the waist with a jacket which was now altogether too small for him. Farquhar clearly heard the question being put to him.

'If you please, sir, have you ever before been in this part of Neptune's dominions?'

The look of surprise on the boy's deeply tanned face was evident, his right hand casually reaching up to brush aside the mop of brown hair – now damp with sweat – from his forehead.

'I have not,' he replied simply.

'If you would be so kind then, Mr Fury, as to accompany us to the fo'c'sle, we have a tub set up with which to mark the special occasion.'

The request was made perfectly respectfully, although even Farquhar could detect the underlying hostility of the seaman. It was obvious that this was an officer not liked by the men. The young man's eyebrows came together in obvious confusion.

'And what special occasion is that, Davies?' he asked of the leader.

'Why, crossing the equator, of course, sir,' the man Davies replied with a look of small surprise.

'I see. And then what is the tub for?'

'It is a tradition, sir, for those who have never before crossed the line, to immerse themselves in a bathing tub of sea water to pay homage to the God Neptune.'

The lad shook his head slowly before replying.

'In that case, I decline. I have no wish to be immersed, thank you.'

Farquhar was surprised at the arrogance with which the young man gave his reply, and it was perhaps the reason for the crew's obvious dislike.

The leader of the three seamen, Davies, hesitated before persisting. It was unwise for common seamen to argue with officers, no matter what the occasion.

'But it's tradition, sir. It'll be bad luck if you don't.'

'It is hardly commensurate with the dignity of a King's officer to frolic on deck in a tub of sea water. Now let's hear no more of this nonsense.' The reply was given with an air of authority which belied his youthful appearance. Farquhar was in no doubt that Mr Fury considered this an end to the matter.

There followed a moment of silence as the three seamen stood looking at the young man sullenly, obviously reluctant to persist further even against a young midshipman, but the strength of tradition ensuring they made no immediate attempt to leave at this second refusal. A despairing glance by Davies over to Barber, who was keenly watching events, prompted the captain's intervention.

'Even the captain of one of the King's ships cannot easily go against tradition, Mr Fury!'

His young officer did not take the hint, but merely looked a protest before finally finding his voice.

'My apologies, sir, but I will not do it,' he stated resolutely.

'You will not do it, Mr Fury?' Barber exclaimed indignantly and with rising volume, straightening up to his full height. His features became sterner as he spoke.

'I do not believe it forms part of my duty, sir,' Midshipman Fury replied unabashed.

Farquhar himself flinched at that response and he could see Captain Barber's features stiffen perceptibly.

'Your duty, sir!' Barber repeated. 'Do you presume to tell me, sir, what your duty is on my own quarterdeck?'

His tone was icy now and Farquhar was sure that Fury could sense he had gone too far.

'No, sir,' Fury replied quickly, backtracking fast in an attempt to diffuse the situation. 'I—'

'I think you need reminding, Mr Fury, of who commands here,' Barber interrupted him. 'Bosun!' he shouted, in response to which came hurrying over a stocky man, his neck nearly as thick as one of the *Amazon*'s twelve-pounders down on the deck below. The speed of his response betrayed the fact that he had been standing close by witnessing the scene, as indeed were many of the crew Farquhar could see.

'Sir!' the bosun reported, knuckling his forehead.

'Mr Harrison,' the captain greeted him, 'it seems Mr Fury is in need of being reacquainted with the gunner's daughter. You have your cane?'

'Aye, sir,' the bosun replied with a half-stifled grin, holding up the short black stick clutched in his right hand which Farquhar had seen him use liberally on several occasions before to 'encourage' the men to their duty. Even so, he seemed uncommonly enthusiastic at this opportunity.

'Then be so kind as to give him a dozen, Mr Harrison. And lay 'em on!'

The young Fury was led over by the bosun to the nearest cannon, which just happened to be that nearest to where Farquhar was standing. He caught Fury's eye as he passed, the resignation within only too apparent, but mingled perhaps with a hint of defiance. Not a sign of further resistance came from the midshipman, however, as he silently bent over the breech of the gun.

From Farquhar's view of proceedings, it certainly looked as if the bosun took the captain at his word, each stroke being delivered with vigour. A quick glance around showed that all the men on deck had stopped to watch the punishment and each man certainly seemed to be enjoying Fury's discomfort. To the young man's credit, apart from a stifled grunt after the first blow had landed, he did not utter a sound during the whole punishment, the only evidence betraying the pain of the strokes being a slight convulsion of his rear as each of the twelve landed.

At last the bosun stood back.

'Twelve, sir!' he announced with apparent satisfaction to the captain, who had been witnessing the punishment from a short distance away.

'Very good, Mr Harrison. You may go about your duties now.'

The bosun withdrew to leave all eyes on the young Fury as he gingerly straightened himself up. Farquhar could see as he turned his face that the features were still contorted with pain, but there was no sign that he had shed any tears during the beating.

'Now, Mr Fury,' the captain began, 'you will oblige me by demonstrating your love of tradition, if you please.'

'Aye aye, sir,' Fury replied, understanding the captain's

meaning and making his way forward, all further resistance beaten out of him.

Farquhar watched him from where he stood as the boy reached the fo'c'sle and slowly peeled off his uniform – taking particular care with the removal of his breeches – until he stood there completely naked.

There was a distinct atmosphere of pleasure from the men around the tub, perhaps at being the cause of this young man's pain and embarrassment. Fury turned and slowly stepped into the tub, showing as he did so his posterior, which even at a distance Farquhar could see was red-raw.

He immersed himself in the tub of water quickly and showed no sign of the pain he must have felt as the salt water covered his injury. In fact, to his credit, he suffered the ordeal with remarkable goodwill, plunging his head under the water and staying in the tub for several minutes splashing about, so that – in the current heat – Farquhar began to feel almost envious. Finally he got out and was grudgingly passed a towel by one of the seamen nearby.

'Mr Fury!' the captain called, as Fury began to make his way below with his clothes under his arm.

'Sir?'

'After you have regained your uniform I expect to see you back on deck until your next watch, not skulking about below like a Frenchman!'

'Aye aye, sir,' Fury replied, disappearing down the ladder.

It was a full twenty minutes before Farquhar, still standing by the larboard bulwark covered in sweat, became aware of the presence of young Midshipman Fury, standing further aft looking down at the sea as the ship swept on its way. He shuffled himself along without losing his footing until he was next to the lad, who evidently was so engrossed in his thoughts as to not notice his presence.

'Mr Fury, is it not?' Farquhar asked.

Fury looked up with a start. 'It is, sir,' he replied simply, looking sideways at him.

'And how do you do today, Mr Fury?' Farquhar continued, determined to strike up a conversation. He was well aware that the question was idiotic given what he had just witnessed.

'Very well, sir, thank you.'

'I was almost envious, Mr Fury, to see you in that tub. This damnable heat is unbearable.'

Fury showed no hint of embarrassment at this mention of his ordeal.

'You should take a turn aloft, sir,' he replied. 'The breeze is much more refreshing up there.'

Farquhar stifled a chuckle.

'Not a chance, Mr Fury, not a chance! I should get a nosebleed before I reached the top.' He looked up at the mainmast and shuddered despite the heat.

'You would get used to it presently,' Fury observed with a confidence perhaps borne of experience. 'My first time aloft I had to be lowered down by a tackle rigged to the main topmast head.'

'You would not think it, to look at you now,' Farquhar said with genuine surprise. He had seen Fury scampering aloft with the other 'young gentlemen' with an amazing disregard for danger. 'You gentlemen climb aloft like monkeys. It is a wonder you do not kill yourselves. Then where would the future of the service be?'

'I am of the firm opinion, sir, that the quicker I move aloft, the less time I have for losing my footing.'

A small pause for silence followed while Farquhar digested this debatable theory.

'And how long have you been in the service now, Mr Fury?' he asked finally, thinking it best to change the subject.

'Eight months, sir.'

'Only eight months? I would have thought it was longer, judging by your competency.'

'No, sir. Just eight months, although it seems more like a lifetime. The first few weeks were the most daunting. Fathoms and fathoms of rope in every direction for every conceivable use. It was sheer embarrassment which drove me to study my new profession.'

'Embarrassment, Mr Fury?'

'Aye, sir. At having to give orders to men twice my age and with vastly more experience than me.'

'Ah, I see. And how old are you?'

'I shall be seventeen at the end of this month. Far too old to start a career in the service, some would say.'

'Nonsense, you have plenty of time ahead of you. May I ask what prompted you to join in the first place?'

'I did not actually have much say in the matter, sir. Captain Barber is my uncle, and he promised my mother he would take me to sea to instil some discipline into me. I believe my mother was growing anxious with my constant fighting at school. None of my doing, I assure you.'

Farquhar stared at the boy's nose which was slightly crooked at the bridge, the only blemish on otherwise symmetrical features and perhaps as a result of one of those fights.

'And you enjoy it?' he asked.

'Certainly. Although the master's navigation classes can be painful. Mathematics is not something I can claim to enjoy.'

'From what I have been able to observe, Mr Fury, the master seems perfectly satisfied with your navigation.'

'It is quite sufficient now, certainly – purely out of necessity. During my first two months' service I was mast-headed by the captain several times for my ineptitude. In one week alone my calculations had us somewhere in the Indian Ocean on the Monday, the western Atlantic on the Wednesday and mainland Russia on the Saturday!'

'And what was your actual position?'

'We were running southward past the Bay of Biscay at the time, if my memory serves me. We were given a short cruise to get the men in order. The rest of my service was spent mostly at anchor in Spithead – a most uneventful time.'

Farquhar nodded and looked down at the water churning past. Another small silence ensued while Farquhar mentally phrased his next question. He was aware that the question could be thought importunate, but after two months at sea his curiosity was getting the better of him.

'Forgive me, Mr Fury, I do not wish to pry, but the men seem to bear some hostility towards you.'

Fury grimaced slightly.

'Yes, sir, they do.'

Farquhar felt sufficiently snubbed by the flat response not to risk further prying. It was Fury himself this time who broke the silence.

'My father was Charles Fury.'

Farquhar looked at him, aware that Fury evidently thought that name would explain everything.

'Charles Fury?'

Fury sighed, as if sick of explaining the story.

'Charles Fury was in command of HM brig *Wasp* in the year eighty-three.'

Farquhar silently mouthed the word 'Wasp', realising the name was vaguely familiar to him and trying to drag the reason from his memory. Fury saved him the trouble by explaining further.

'The crew of the *Wasp* mutinied in September of that year, killing all the officers and taking the ship into Martinique where they handed her over to the French.'

Farquhar remembered now. It was said that the *Wasp* sailed into Martinique with the body of Charles Fury still hanging from the yardarm. The incident had been a major embarrassment to the navy at a period when they were still at war with the French. Not least because further rumours had subsequently suggested that Fury had been mad at the time of his death. To Farquhar's knowledge, none of the mutineers had ever been captured. He looked at the younger Fury, wondering what he could say.

'You cannot be blamed for your parentage.' It was a feeble defence, he knew.

'Nevertheless,' Fury continued, 'the men see me as a bad omen. There are no men on earth more superstitious than seamen.'

Farquhar was frustrated in his attempt to reply by another of the ship's young gentlemen calling out to his companion.

'How do you fancy another rematch, John?'

Fury looked at the boy, his face breaking into a shy smile. He was no doubt glad of the interruption.

'Not at the moment I'm afraid, Charles. I've only just had

a rendezvous with the gunner's daughter – even you would be able to beat me in my current state!'

'Bah! Excuses, John. I have the beating of you any time you choose,' came back the reply.

'Tomorrow then, and I shall be glad of a newly patched pair of breeches!'

He turned back to Farquhar, the smile still lingering and lighting his face up with a startling animation. Farquhar could guess that, no matter how strained Fury's relationship with the men, he was at least popular among his own messmates.

'A small competition we are engaged in, sir,' Fury explained, 'to see who can climb the rigging and get back down on deck the fastest. We choose different masts each time and the loser has to perform a chore of the winner's choice. It just so happens that several of my pairs of breeches are in some urgent need of repair.'

'I see,' replied Farquhar. 'And what will be the mast tomorrow?'

'I think I will choose up to the main topgallant lee yardarm and back, tomorrow. Mr Roxborough has a particular dislike for the lee yardarms, I believe.'

The sounding of eight bells and the piping of the watch below saved Farquhar a response.

'If you will excuse me, sir,' said Fury. 'I have the next watch.'

Farquhar watched him walking uneasily away and then, looking up at the swaying yards high above, shuddered again at the thought.

Chapter Two

Midshipman Fury had cause to break his word the following day. He found himself so stiff from his punishment that he could barely walk the deck, never mind scramble through the rigging.

Fortunately his shipmate, Midshipman Charles Roxborough, could well sympathise with his plight. He had suffered the same punishment himself only two weeks prior for nearly knocking down the first lieutenant in his rush to get on watch in time.

Thus Fury spent the first half of the morning gingerly walking the deck, trying to loosen up his sore limbs. Occasionally, to break the monotony, he would stare overboard to watch the numerous flying fish darting in and out of the water alongside, seemingly following them on their journey south. For all their number, however, none seemed to be interested in taking the bait which was hanging down in the water from a line attached to the ship's taffrail.

Eventually came the shout for all the 'young gentlemen' to congregate on the quarterdeck for the regular class from the master, Mr Hoggarth. Fury swore under his breath as he made his way aft – he had completely forgotten about the class. By the time he had hobbled along the gangway and reached the quarterdeck, six stools were ready, waiting along with an ever-impatient Mr Hoggarth. One glance showed that each of the other five midshipmen wore the same look of displeasure as Fury.

The master's classes were never welcome, especially when it was a fine day with the sun beating down from a cloudless blue sky and a beam wind for the *Amazon* to thrash along on. Sitting on the stool reminded Fury immediately of his delicate condition, and every movement of the ship exacerbated the pain.

He struggled through the calculation the master had set them and handed his slate back to Mr Hoggarth along with the other midshipmen when it was asked for.

'Well, well,' Hoggarth began, after taking some time to study the solutions given to him. 'I am amazed, gentlemen,' – there was the slightest stress on the word 'gentlemen' – 'that on such a fine day and with dinner not twenty minutes off, you should contrive to come to the correct answer!'

They were all smiling now, pleased at receiving the approbation of the master, albeit sarcastically.

'With one notable exception,' he continued. 'Mr Fury!'

Fury looked up sharply at the mention of his name.

'Tell me, sir,' Hoggarth demanded, 'did we, or did we not, pass the Canary Islands some weeks back?'

A hasty trawl through his memory brought a faint recollection of the mention of it some time back as a small hump of land slowly slid astern.

'I believe we did, sir,' he replied.

'Then pray tell me, how could we possibly still be there? For that is where your calculation puts us, Mr Fury!'

31

Fury was about to raise the possibility of their having sailed round in circles since they had last been there, but managed to bite his tongue – he would not welcome another meeting with the bosun's cane at this time. Instead he waited in silence, confident that the master did not really expect him to answer the question.

'I'll warrant you've had other things to occupy your mind?'

Fury did not know exactly to what Hoggarth was referring, but saw the opportunity and took it.

'Yes, sir.'

'Very well, I shall overlook the miscalculation for now. But it is dependent upon your future good performance.'

'Yes, sir.'

He had been sure ever since he joined the ship that Mr Hoggarth was more severe on him than the other mid-shipmen, perhaps because he shared the men's hostility over his father. Nevertheless Hoggarth seemed satisfied on this occasion, and quickly moved on to a short narrative on hold stowage and the effects of different types of trim on a vessel's sailing qualities. At least that was what he announced he would be talking about, for Fury did not actually listen to him. Instead he allowed his mind to wander during this time until the scraping of stools and the rising of his messmates informed him the class was now over.

Relieved, he rose gingerly to his feet, the protests in his stomach telling him better than any watch that dinner was not far off. That his stomach was correct was confirmed moments later by the sound of eight bells and the piping of the hands to dinner. Fury began eagerly to make his way below but was stopped by the master before he had even reached the quarterdeck ladder.

'A moment, if you please, Mr Fury.'

Fury turned round in exasperation but managed to curtail his reply to a polite 'Sir?'

'You are still in some pain I take it?' Hoggarth asked.

'It is nothing, sir.' Fury guessed that reply gave him the best chance of getting below to his dinner before it was cold.

'I hope you have learned a valuable lesson this morning, Mr Fury.'

'Sir?' he repeated.

'If ever you are fortunate enough to rise to command, the safety of your ship and your men will depend upon your accuracy in ascertaining your position. The circumstances in doing this may not always be favourable – you may have many other pressing matters weighing on your mind. Nevertheless you must always concentrate fully on your navigation if you are to survive – physically or professionally. Do you understand?'

Evidently the master considered his incorrect calculation was as a result of the pain he was suffering due to his recent punishment. Fury himself was convinced it was merely down to adding the figure for refraction instead of subtracting it – a simple error which anyone could make. Nevertheless he took the point.

'Yes, sir,' he replied, anxious to get below and have his dinner.

'Good. Then bear that in mind in future. Now off you go.'

Fury turned and hurried to the ladder leading down to the upper deck as fast as his sore posterior would allow him.

It was a further two days before Fury felt able to move freely once again so that he could oblige Midshipman Roxborough in his challenge. Again the sun was shining brilliantly, although there were at least some light, wispy clouds to be seen to break the monotony of endless blue across the sky.

Neither officer being on watch, both Fury and Roxborough had elected to leave their uniform jackets below for what they knew would be a demanding task, especially in such heat. And so the two of them stood by the ship's bell on the fo'c'sle with Midshipman Turner in company to keep the time.

'Well, gentlemen,' announced Turner, 'who shall be the first to go?'

'It is my turn, I believe,' stated Fury eagerly. He was anxious to get his turn finished before the captain arrived on deck, knowing as he did the captain's dislike of childish games.

'You are both clear on what is required?' Turner asked, not waiting for a reply before continuing. 'Up to the main top-gallant yard and then out along the lee yardarm before descending again. The watch will stop when you arrive back at our current position.'

Both young men nodded their understanding.

'Very well then. John, when you are ready, we shall begin.'

Fury stared forward along the gangway, waiting for the time when it would be free of the men on watch. His thin shirt was already sticking to him, the beads of perspiration on his forehead trickling down his face before being brushed away irritably.

It took only seconds before the gangway was empty and Fury seized his opportunity, hurrying over to the weather gangway and moving aft towards the quarterdeck before flinging himself over the bulwark and into the main channel.

Grabbing high at the shrouds rising above he hauled himself up out of the channels and rapidly began to climb, the heel of the ship from the wind ensuring that his climb was less vertical than it otherwise would have been. He was near the maintop in a flash, the large, square platform protruding out above his head with the futtock shrouds extending out to the edges of the platform. For a few daring seconds he hung out and backwards as he climbed the futtocks and hauled himself over the edge of the maintop. No time to exchange pleasantries with the two men sitting there as he carried on up the smaller shrouds leading up from the maintop to the topmast above. This same journey was repeated until finally he reached the topgallant masthead with the topgallant yard slung across.

The yard was braced round at an angle to ensure the sail caught the wind fully, and Fury quickly but carefully transferred his feet from the rigging to the footropes slung underneath the yard. With the ease of long practice he edged himself along with his feet braced back and his arms over the yard itself to keep from losing balance. He soon reached the end of the yard, pausing only momentarily to look down at the white-topped waters of the Atlantic over which he was standing, before making his way back in towards the mast without a thought spared for the beauty of the scene he had just witnessed. Back to the mast and he grabbed the backstay with both hands, wrapping both his feet around the thick rope and sliding down hand over hand as quickly as he could.

The backstay, hardly the method an officer ought to use to descend the rigging, was nevertheless much quicker than the shrouds and took him right down to just aft of the main channel where he had begun his ascent. A nimble hop over the bulwark took him back on to the gangway and moments later he was back with Turner and Roxborough on the fo'c'sle.

'Four minutes and nine seconds,' Turner announced, looking at the stopwatch as Fury tried to wipe the tar off his hands. 'Quite impressive, John.'

Fury looked over at Roxborough.

'I shall go and see if the sail-maker has a darning needle for you, Charles, while you are aloft!'

'Do as you wish, John, for I shall be back on deck within four minutes,' Roxborough retorted good-naturedly. 'Are you ready with that watch, Patrick?'

'When you are,' Turner replied.

Roxborough stood in silence for a few seconds, breathing deeply and judging his time before he was off.

Fury watched him take exactly the same route as he had and his confidence wavered as he saw the speed with which Roxborough scrambled up the shrouds. He had reached the main topgallant yard now and was busy transferring himself to the footropes slung underneath while Fury glanced at the watch. It would certainly be tight, he thought, as he transferred his gaze back aloft to where Roxborough was just reaching the yardarm.

Fury staggered slightly, caught off balance as the *Amazon* ploughed into a rogue wave before rising her bows more sharply. He looked up instantly and stared in mute horror as one of Roxborough's feet lost contact with the footrope and he began falling backwards away from the yard. Even as he watched he was sure Roxborough would reach out with his arms and grasp the yard, but the boy seemed to freeze. It felt as if a cold hand was clutching at Fury's heart, squeezing it so tight that it stopped beating, as he watched Roxborough begin to drop, before getting his right foot caught up in the footrope to leave him dangling there upside down momentarily, arms flailing desperately. For one moment, one blessed moment, it looked as if that footrope would save him. And then he fell – not making a sound – as Fury and Turner watched, rooted to the spot. The splash as he hit the water close by to leeward jerked Fury at last out of his trance.

'Man overboard!' he bellowed, rushing over to the *Amazon*'s side and keeping a firm sight of Roxborough flailing in the water. A number of shouts echoed round the deck now as the officer of the watch gave the orders which brought the *Amazon* flying up into the wind to slow the way off her.

Time seemed to pass quickly as Fury tried to keep his eyes on where Roxborough had landed, although the distance had increased now and he could only see what he thought to be a head above the water, disappearing regularly as the long Atlantic swell washed over him.

'Lower the cutter there! Handsomely now!'

Fury became aware of the order which sent the men hurriedly lowering the cutter from its position stowed amidships on the booms. By the time the cutter splashed down into the water alongside, the boat's crew had already assembled and were scrambling over the side into her.

Lieutenant Carlisle took the tiller and the cutter swung out from the lee of the *Amazon*'s side as the men bent furiously to their oars.

'Larboard three points!' Fury bellowed, pointing with his arm to where he judged Roxborough to be. Carlisle followed the direction of his arm and nodded his understanding as he swung the tiller over to send the cutter in the required direction.

The wait which followed was the most anxious Fury had ever experienced, even more so than when he had waited on the stone quay at Portsmouth before first joining the *Amazon*. The cutter danced over the swell waves with agonising slowness until at last he could see the men laying on their oars. The boat itself was blocking his view but some of the men seemed to be leaning over the side and dragging something up into the boat. Shortly afterwards the oars were back in use and the cutter was heading, beetle-like, back towards where the *Amazon* was slowly drifting down upon them. Fury made his way to the quarterdeck to await the return of the cutter with relief surging through him.

'What happened, Mr Fury?'

Fury turned round, startled, to see Captain Barber studying him.

'Mr Roxborough was on the main topgallant yard when we hit a rogue wave, sir. He lost his balance and fell.'

'He was not on watch, was he?' Barber asked.

'No, sir.'

'Then what was he doing on the yardarm? I hope you were not engaged in another of those idiotic races again, Mr Fury. It will go harsh on you if you were!'

'No, sir,' Fury lied, 'I believe he wished to check the boltrope on the main topgallant sail, sir.'

He told the lie more to protect Roxborough from further punishment than himself – the lad had suffered enough today already. Any reply from Captain Barber was cut off by an announcement from Lieutenant Douglas that the boat was alongside.

Fury turned to the entry port to see that a tackle had been rigged from the main yardarm and men were now hauling away. Lieutenant Carlisle appeared on deck a moment before the limp body of Roxborough was hauled up. With the help of several men the boy was brought inboard and laid on the deck where the surgeon, Mr Pike, immediately bent over him to give him treatment.

'I'm sorry, sir,' Carlisle was saying to Captain Barber as Fury moved forward towards his friend. 'There was nothing we could do. I think he was dead when we reached him.'

The words did not fully register until the surgeon rose to his feet shaking his head, his melancholy face turning and looking at Fury with sympathy.

Roxborough was lying there on the deck in front of him, his face blue and the water dripping on to the deck from his lifeless body.

It was a full twenty minutes before Fury became fully conscious of his surroundings once again, sitting at the mess table on his own, with no recollection of how he had got there.

The next day, it having being announced to the officers and crew of the *Amazon* that the funeral would take place at two bells in the forenoon watch, the bosun and his mates hurried throughout the ship rousing every man.

'I'm telling you, the boy's a Jonah. You all know what happened to 'is old man. An' now poor Mr Roxborough has choked it.'

The three men around the speaker solemnly nodded their agreement.

'Come on! Rouse up! Everyone on deck for the service.'

The strong voice of the bosun interrupted their chatter. The men silently joined the rest of the off-duty watch filing up to the deck above.

By the time Fury gained the quarterdeck the crew had all been gathered along the gangways and down in the waist, with the officers standing stiff and sombre on the quarterdeck and the bright scarlet of the marines in contrast behind them. With the ship hove to, only the lookouts aloft were obliged to keep their concentration on their duty at this particular time.

Captain Barber reached the quarterdeck with his Bible tucked under his arm, and a quick nod from him to Harrison, the bosun, led to the shouted order 'Orf hats!'. The bosun's mates now came along carrying the body of Roxborough, lying on his mess table – that which Fury himself had sat at, in fact – and hidden beneath the red ensign draped over him.

The sail-maker had been busy the previous day sewing the wretched boy up in his hammock with two round shot at his feet, the last stitch being put through his nose as a final assurance that he was indeed dead. They had reached the standing part of the foresheet now, on which the table was rested while they waited patiently for the captain to conduct the service. Captain Barber cleared his throat. Fury's eyes were concentrating on the body of his friend so intently that he only subconsciously heard the captain begin.

'In the sure and certain hope of the resurrection to eternal life through our Lord Jesus Christ, we commend to Almighty God our shipmate Charles Roxborough and we commit his body to the deep to be turned into corruption. Ashes to ashes, dust to dust. The Lord bless him and keep him. The Lord make His face to shine upon him and be gracious unto him. The Lord lift up His countenance upon him and give him peace. Amen. Amen.'

The crew solemnly repeated the two 'Amens' before the two bosun's mates – holding the mess table upon which the body was laid – upended the table while keeping a firm hold on to the ensign, to send the body slipping from beneath it into the sea. The sound of the splash as the body hit the water and sank quickly brought Fury momentarily out of his reverie. A moment later came the bosun's powerful voice again.

'On hats! Dismissed!'

The crew quickly began to disperse but Fury stood motionless, blankly staring ahead as if in a daze. Then, as if awoken from his trance and unaware of the eyes upon him, he slowly put on his hat and walked with deliberation towards the quarterdeck ladder leading to the deck below.

'Mr Fury!'

Fury turned, one leg poised over the top of the ladder as he prepared to descend.

'Sir?'

Lieutenant Carlisle was looking at him with sympathy.

'The captain would like to see you in his cabin when it is convenient, Mr Fury.'

'Yes, sir,' Fury acknowledged, sighing to himself as he made his way down the ladder and hurried aft.

The marine sentry announced his arrival as he passed through the captain's dining cabin and reached the day cabin, where Barber was sat at his desk. Fury took off his hat and stood to attention, hoping that the interview would be quick so that he could get back to his mess again and wallow in his grief.

Finally Barber looked up at him from behind the desk, his cold eyes showing no sign of sympathy or compassion.

'Well, Mr Fury. What have you to say for yourself?'

Fury shifted his feet nervously, feeling awkward and unsure as he stood with his head cocked to one side to avoid hitting the deck beams above.

'Sir?'

'Your behaviour, Mr Fury. It is entirely unacceptable.'

'I'm sorry, sir,' Fury offered, not quite sure what he was apologising for.

'Sorry? Sorry?' Barber repeated, raising his voice as he began to lose his temper. 'Poor Mr Roxborough is dead and all you can say is sorry?'

'S-sir,' Fury stammered, horrified that Barber blamed him for the death of his friend. 'It was an accident, sir.' It was a paltry defence, and Fury knew it.

'An accident that would not have happened if you had not been engaged in another of your idiotic races!'

'Sir, Charles fell as he was checking on the –'.

'Silence! Do not lie to me again. We both know Mr Roxborough was not checking the boltrope on the main topgallant sail. I am not a fool, Mr Fury.'

Fury stood in silence, looking down at the deck with the tears beginning to sting his eyes. He clenched his teeth to fight them back and looked up at Barber, still watching him coldly.

'Your behaviour since you came aboard the *Amazon* has been childish and irresponsible,' Barber continued, apparently satisfied that he had got his point across regarding Roxborough's death. 'You are an officer in a King's ship, Mr Fury. This is not a game. If you wish it I can have you discharged once we reach Portsmouth again so that you may return to Swampton and be with your mother.'

Fury shook his head vigorously, unaware until this point how appalling that thought sounded. He had grown fond of his life on board the *Amazon*, despite all the hardships, and he had no wish to return to the little village of Swampton where he had grown up with his mother and brother. He doubted if he could ever settle for a quiet life ashore again.

'No, sir.'

'Are you sure, Mr Fury? It can be easily done.'

'No, sir,' he repeated.

'The thought of scraping around for a living in a small village does not appeal to you, eh? Perhaps you do not realise how lucky you are to have been given this chance. I have no doubt that your brother Richard would have jumped at such a chance, had he been old enough. You have an opportunity to make something of yourself here, Mr Fury. To eradicate a stain which hangs over your family. Is this how you intended to achieve that?'

'No, sir.'

'I am relieved to hear it. Then perhaps your conduct in the future will reflect that fact.'

'But, sir – the men.'

'What about the men?'

'They treat me like a pariah, sir. They all know about my father and they will never trust me because of it.'

'Nonsense! You have to earn men's trust, Mr Fury, and their respect. You have treated the crew with nothing but arrogance and condescension since you arrived on board. These are the men you will have to trust with your life if you ever go into battle, to stand side by side with and know that they are willing to follow your orders, even if it could mean certain death. Did you think that your rank gave you free entitlement to their loyalty?'

'No, sir.'

'Well then, I suggest you begin trying to earn it, Mr Fury.'

'I'll try, sir.'

'Good. I am giving you a second chance here, so I suggest you take it. It will not be easy to convert the men from their beliefs – sailors are a superstitious breed at the best of times. But if you apply yourself to your duty and treat them with fairness and respect, then you will go a long way towards achieving your goal. Remember Mr Fury, it is always better to lead men rather than drive them.'

There was a brief silence in the cabin while Fury digested all that he had been told.

'Yes, sir. I understand.'

'Mark me, Mr Fury, if you are not as good as your word I shall have no compunction in having you discharged and sent home in disgrace.'

'I shall keep my word, sir.'

'Very well. You are dismissed.'

Fury saluted and left the cabin, his head still spinning from the shock of the conversation and the import of what he had been told. His neck was feeling stiff and sore from the prolonged effort of tilting it while he was in Barber's cabin, and he began to massage it as he made his way below to his quarters in the gunroom.

A couple of seamen were in the process of removing a sea chest as he arrived, under the supervision of Lieutenant Scott. Fury caught sight of the inscription on the lid as they passed him, recognising it immediately. It was Roxborough's.

His conversation with the captain had thrust the death of Roxborough temporarily from his memory, and the sight of the poor boy's sea chest brought the threat of tears flooding back. He clenched his teeth again to fight the urge, feeling the bitter taste of unfairness at the thought of his own second chance, while his friend lay rotting at the bottom of the ocean. The thought of it helped steel his resolve to make the most of it.

Chapter Three

It was almost two months before they reached their objective, gliding slowly into Bombay harbour under topsails alone, with a gentle land breeze barely enough to give them steerage way.

Those two months since Roxborough's funeral had passed uneventfully, each day merging with the next in a monotony of bright sunshine and clear skies. Even the Cape of Good Hope, an area where tempests were commonplace, had passed with no more than a distant glimpse of the southern tip of Africa over on the *Amazon*'s larboard beam.

Fury had spent much of that time looking over the side where the master, Mr Hoggarth, had told the midshipmen that it was possible to see where the Atlantic Ocean met the Indian Ocean by the slight change in the colour of the sea. He had finally given up, reflecting perhaps that it was only discernible at a distance.

A black mood of depression had cast itself over him for two full weeks after the funeral, caused perhaps by the guilt he had felt at having been partly responsible for Roxborough's death. He had somehow weathered the storm though, emerging from that mood with a vow to throw himself into his duty, not only because of Barber's threats, but also as some kind of punishment to ease his conscience over the death. It was as if he had aged ten years in the space of a month, as the master had commented to the first lieutenant one evening. In any event the result was that he had not received one single beating since, nor indeed even a mast-heading for some slight misdemeanour.

Now he stood on the fo'c'sle, a spyglass to his eye in silent study of the city as they crept in, looking more like a vagabond than a King's officer with his uniform coat worn and patched. The absurdly ill-fitting coat was a testament to the spurt of growth he had experienced in the five months since leaving Portsmouth, a spurt which had taken him to the lofty heights of five feet and ten and a half inches.

The city of Bombay itself as he scanned left and right seemed to be spread over several islands just off the mainland, a sprawling mass of whitewashed housing stretching back beyond his sight. The bay was dotted with a variety of vessels, mostly small local craft and certainly nothing as large as the *Amazon*.

He started as a gun went off nearby, quickly realising that it was the first gun of their salute to the fort on the hillside over to his left. As soon as the *Amazon* had completed her salute, the thunder of the fort's reply came echoing across the water, leaving Fury pondering over how he would react when he first experienced guns fired in anger.

He studied the lofty embrasures of the fort through his glass, the grey stone walls looking imposing high up on the hillside overlooking the bay as the *Amazon* swung round slowly into the wind. The thick undergrowth dominating the lower hillside had made an attempt to scale the walls of the fort, but had seemingly been defeated about six feet up.

Above that Fury fancied he could see cracks in the stonework where age, or perhaps attack, had weakened the wall.

A shouted command from Lieutenant Douglas sent the anchor plummeting down into the clear water of the bay with a loud splash as the *Amazon* began slowly to drift backwards, before another shouted command sent the hands hauling on bunt and clew lines to bring the canvas up to the yard where it could be furled. With the *Amazon* swinging safely at anchor, Fury abandoned his scrutiny of the shore and turned to walk aft along the starboard gangway to the quarterdeck.

Captain Barber was standing on the quarterdeck, looking stiff and uncomfortable in his thick uniform coat under the glaring sun.

'Where is Mr Farquhar?' he asked of the first lieutenant irritably.

'He should be along presently, sir. I sent Mr Turner to fetch him five minutes ago.'

Fury marvelled that, after nearly five months to prepare for this moment, Farquhar could still contrive to be late when the time arrived.

Barber was looking round the ship, pausing to note the men's efforts in hoisting out his gig, now in the process of being lowered down over the side from tackles rigged at the fore and main yardarms. He turned back to Douglas, standing next to him.

'Once I have left you may set an anchor watch, Mr Douglas. The rest of the men can have the remainder of the day off. We will begin preparations for reprovisioning the ship tomorrow, after which time I will arrange for the men to take some leave on shore by divisions.'

'Aye aye, sir,' Douglas replied.

'And make sure the men are aware that continued shore leave is dependent upon their good behaviour.'

Douglas was interrupted in his reply by the arrival of Mr Farquhar on the quarterdeck.

'Ah, there you are, captain! My apologies for keeping you waiting, sir.'

'It is no matter, sir,' Barber replied, doing well to hide his impatience. 'You have everything?'

Farquhar pointed behind him to where a large chest had just been placed on the deck.

'My servants have brought up my baggage, captain. I do not believe there is anything else I have forgotten.'

Barber nodded his head in satisfaction and turned to Douglas.

'Mr Douglas, have Mr Farquhar's chest hoisted into the gig and assemble the boat's crew.'

The first lieutenant obliged, leaving Farquhar enough time to make his farewells. He came over to Fury and held out his hand.

'Take care, Mr Fury,' he announced.

'And you, sir,' Fury replied sincerely, pumping his hand vigorously.

'As far as I can see you have improved considerably since we set out from Portsmouth,' Farquhar continued, 'although I admit I am somewhat of a novice in naval matters. I have no doubt that if you keep improving at the same rate throughout your career, you will soon be an admiral!'

Fury smiled at the thought.

'Thank you, sir.'

Farquhar turned away and said his goodbyes to the remainder of the *Amazon*'s officers, who were now all gathered on the quarterdeck to see him off. Fury was left to reflect on the remarkable change in the man over the last two months, which had resulted in this turnout for his farewell. If he had left the ship somewhere on the west coast of Africa, it was doubtful if anyone would have even noticed his departure, much less regretted it.

Fury moved over to the ship's side for a better view as Farquhar, his baggage now safely stowed in the stern sheets of the gig, made his way as elegantly as he could manage down the side, closely followed by Captain Barber. A moment later and the boat was skimming over the water towards the shore.

It was more than three hours before the return of the gig was reported to Lieutenant Douglas, sat in his small cabin with the dim light from a hanging lantern casting flickering shadows over the open pages of his journal.

'Call the side boys,' he ordered curtly to Midshipman Marsden, who had brought the news. Marsden hurried off and Douglas rose to make his way on deck, closing his journal and swatting irritably at a fly which had been pestering him for the last twenty minutes. The sun was dipping below the western horizon as Douglas reached the quarterdeck, a quick glance overboard showing the gig still some fifty yards off.

The side boys were soon standing by the entry port, ready to hold out the side ropes from the ship's side to aid the captain in his climb up from the boat below. Douglas stood some way back, waiting to receive his captain on board.

The gig was out of sight now, hidden below the bulwarks as it neared the *Amazon*'s side. Faint noises drifted up as the bowman hooked on, and a moment later the captain's head appeared at the entry port, the pipes immediately twittering until he had gained the deck.

'Welcome back, sir,' said Douglas, touching his hat.

'Thank you,' replied Barber, returning the compliment. 'Anything to report?'

'Nothing, sir; everything has been quiet. I trust you had an enjoyable visit?'

'Unfortunately not, Mr Douglas. It would perhaps be better if you joined me in my cabin.'

Douglas followed him with more than a little curiosity as Barber led the way down the companion ladder and aft to his suite of cabins.

'Please take a seat.'

Captain Barber proffered a chair as they reached the large day cabin stretching across the entire width of the ship, the stern windows showing a sky of darkening purple beyond as dusk gradually settled. Barber peeled off his heavy jacket with a sigh. The sweat was beading his face and his shirt was sticking to his back as he turned to the decanter on the sideboard.

'A glass, Mr Douglas?'

'If you please, sir,' Douglas replied, suppressing his impatience. He waited in silent frustration while the drinks were poured and his glass handed to him.

Finally, seating himself behind his desk opposite Douglas with his glass of wine in hand, Barber began.

'Mr Farquhar will be officially taking up his appointment as Governor of Bombay tomorrow morning. His predecessor was kind enough to bring us both up to date with current affairs here.' He took a sip of his wine with what seemed to Douglas to be painstaking slowness before continuing. 'It seems we have a bit of a mystery. Several ships of the East India

Company have disappeared over the last few months, both going to and from Bombay. The current Governor thought it prudent to despatch the Company's flagship, the *Earl of Mornington* of twenty-four guns, along with another of their warships, the *Otter* of eighteen guns, to patrol to the southward for one month to see if they could sight anything. Unfortunately these two ships are now over a week late themselves in returning to report.'

'Pirates, sir?' suggested Douglas.

'Unlikely,' replied Barber. 'Certainly there are no pirates in this region who have the strength to overpower the *Earl of Mornington* or the *Otter*, if in fact these two have been taken. Doubtless they will turn up soon safe and well, but the Governor is under pressure from the East India Company to resolve the matter. Therefore I have agreed to proceed to the south immediately and cruise for two weeks in search of them.'

'I see, sir.'

Douglas knew very well that Captain Barber's orders required him to return to England 'with all despatch' once they had delivered Mr Farquhar and completed their stores again.

'We still have sufficient stores for a short cruise?' Barber asked, following Douglas's own train of thought.

'Yes, sir. Beef and pork for a month at least.'

'Water?'

'Six weeks on full rations.' Douglas felt relieved that he had been studying the purser's reports only the day before, so that the answers came without hesitation.

'Very well then. We shall weigh anchor at first light tomorrow. The men's shore leave shall have to wait until we return.'

'Aye aye, sir.'

Douglas drained his glass and rose from his chair.

'I will make the necessary preparations now, sir, if you will excuse me.'

He walked out of the cabin, leaving Captain Barber looking out of the stern windows at the approaching dusk, silently pondering these new, unexpected events.

The next day at dawn the *Amazon* weighed anchor and crept out of the bay, swapping salutes with the fort as she went. An expectant buzz of excitement had swept round the ship once the crew had found out there was a possibility of action and prize money ahead, even if it did put an end to all possibility of shore leave for the present.

In a service where monotony and routine were prevalent, the thought of action – even with all its possibilities of death or mutilation – gave men a spring in their step, almost as if they considered it as a reward for their months of dutiful obedience. Or so it seemed to Fury as he carefully observed the men on watch go about their business of setting or taking in sail as the conditions demanded.

In his own case he was unsure, not having seen any kind of action before. He plied the second lieutenant, Mr Scott, almost continuously during their first watch together after standing south. Scott had seen action some years before against the French during the American war. Fury listened with growing scepticism, quietly dismissing the vast majority of what he was told, believing Scott was exaggerating when he spoke of the dreadful noise and smells and sights that could be expected.

Nevertheless, the seeds were sown, and Fury found himself wondering whether he would be able to stand it. He could not quite distinguish whether it was physical fear which was worrying him – the thought of suffering serious injury or death was quite alarming – or whether it was more the fear of letting down his captain and the rest of the men when the moment came.

He spent some time during that first day out of Bombay trying to analyse this, but to no avail, eventually giving up and throwing himself into his duties and his studies to keep his mind occupied.

The first few days of their passage south also saw a gradual decline in the men's excitement as the contrary weather sucked it from them. Southerly winds – unusual in that part of the world – reduced the *Amazon* to beating southward close-hauled, clawing her way to windward inch by inch.

On the fourth day, just before dawn, they lost the wind altogether and lay becalmed. Barber immediately ordered all the boats out to tow the *Amazon* along – backbreaking work for the men as Fury witnessed first hand, sitting in the stern sheets of the second cutter, watching as the men strained every sinew at the oars for little or no visible gain, the relentless sun blistering the backs of those careless enough to dispense with their shirts.

Just prior to sunset a cat's-paw of wind was sighted by the mainmast lookout, the report of which sent the men to sheets and braces, eager to trim the yards in time to get the most from the breeze. What breeze there was came from the west, steadily increasing so that by dawn the next morning they were bowling along southward with the wind abeam, making over eight knots.

It stayed like that for the rest of the journey – seven days – until finally they reached the position that Captain Barber had decided to be the most suitable place to cruise. It was at this point that Barber ordered the men's daily gun drill to be increased, whether to keep them busy and break the daily monotony, or because he seriously expected some action, Fury could only guess. Whatever the reason, Fury, stationed in temporary command of Lieutenant Carlisle's division of main deck guns while Carlisle was in the sick bay with a debilitating fever, could see that the men enjoyed it, particularly when allowed to fire off a round or two at one of the empty casks dropped overboard for target practice. The times between reloading for each broadside gradually diminished as the hours of training bore fruit. The reduction was also roughly in line with the decline in the men's optimism as the days passed and no pirate or other enemy was sighted.

'Sail ho!'

The shouted report came early in the afternoon watch on the tenth day of their search, as the *Amazon* ploughed along to the west with a quartering wind. Fury, standing on the quarterdeck as the shout came down from the foremast lookout, could sense immediately the buzz of excitement around the ship.

'Four points off the larboard bow,' continued the lookout, 'heading north. There may be another sail abaft her!'

Fury watched silently as Captain Barber gave the orders which saw the *Amazon* alter course to the sou'west to intercept the strange sails. The speed with which they converged on the two vessels – for two of them there were – meant that they were visible to the naked eye after only a short time. Not long after came another shout from the man aloft.

'They're both flying East India Company colours, sir! The front one looks like a merchantman. The sail abaft her looks like she could be a sloop – maybe the *Otter*!'

Fury smiled inwardly at the groans from some of the men at this news that the ships were friendly. Or was it relief? He could not tell. He remained where he was nevertheless, hoping to be on hand if the captain wanted any officers to go aboard the *Otter* for news.

Slowly they approached, Barber waiting until they were no more than half a mile away before ordering the *Amazon* back on to her original westerly course. The East India Company ships altered course to somewhere north of west in response, so that they were converging on the *Amazon* and would eventually be close enough that Barber could use a speaking trumpet to converse with the lead ship.

It did not take long before they were within a quarter of a mile of them, so close in fact that Fury could see an officer standing on the deck of the lead ship waving gaily at them. He waved back, staring so intently at the little figure that he did not register the movement along her hull which signified the opening of her starboard gun ports.

Chapter Four

The thunderous roar of a broadside echoed across the turquoise water, shattering the silence. Fury stared across in disbelief at the lead ship, just emerging from the smoke of that first salvo as the sou'easterly wind whipped it away. Almost immediately another broadside came crashing into the *Amazon*, sending showers of splinters scything across the decks.

Confusion and terror momentarily paralysed the young midshipman as he stood watching the merchantman by the larboard quarterdeck bulwark, so much so that it took him some moments to realise that there was no new smoke emerging from her gun ports, indeed as far as he could recall she had not yet run out her guns again after her initial broadside. Where had the second broadside come from?

He spun round to see the dull outline of her consort, presumably the East India Company sloop *Otter*, ranging up on the larboard quarter about a cable's length distant, the sharpness of her features dulled by the smoke from that last broadside as it passed ahead of her towards the *Amazon*, obscuring his view somewhat.

He looked up above the smoke at her masthead to see that the East India Company's ensign had now been replaced by a flag he had never seen before, presumably raised at the last possible moment before firing to provide legitimacy to the attack.

Only a few moments had passed since that first broadside had bellowed out, but it seemed like hours to Fury, and he guiltily realised he had done nothing but stand stock still the whole time. His first sight of action since joining the navy nearly fifteen months before, and here he was in a state of terror with not a thought about his duty.

He tried to regulate his breathing in an effort to calm himself. Strangely, the face of Midshipman Roxborough floated into his head. He swept the image aside hurriedly, struggling for clear thought. What was it the captain had told him when he had first joined the *Amazon*? A good officer should always lead by example. No matter what the situation, always stay calm and never stop thinking.

His brain was clearing now and he was becoming aware of shouts about the deck – not in panic, but with a cool, calm authority. His heart was racing and his body tensed to avoid shaking uncontrollably. With a deep breath he slowly released his grip on the larboard bulwark and turned inboard to make his way towards the quarterdeck ladder leading down to the main gun deck, which was his station in battle under the command of Lieutenant Scott. Even as he walked – calmly, deliberately, so as not to betray the nervousness he was feeling – his mind was racing.

He looked across at his uncle, Captain Barber, who was now standing by the wheel, still shouting the orders that sent the men to their quarters and turned the *Amazon* into what would be a formidable adversary given a chance. Even outnumbered two to one, the enemy would stand little chance against a thirty-two-gun frigate, albeit one of the older twelve-pounder classes.

Their first attacker was a merchantman, not a ship of war, even if she did look like one of the larger ones – he spared her another glance – almost as big as the *Amazon* herself. Her guns were placed there more as a deterrent against small privateers than as an effective defence against a trained warship. As for the sloop – he turned to get another glimpse of her – he could see she had nine ports on each side. One of the new eighteen-gun ship rigged sloops, probably carrying twenty-four-pounder carronades. Still no match for the *Amazon*, at least not on her own.

The enemy must have been hoping to rely on the element of surprise to gain enough of an advantage to enable them to overpower the *Amazon* before they could mount an effective defence. That being the case, they had opened fire a little too early to take full advantage, allowing Captain Barber just enough time to get the men to quarters.

Still, if they could close quickly with *Amazon*, bringing some of those great twenty-four-pound smashers into use – tearing through two feet of solid timber from thirty yards – then board from different sides to divide *Amazon*'s forces . . . Fury dragged his mind away from the thought; the result didn't bear thinking about. Whatever their tactics, they would need to be pretty well manned to stand a chance against the two hundred or so crew that the *Amazon* was carrying according to last Sunday's muster.

He reached the top of the quarterdeck ladder at last, the bile already beginning to rise in his throat. His fear was gripping him tightly, and he was suddenly afraid he would suffer the ignominy of vomiting in full view of the quarterdeck. He stood aside to let the last of the gun crews up whose job it was to man the quarterdeck six-pounders.

More loud roars, becoming more ragged this time as the faster gun crews reloaded before their fellows, told him that the merchantman was commencing with her second broadside. Screams erupted nearby. He turned to see a seaman writhing on the deck, clutching grotesquely at one of his legs which was no longer there as the blood flowed from the stump into a growing pool on deck. Strange that the only thing Fury could think of was how upset the first lieutenant would be when he saw the stain on his usually pristine deck. More crashes, this time accompanied by the sickening sound of tearing wood, and he was suddenly staggering sideways, trying in vain to keep on his feet as the deck came up to meet him.

Oak, best British oak – Fury examined the grain as he lay there, a slightly disconcerting feeling arising as he began to wonder why it was turning red. He turned his mind away from the texture of the wood and tried to focus on the source of the wound. A faint recollection of a sharp pain under his mouth before he was knocked off his feet brought his hand up to his chin – he could feel a loose flap of skin there, and the hand that he brought away was warm with blood.

'Sir . . . sir – are you all right, sir?'

The voice seemed to come from somewhere above and Fury rolled over to find a seaman stooping over him, a look of genuine concern on his face.

'Yes – yes, I think so,' he replied, allowing himself to be helped to his feet. A sharp pain shot through his head. Had he hit his head on the deck?

'Just a small splinter wound, sir. T'aint nothing more than a scratch,' the man reassured him.

Fury suddenly realised that this was the first time one of the crew had shown him a kindness, and he opened his mouth to utter his thanks, but he was too late. The man had already hurried off to his station at the quarterdeck guns.

As Fury stood there gingerly checking the rest of his limbs, a slow rumbling from below suggested at least one gun crew was at work and preparing to fire. The sound of it recalled his thoughts guiltily back to his duty, so he hurriedly descended the quarterdeck ladder to the main gun deck, not even realising his feeling of nausea had vanished.

He passed the marine drummer – little more than a boy – still standing at the foot of the ladder and banging out the slow beat that always accompanied the men's rush to their allotted battle stations. Another deafening roar invaded his senses, this time much closer at hand and accompanied by a tongue of flame and the violent recoil of one of the main deck twelve-pounders on the larboard side. The remaining gun crews on the larboard side were in various stages of loading, helped by the crews of the unused starboard side as Fury picked his way along the deck and finally sought out Lieutenant Scott.

'Ah, Mr Fury! Good of you to join us at last,' Scott said, sarcastically. 'Well, you've been itching for some action for months, but I'll wager you'll have had your bellyful before this day is out – if we live to see it!' He rubbed his hands as though in glee, Fury noting his eyes light up in anticipation before he continued. 'Take charge of Mr Carlisle's division and fire as they bear – but mark you, Mr Fury, remember what you've been taught and make sure each shot counts.

Aim for the hull and if I see any wild shooting I'll make sure the gun captain is flogged tomorrow!'

'Aye aye, sir,' Fury gulped, remembering suddenly that Lieutenant Carlisle was still incapacitated with fever.

He walked forward to join his division while subconsciously going through the gun drill, more to keep his mind busy than anything else. He approached the foremost section of guns just as most of the crews were toiling to run them out preparatory to firing them for the first time in anger since he had been aboard.

'Right men!' he shouted, grateful to have something to concentrate on at last aside from the thoughts of death and mutilation. 'You all know the drill. Gun captains, aim for the hull and fire on the down roll.' One or two irritated glances were flashed his way, but Fury was unaware of such trivialities.

He walked to the nearest open gun port and peered out, seeing their first assailant, the merchantman, about a cable's length away.

'There she is, lads – concentrate on her and we'll take care of *Otter* later. All ready?'

A small pause while each of the gun captains nodded their agreement as the rest of the crews backed away from the recoil path of the guns.

'As they bear . . . fire!'

Fury just managed to remember in time to jump out of the way himself as the guns spurted orange tongues and leapt back against the restraining breech ropes like wild beasts, the smoke from the discharges being blown back through the ports, blotting out any sun streaming in through the open ports and stinging the eyes with the sulphurous vapours.

'Sponge out,' he coughed, suddenly wishing he had a neckerchief tied around his ears like the rest of the crews to block out the deafening thunder.

He watched through the thinning smoke as the sponges were rammed down to the bottom of the chambers and twisted to ensure no still burning embers remained, before being withdrawn. His eyes were streaming from the smoke and stinging fiercely.

'Reload!'

The cartridges were taken out of the wooden containers brought up from the powder room by the powder monkeys, inserted into the muzzles and rammed home. Next came the first wad, followed swiftly by the twelve-pound balls, the smoothest and roundest that could be found from the shot garlands, rolled in to rest on the wad before the second wads were inserted and rammed home to stop the cannon from tumbling out of the muzzle as the ship pitched and rolled. The gun captains now took over, pricking the cartridges down through the touchholes, before pouring powder down the hole from their powder horns.

'Run out!'

The men threw their weight on the gun tackles to haul the guns out of the ports by main force, while others stood by with crowbars and handspikes to train the guns round on to their target once again.

'Cock your locks!'

Everyone stood back, the gun captains holding the lanyards attached to the locks to fire the guns, waiting for the order.

'Ready . . . fire!'

As if in one smooth movement each gun captain tugged at the lanyard and the guns belched fire and smoke once again. The men automatically set about reloading at a frantic pace, eager to fire as many rounds as possible into their first adversary before she left their arc of fire.

'Men – fire when ready!'

It was now that all those hours of practice bore fruit, and Fury was thankful for it. The constant drills allowed the crews to perform their tasks like automata, leaving Fury able to walk over to the nearest gun port once again to check the condition and location of the enemy ships.

Such an invigorating feeling as he thrust his head out through the gun port and sucked in the clean, fresh air while glancing slightly astern. *Otter* had by now sheeted home her courses to narrow the distance between the protagonists, the weather tack of the main course clewed up to prevent it blanketing the fore course as she brought the wind back on to her larboard quarter after yawing to fire her second broadside. Second broadside! Fury was shocked to realise that he had not even noticed the second broadside, so intent had he been on the job in hand.

He shifted his gaze over to their immediate target, the merchantman. No more attention was needed towards *Otter* for the moment – the aftmost gun crews would give her a hot reception as soon as their guns would bear.

The merchantman was still about a cable's length away broad on the larboard beam, under topsails only and seemingly content to trade broadsides with the *Amazon*. Even after two broadsides he could see they had hit her hull several times, jagged holes having appeared near the waterline. Two of her foremost gun ports looked like one big hole as numerous shot had smashed into the same area, piercing the hull and possibly knocking the guns out of action while killing or maiming God knows how many men on its path of destruction. Even as Fury watched, some of the empty ports began filling as the crews ran the guns out again for another deadly broadside.

'Lord, for what we are about to receive . . .' he thought grimly.

He was startled as a hand gently touched his shoulder, only just having the sense to keep his head from hitting the top of the gun port as he turned inboard to see the gun captain of number four gun grimacing at him with sweat pouring down his face, the rag tied round his head preventing it from getting into his eyes.

'Begging yer pardon, sir, but we'm ready to run out agin now, sir.'

'Yes, yes, of course,' Fury replied quickly, standing aside to enable the crew to haul the gun out again prior to firing.

Clearly number four gun had one of the more efficient gun crews working her, as the rest of his division were still in varying stages of reloading after their last broadside. The gun captain stood aside, lanyard in hand, ready to fire.

A distant bellow was followed by what seemed to Fury like a full minute of silence, then the whole ship's side nearby appeared to disintegrate in a shower of splinters, a sharp twang sounding as the ball hit number four gun, lifting it off its trucks and flinging it aside into the waiting gun crew. The ball itself must have ricocheted off its course but Fury had no idea in which direction.

He wondered why the gun captain was still standing there, lanyard in hand, when there was no longer a gun to fire. It took some moments to realise the man no longer had a head – taken clean off at the neck by the last deflected shot. Fury wondered for a moment if by some absurd freak of nature the man was still alive, standing there as he was like some grotesque, headless statue. That thought was dashed seconds later as he finally dropped to the deck in a heap, blood swelling from that gaping hole in his neck.

More crashes and screams around told him the rest of the enemy's broadside was doing its work as he quickly shouted orders to the remaining crews in his division.

'You men, avast there – get that gun secured at once!'

He pointed towards number four gun which was still on top of two of its former servers, one of whom was screaming in agony as he looked at what was left of his crushed legs, the other silent, the life squeezed out of him.

The men hurried to work on securing the dismounted gun; the terrifying thought of twenty-nine hundredweight of iron rolling about the deck, knocking men over like skittles, was a powerful incentive. Lucky that the weather was fine and so there was not much of a sea running, but even so Fury was shocked to realise that a small part of him was actually feeling a little grateful that the gun was kept steadier by the men it was lying on.

He looked around at the rest of the men in his division, endless drill at the guns ensuring that throughout all this carnage and confusion they were still efficiently reloading and firing their charges, while all around them former messmates, friends, lay dead or wounded.

'Hopkins – take Johnson and get these bodies out of the way of the guns, then see the wounded are taken below to the cockpit.'

'Aye aye, sir,' Hopkins replied, the two men from the starboard watch abandoning their work assisting the crew of number six gun, larboard side, and getting to work on clearing the deck.

Fury walked over to the nearest water butt and thrust his head into it to try and clear his brain, the water immediately stinging his chin to remind him of the wound he had received during the first broadsides. He stood up and tried to shake the water off, feeling slightly more refreshed even though his head still hurt like the very devil as he shook it.

'Sir!'

Who on earth was this pestering him now? Could no one leave him alone for even a second? He turned round to see one of the quarter gunners – what was his name? Jenkins, that was it – facing him.

'Yes, Jenkins, what is it?'

'It's Mr Scott, sir – he was cut in two by a shot from the last broadside.'

'My God!'

It was not so much the shock of hearing that Lieutenant Scott had been killed which brought forth the exclamation, but the realisation that he was now in command of the gun deck until the captain saw fit to replace him.

'Very well, Jenkins, thank you,' he replied.

The effort it took to keep control of himself and appear calm after his initial outburst helped to steady his nerves, and by the time Jenkins had knuckled his forehead and made his way aft back to his gun, Fury was fully in control again.

More crashes close at hand told him all of the larboard gun crews were firing as their guns bore, aided by the crews of the unused starboard batteries. Fury's brain, working feverishly, could think of no further orders which needed to be given immediately, so he started to make his way aft.

Reaching the waist, he paused to look up at the set of the sails, stark and clear against the cloudless blue sky. *Amazon* was now under topsails alone. The captain must have ordered reduced sail as soon as the attacks started, because when he had been on the quarterdeck she had had her fore and main course set also, as well as the outer jib.

He caught sight of Marsden, the most junior of the six midshipmen on board *Amazon*, as he passed the waist. He was little more than about thirteen years old and looked a pathetic sight, standing there out of the way of the gun crews with smoke-blackened features and tears rolling down his cheeks. He had joined the *Amazon* just prior to her leaving Portsmouth nearly six months back and he was obviously completely lost and terrified in the current situation. Sympathy suddenly swept over Fury and he knew the best thing for the boy was to be kept busy.

'Mr Marsden!' he shouted.

'Ye–yes, John?' the boy stammered in reply.

'Lieutenant Scott has been killed and I am now in command of the gun deck. I shall need a messenger to pass word to the captain. Do you think you are up to it, Mr Marsden?'

Funny that until recently he and Marsden had played together in the midshipmen's berth along with the other 'young gentlemen', and now here he was talking to the youngster as if he were his father.

'Yes, sir, I can do it.' The 'sir' seemed to slide off Marsden's tongue with no effort whatsoever.

'Very well then. My compliments to the captain and please inform him that Lieutenant Scott is dead, and I have taken command of the main deck batteries until I receive further orders.'

'Aye aye, sir,' Marsden replied, turning away towards the ladder leading up to the quarterdeck.

'Mr Marsden!' Fury shouted, making the boy turn round abruptly. 'It is customary to repeat the message back to ensure there is no confusion.'

'Yes, sir. Your compliments to the captain, and Lieutenant Scott has been killed, leaving you in command of the main deck guns until further orders.'

'Very good, Mr Marsden, carry on.'

It was good to see that the child who went up to the quarterdeck was no longer crying and looked much more in control of himself. Fury was glad that he had trusted him with the task. His uncle had been right, he thought – it was always better to lead men rather than drive them. Now all he had to do was ensure the guns were fired efficiently until he received further orders from the captain.

Fury made his way to the nearest gun port and pushed his head through, squinting at the brightness of the sun reflecting on the water. He could see the merchantman clearly, still abeam and possibly head reaching slightly, but making no visible attempt either to close or disengage. Her hull was scarred and holed, showing where she had been hit by *Amazon*'s broadsides. Even as he watched, one or two of her guns were fired, much more raggedly than before, betraying the damage she had suffered. He could not see where the balls landed – certainly not in the *Amazon*'s hull – but some faint tearing noises from above told him they had probably been aimed at the rigging and had shot holes in some of the topsails.

He looked further aft at the *Otter*, now under topsails and jib like her consort, and now much further forward than her last position, so much so that *Amazon*'s aftmost guns were traversed as far round as possible and were trying to reach her – unsuccessfully at the moment judging by the look of the splashes just in front of her bows, gently rising and falling as she ploughed forward. It would not be long now before she was in range, Fury judged, beginning to turn inboard again.

He abandoned his turn and quickly thrust his head back out of the port. Something had caught his eye just as he had turned away. He looked again over at *Otter* – was there something? Yes! She was gradually coming before the wind. He watched as her bow turned slowly until it was pointing straight towards him in the *Amazon*, her bowsprit and jib boom extending out and upwards in front of her. Round and round she came, bringing the wind on to her starboard side, the men at the braces hauling to bring her yards round sharp up on the new tack. It was perfectly obvious to Fury what her plan was – it had been obvious as soon as he had seen her bows begin to swing. She was now sailing at right angles to *Amazon* and, if things remained the way they were at present, it would not be long before she intersected their wake, leaving the *Amazon*'s stern vulnerable to a deadly raking broadside which would sweep down the whole length of the deck, carrying away anything which it found in its murderous path.

He turned inboard again, feeling suddenly impotent. There was absolutely nothing he could do to stop it – his responsibility ended with ensuring the guns were fired. He could have no influence whatsoever on the handling of the *Amazon*. It occurred to him that the thought of that raking broadside sweeping the deck after the carnage he had witnessed from just a single ball left him strangely unmoved. Perhaps his initial fear at the beginning of the action was more due to the fact that he did not know what to expect. Most people's fears stemmed from ignorance – the unknown. Now he had seen action he knew exactly what to expect – he knew that a cannonball swept aside men with no regard for rank or colour or nationality. If it was his time next, there would be nothing he could do to stop it, except hope it was mercifully quick.

'Sir, sir!'

Here was young Marsden rushing towards him as if the hounds of hell were on his tail. He must have come straight from the captain on the quarterdeck.

'Yes, Mr Marsden, what is it?'

'The captain sends his respects, sir, and he will be hauling our wind shortly to pass between *Otter* and her consort, and would be obliged if you could have both larboard and starboard guns loaded and run out.'

'Very well, Mr Marsden, thank you.' Fury stopped himself from turning away as he remembered one last point. 'Is he sending another officer to command the guns, Mr Marsden?'

'I'm sorry, sir, he said he couldn't spare anyone at the present time, but he is confident you will do your duty.'

'Thank you, Mr Marsden,' he replied, trying to make it sound as if he had just been told his supper was ready, and not that he was now responsible for the entire deck – men, guns and all. 'It would be best if you were to remain alongside me for the remainder of the action, Mr Marsden. I may need more messages delivering to the captain.'

'Aye aye, sir,' Marsden replied, trying hard to conceal his relief at being allowed to remain with his messmate.

*   *   *

Captain Barber stood by the wheel, hands thrust behind his back and legs apart to balance himself as the *Amazon* gently pitched and rose through the clear Indian Ocean, a creamy wake leading aft the only evidence of where she had come from. His demeanour bespoke a man of confidence. Confidence in himself, in his ship and, most importantly of all, in his men. It was borne from years of drill, years of discipline, of backbreaking work, and it was so engrained now that Barber took it for granted.

He looked up frequently at the set of the sails and felt the wind on his face, using all his years of experience to judge the right moment for the manoeuvre. The *Otter*'s attempt to cut across *Amazon*'s stern had been poorly timed. She had been much too far to windward when she changed course, meaning that there would be several minutes before she reached the *Amazon*'s path, ample time for the *Amazon* to counter the move. All his initial orders had been given as soon as he saw the *Otter*'s head swinging slowly towards them, and the men now stood by their stations, ready for the orders which would bring the *Amazon* round close-hauled on the larboard tack.

'Ease down the helm,' he growled to the quartermaster standing by the wheel.

The quartermaster gradually turned the spokes of the wheel through his fingers and the *Amazon*'s head began to swing round, heading more and more towards the merchantman, still surging along and firing ragged broadsides. The jib sheets were eased off and the men were busy hauling on braces to bring the yards round as the *Amazon*'s head turned closer to the wind.

'Helm's a-lee, sir,' said the quartermaster finally as the rudder was put as far over as it would lie.

'Ease off fore topsail sheets there!' shouted Barber, the fore topsail immediately spilling the wind, giving the *Amazon* still more turning power as she came up close-hauled on the larboard tack.

Another shouted command from Barber moments later saw the fore topsail sheeted home once again, the sails shivering slightly as she got a little too close to the wind, before the quartermaster eased off slightly and reported to the captain.

'Full and bye, sir.'

'Very good, keep her at that.'

The *Amazon* and *Otter* were now on opposite courses, about half a cable's length from each other. The *Otter* had no choice now but to remain on her present course until the *Amazon* had passed. Any attempt to manoeuvre would expose her vulnerable bow or stern to a raking broadside from the *Amazon*. Barber raised his glass to his eye and looked forward to where the merchantman was still ploughing along. She was fine on the *Amazon*'s starboard bow now and Barber could see her name emblazoned across her stern – *Bedford*. He snapped his glass shut, aware that all he could do now was wait.

The starboard side gun crews hurried across from the larboard side as Fury gave the orders for loading and running out the starboard battery. The muzzle lashings which kept the guns securely fixed to eyebolts just above the port lids were taken off, while the quoins were pushed in to depress the gun barrels allowing the guns to clear the opened ports, thus showing the *Amazon*'s full set of teeth. The lead aprons over the touchholes were removed and the tompions were taken from the mouths of the guns, while men from each crew laid out all the equipment they would need to serve their pieces – handspikes, sponges and worms.

'Larboard side crews!' shouted Fury. 'I want all guns double-shotted, half-charge. Starboard side crews – guns single-shotted only.'

The larboard side would pass the *Otter* far closer than the starboard side would pass the *Bedford*, which would be sailing away from the *Amazon*. Fury had spent months poring over his copy of Falconer's *Marine Dictionary* and knew very well that double-shotting the guns was only useful for short-range gunnery as the two balls interacting inside the barrel were likely to throw the aim off.

He walked over again to the nearest gun port on the larboard side and looked out to see *Otter* up ahead and surging towards them, her bow slicing gracefully through the turquoise waters. It would not be long now before the two ships crossed.

'Larboard side guns – stand by to fire as your guns bear!'

The men were all stood by their guns, ready for the word. Complete silence reigned as the gun captains stooped, lanyards in hand, ready for the *Otter* to appear in their sights. Boom! The forwardmost gun fired, followed swiftly by the next, until the whole battery had unleashed a rippling broadside, the guns leaping back in recoil and threatening to tear across the deck until stopped by the straining breech ropes. Fury could hear the more distant roar of the *Otter*'s carronades, followed almost immediately by crashes and screams closer at hand as the huge twenty-four-pound balls came smashing into *Amazon*'s hull.

The first crews to fire were frantically reloading in an attempt to fire again before the *Otter* passed, but Fury knew it would be too late – the *Otter* heading on an opposite course would be gone far too quickly. He peered out at her. Even after one broadside, albeit double-shotted, she showed visible signs of damage, particularly to her hull. It looked like the larboard rail on her tiny quarterdeck had been utterly destroyed, the flying splinters possibly scything down the officers stationed there.

As he turned away, he could see *Otter* beginning to wear round to bring her back into a position to engage *Amazon*, and he quickly dashed to the starboard side to look out of the nearest gun port there. There was *Bedford*, her side slowly shortening as the *Amazon* continued on course to cross her stern. He could not help but wonder why she made no attempt to turn and avoid the raking fire which she must know was to follow shortly.

'Steady, lads, steady. As you bear, and make each shot tell!' he shouted.

Again, the forwardmost gun barked out first as the *Amazon*'s bows crossed *Bedford*'s wake, followed by a series of heavy crashes from the rest of the guns as each one bore in turn. The stern windows of *Bedford* disappeared after the first shot, disintegrating instantly as the ball smashed through it on its murderous course along the full length of her deck. Fury was certain he could hear screams from across the water, even from this distance and over the sound of the *Amazon*'s broadside, as men were cut down, helpless at their guns, as the *Amazon* slowly passed.

He reached the aftmost gun having unconsciously run down the whole length of the main deck keeping pace with the firing, and he suddenly realised he was jumping up and down with joy as *Amazon* finally passed her – no, perhaps joy was not the right expression – intense satisfaction mixed with excitement maybe. Even so he was shocked. He had always thought of himself as compassionate, yet he did not feel a smidgen of emotion at the thought of those men across the water dead or dying.

He glanced around to find a number of the men at the guns were looking at him and grinning broadly, showing that his childish prancing had not gone unnoticed by at least some of them. He made an effort to pull himself together, his face turning crimson with embarrassment beneath the black powder burns. He strode off to the nearest gun port, cursing himself under his breath for his childishness. As he glanced out, he could see the *Amazon* was beginning to turn in an attempt to get abeam of the *Bedford* once again and engage, this time from windward. Still, it would not take *Otter* long to reach them again with a beam wind. Would it give *Amazon* enough time to finish off *Bedford* before the two could join forces again?

They had almost finished their turn now, the wind coming on to the larboard quarter once more. The captain must have ordered the helm put up as soon as they had passed *Bedford*'s stern. Already the guns from the starboard side were firing again, only this time the *Bedford* was able to reply, crashes from further forward and from aloft telling where she had struck as the *Amazon* ploughed along in an effort to get abreast of her in preparation for boarding.

Chapter Five

Fury became vaguely aware of someone at his side and turned around to find the familiar tanned face and distinctive yellow hair of Midshipman Turner, one of his messmates, whose station in action was on the quarterdeck alongside the captain.

'The captain sent me down with a message, John,' Turner said, looking around him at the damage and the bodies. 'We'll be luffing again shortly to avoid having the *Otter* crossing our stern and he'd like the larboard guns ready for firing as she comes up with us.'

'Larboard guns, aye, Patrick – thank you. Tell me, how are things up on deck? The view from here is limited unfortunately.'

'Well,' Turner replied, 'the captain and first lieutenant are pacing about as if they're on an afternoon stroll. We've taken some minor damage aloft – sheets parted, sails holed – that type of thing. They seem to be aiming more for the hull, but then,' looking around again, 'you probably know more about that than I do!'

'How does the *Bedford* look?'

'She looks pretty knocked about, as you'd expect, although

it's surprising how well she's firing still, all things considered. My God, John!' he suddenly exclaimed, 'you're damned lucky to be down here in command of the whole deck like this. Better than running back and forth for the captain like me, I'll warrant!' he added, a touch of envy creeping into his voice.

'Possibly,' Fury replied noncommittally, looking over at the remains of Lieutenant Scott, a bloodied mess distinguishable only by the stockings and buckled shoes he wore. 'Well,' he said, shaking off his sudden melancholy, 'you had better be getting back to the captain or he'll have you kissing the gunner's daughter tomorrow!'

'Aye, that he will,' Turner replied, grinning broadly. 'Take care, John!' he shouted as he headed back towards the quarterdeck ladder.

Fury turned back to the job at hand.

'Larboard crews!' he bellowed. 'Stand to your guns. We'll be luffing up alongside *Otter* presently and I want three broadsides in two minutes from every gun!' He looked significantly at his pocket watch to reinforce the order.

Looking out of the nearest starboard gun port he could see the *Bedford* was shooting ahead, already out of the arc of fire of the *Amazon*'s aftmost guns. He hurried to the waist and looked up to see that the main topsail yard had been hauled aback by the men at the braces. The *Amazon* had quickly lost headway as the captain had heaved her to, main topsail to the mast, most likely to avoid exposing her stern to the *Bedford*'s broadside as she turned to the wind to meet *Otter*. As he watched, the yard was braced sharp up again, the main topsail shaking as it passed through the eye of the wind before finally catching the wind and filling, sending the *Amazon* surging forward once more.

Minutes passed which seemed like hours as the captain allowed the *Amazon* to gain sufficient headway before ordering the quartermaster at the wheel to put the helm over to starboard, gradually sending her head towards the wind. Fury rushed over to the larboard side now to see *Otter* ranging up on the *Amazon*'s quarter, gradually coming up to them as *Amazon* steadied on her new course, the wind on the beam.

'Steady, lads, steady.'

The range was little more than pistol shot as *Otter* came up, ideal for those great twenty-four-pound carronades she carried. The next twenty or thirty seconds would be interesting, Fury thought, suddenly realising with a shock that he might not live that long.

'Fire as your guns bear!' he shouted, the sentence hardly finished before the first gun bellowed out, spitting fire and smoke. The deeper roar of the *Otter*'s carronades in reply was easily recognisable, followed shortly by the now familiar crashing noise as the balls tore through the *Amazon*'s wooden side, sending showers of deadly splinters twenty feet across the deck until stopped by something or somebody.

Smaller bangs, seemingly insignificant amid the general thunder of the great guns, told him that the marines were at work in the *Amazon*'s fighting tops, firing their muskets down at the men on *Otter*'s quarterdeck. The time seemed to be passing quickly now as *Amazon* and *Otter* sailed along side by side, broadsides crashing out in a melee of smoke and thunder, the deck heeling slightly to each discharge. It seemed to Fury that their rate of fire was markedly superior to their opponents', although the *Otter*'s larger carronades were doing their share of damage. He was amazed at how men could survive amid such carnage, with shot crashing into the hull and splinters flying in every direction.

'Mr Marsden.' He turned to the young midshipman who was still standing at his side like some faithful dog. 'Please give my compliments to the captain and—', his sentence was cut short as a large crash was followed instantaneously by the fragile body of the youngster being flung to the deck.

It took only a moment for Fury to reach him, bending down beside the stricken boy as he grasped the situation. What had presumably been a splinter had completely lacerated Marsden's stomach, Fury realising with horror that the bloody entrails lying on the deck next to him were the wretched boy's intestines. He was struggling to hang on to life for a few moments more, his face now white with loss of blood.

'John . . .'

He was almost too weak to speak, the words coming in a whisper. Fury knelt closer to hear him.

'Don't try to speak, Andrew. We'll get you to the surgeon as soon as possible', knowing even as he said it that it was hopeless.

'No need, John,' Marsden whispered, 'I'll not last much . . . longer. Write to . . . my . . . family will you . . . John? Tell them . . . I did my . . . duty.'

'Aye, I'll tell them, Andrew,' Fury replied, his own voice little more than a whisper.

'It's getting awfully . . . dark.' The last word was dragged out with a sigh as his last breath was forced from his limp body, his head finally lolling to one side.

Fury stood up slowly, oblivious to the crashes and the thunderous broadsides that still went on around him. His white cotton breeches were completely blood-soaked – Marsden's blood must have spread across the deck as he knelt down beside him. He had only been a few years younger than himself. Now he was dead, killed in some small action which probably wouldn't even get a mention in the *Gazette*. Fury could feel a sudden anger towards the enemy welling up inside him, as he took a last look at his friend.

'My God!'

The voice startled him and he turned around to see Midshipman Turner, standing staring at the body of Marsden with a look of wide-eyed horror on his face.

'The poor boy,' Turner muttered, seemingly unable to take his eyes away from the sight.

'Yes,' Fury replied absently, following the gaze of Turner. 'You have a message, Patrick?' he asked, recalling himself to his duty and looking at Turner.

'Yes.' Turner managed to tear his gaze away from young Marsden and back to Fury. 'The captain intends to go on board *Otter* soon, and would be obliged if all boarders could take their stations up on deck. You are to continue to fire until our men have boarded, at which time you are to man the starboard side guns in the event of the *Bedford* coming up alongside us.'

'Very well,' he replied, forcing a smile as he added, 'you'll get your chance of glory now, eh Patrick?'

'Hopefully, and not a moment too soon.'

Turner waved a farewell as he hurried back towards the companionway leading up to the quarterdeck, leaving Fury staring after him for a moment, wondering if he would see his friend again.

He turned to the crews serving the guns, trying to shake off his sudden morbid thoughts.

'First division of boarders,' he shouted, 'we will soon be boarding *Otter*! Take your positions up on deck.'

Simultaneously one or two men from each gun, who were also down as boarders on the ship's watch and quarter bill, left their guns and headed for the arms chest under the command of the master-at-arms. The crowd which gathered round the chest slowly diminished as men emerged carrying their own choice of weapon, most favouring the standard navy-issue cutlass, some others opting for the long pike or the tomahawk, before disappearing up the ladder to the quarterdeck to receive their final orders.

Fury was satisfied to note as he paced the deck behind the toiling crews that this transition took place with no noticeable slackening of fire. The fewer men who remained at the guns worked automatically to fire and reload as if it were instinctive, evidence that the endless hours of drill on the outward voyage were now bearing fruit. Sponge, reload, ram, run out, and fire. Over and over again they repeated the drill as the *Amazon* converged on *Otter*, slowly narrowing the gap. For the gun crews there was no longer any need to aim their guns now: the two ships were so close it was almost impossible to miss.

It looked to Fury as if he could reach out and touch *Otter*'s side as he stooped and peered out of one of the ports. Her hull seemed to fill the entire view, broken only by the open gun ports along her side, some of which remained empty as Fury continued to watch her. Possibly those guns had been dismounted by *Amazon*'s twelve-pounders, or maybe she just didn't have enough men to serve all the guns and repel an attack by boarders. Fury neither knew nor cared.

He staggered slightly as *Amazon* finally scraped alongside

her, wild cheering coming from the deck above as the boarders prepared to attack, waiting for the men at the yardarms to secure them to *Otter* so the ships would not drift apart, before jumping down on to the enemy's deck, hacking and thrusting for dear life.

'One more, lads!' he shouted, eager to squeeze another broadside into her before *Amazon*'s own men on her deck would prevent him from firing again.

This last broadside was fired almost simultaneously, *Amazon* heaving up her side to the recoil of the guns.

'Secure the guns!' he shouted. 'Starboard side crews! Stand to your guns, but don't run them out!'

The men of the starboard watch rushed over to the starboard side to man their guns in preparation to receive *Bedford* if she tried to aid her consort, the rest of the larboard crews finally joining them as they finished securing their own guns.

By leaving the guns inboard, there was a chance that he could fool the captain of the *Bedford* into thinking the starboard side was not manned, seeing only a row of empty ports along her side. It would not be an unreasonable assumption by the *Bedford*'s captain, given that *Amazon* was currently locked together with *Otter* and engaged in a boarding action with her. It was most likely *Bedford* would try and come up without being detected, before attempting to board. Fury walked over towards the foremost section of guns, his idea beginning to develop as he walked.

'Right, men,' he said calmly, 'I want you to load with round shot and aim for her hull.'

He turned and made his way further aft.

'You men,' he said, addressing the aftmost section, 'I want

you to load with grape on top of round shot. As she approaches she will likely have men gathered on her upper deck and bulwarks ready to board. You are to aim for these men. Any questions?'

Silence.

'Very well then, carry on,' he ordered, beginning to pace the deck as the men loaded their guns.

Being bowsed together with *Otter* provided a much steadier platform for gunnery and there should be no excuse for the crews not to hit their targets. He strode over to a port and craned his head round to see *Bedford* beating up towards them. How long before she would be up with *Amazon*? Twenty minutes perhaps, he thought. He turned inboard to where the crews had now finished loading their guns.

'Lads!' He raised his voice to address the whole battery. 'No one shall run out or fire until I give the order. After that, fire at will. Understood?'

Nodding heads and murmurs of agreement told him the men knew what to do. There was nothing more he could do now but wait while the battle raged nearby.

With the great guns silent, Fury could clearly hear the clash of steel on steel as the boarders fought like madmen on *Otter*'s deck, intermingled with the occasional pop-pop of small arms as men loosed off pistols point-blank, the only really effective range for the inaccurate navy-issue pistol.

Another, different sound closer at hand. What on earth was that? He turned round to follow it and saw men beginning to climb in through *Amazon*'s larboard gun ports from the *Otter*.

'Men!' he screamed, almost in a panic. 'Repel boarders!'

The crews looked round startled as Fury made the journey to the arms chest in a few bounds. Stooping and reaching down into the chest he felt his fingers close round a pistol and he pulled it out, drawing his dirk from its scabbard at the same time and rushing over to the larboard side where men were emerging from two or three ports, cutlasses in hand.

A terrible feeling of loneliness was all he was conscious of as the first man came lunging towards him, his face disappearing in a bloody mess as Fury instinctively discharged the pistol at point-blank range. No time to think as the next man came at him swinging his cutlass down towards Fury's head, stopped just in time by Fury's raised dirk, the shock of the impact jarring down his arm. Without even thinking, he brought his left hand, still holding the heavy pistol, crashing onto the side of the man's head with a sharp crack. The man dropped like a stone to the deck.

A feeling of relief poured over him as he sensed men at his side now, cutlasses in hand, lunging at the swell of boarders in front of them. Screams and grunts could be heard as men were cut down on both sides. A third man had now come towards him, also armed with a cutlass, a fierce grin on his swarthy face, eyes glowering like a madman's. He paused for only a second before lunging at Fury, arm and cutlass outstretched, point first. Fury had just enough time to step to the right, parrying the cutlass thrust with his own dirk, before swinging the dirk diagonally downwards towards the base of the man's neck at the shoulder. The man was either overcome with fighting madness or else a fool. Fully stretched, his arm extended forward, he did not stand a chance of parrying the swinging dirk as it came down, Fury's arm jarring a second time as the blade sliced through muscle and tissue and bit on the man's collarbone, his screams continuing as he hit the deck.

Fury stood over him, desperately trying to wrench free the blade from the man's collarbone, a sudden movement to his right causing him to look up where another boarder was just beginning to swing his cutlass down towards Fury's head. Releasing his grip on the dirk, he instinctively threw his hands up in a fruitless effort to protect his head, waiting for the killer blow. The close sound of clashing steel followed and, realising he was still alive, he looked up to see that a second blade had parried the man's swing, a seaman thrusting him backwards with brute strength. Fury recognised the man's black hair and huge frame even from the back – Clark, an able seaman in one of the starboard gun crews.

The boarder lunged again at Clark, his cutlass slashing down as before but Clark was too fast, bringing his own blade up as he stepped to the side, slicing open the man's wrist. The cutlass immediately fell to the deck as the nerves in his wrist were severed; his slow glance from his bloody wrist to where Clark stood showed first anger and then fear as he realised he was now defenceless. His gasp as the cutlass point was thrust into his stomach and withdrawn sounded as loud to Fury as the twelve-pound cannon he had been firing, the man slowly dropping to his knees with a look of shock on his face as he stared at his wound, before finally pitching forward on to his face.

Managing at last to wrench his dirk free and nodding his thanks to Clark, Fury turned to discover the fight was over almost as quickly as it had begun. All the boarders, probably around twenty of them, lay on the deck, either dead or badly wounded. The *Amazon* had lost about ten men as far as he could make out, no quarter being asked or given.

'Right, men,' he panted, 'stand to your guns.'

He walked over to the starboard side once more, trying to regain his breath after the last intense struggle. He peered out through the nearest gun port to find the *Bedford* was much, much closer, perhaps half a cable's length away and on a sharply converging course.

'Not long now, lads!' he shouted, half turning as he noticed a rag of a boy awaiting his attention.

'Please, sir. The captain's respects and *Bedford* will be up with us shortly. The starboard battery is to fire as they bear, and he would be obliged if you would send up the second division of boarders.'

'Very well.' Fury turned away to address his gun crews. 'Second division of boarders!' he bellowed. 'Arm yourselves and join the captain on the quarterdeck for further orders!'

A group of men began to move away from the guns towards the arms chest.

'Wait!' he shouted, pausing as they stopped and looked at him. A thought had just occurred to him. 'When you reach the quarterdeck, stay low. I don't want anyone from *Bedford* seeing you too early. Understood? Carry on!'

It would heighten the surprise if *Bedford* was completely unaware that *Amazon* was ready and waiting for them. A large group of boarders standing waiting on the quarterdeck would give the game away as surely as running out the guns too early.

The second division of boarders were filing up the companion ladder now, leaving the remaining crews to wait in silence, the years of strict navy discipline and training taking effect. They were short-handed now that both divisions of boarders had been called, but they had just sufficient to man the guns on one side.

Fury peered out of the port once more from a couple of feet inboard, fearful lest a watchful eye on *Bedford* should see his head poking out of the gun port. He was startled to see how much nearer she was now, probably only fifty yards away.

'Stand by, men! Get ready to run out!'

Fury waited, judging the right time to give the order so that the surprise would be complete.

'Run out!' he shouted. The crews immediately threw their weight on the gun tackles and heaved the heavy pieces out through the ports.

A few moments passed as the men trained the guns round with crowbars and handspikes, finding their respective targets. Finally they stood back and Fury could see the gun captains crouched, ready to fire.

'Fire!' he shouted, that single word almost cut off as the guns were fired almost as one, the combined recoil shaking *Amazon*'s timbers.

'Reload and fire as you bear!' he shouted, stooping to get a further look at her.

She looked badly knocked about by that last broadside, evidenced by the gaping scars along her side. The large party of boarders Fury had seen gathering earlier were still there but looked noticeably smaller, the grape shot having cut them down like a scythe as it swept through them.

She was still coming on bravely enough as he looked, gauging the distance as it gradually diminished – fifteen yards, ten, five, and then she touched at last, scraping the *Amazon*'s side as the two ships were secured aloft. The men were ready to fire again now, the reloading taking slightly longer than Fury had anticipated due to the smaller crews.

'Lads!' he shouted, 'use the water buckets after you fire!'

The men immediately understood his meaning, one man from each crew grabbing a bucket of water and standing waiting next to his gun. Again the guns roared out, spitting flame and smoke, screams from inside the *Bedford* proof of the damage that was being done. The men holding the buckets immediately flung the water out through the ports and on to *Bedford*'s hull to prevent the burning wads from setting her afire as they flew out of the gun muzzles and into *Bedford* at point-blank range. If *Bedford* were to be set alight with *Amazon* and *Otter* both secured to her, every single man on the three ships would be burnt alive.

The men reloaded furiously as the sounds of fierce fighting overhead drifted down – presumably the boarders gathered round *Bedford*'s rail had gained a foothold on *Amazon*'s deck. Crash, the guns went off again, the men throwing out water once more. Not a single broadside had come from the *Bedford*. Indeed, her guns were not even run out, the empty ports staring mutely at him through *Amazon*'s open ports.

Fury tried to place himself in the position of the enemy commander. By firing broadsides into *Amazon* there was a risk that he could kill some of his own men, not to mention the fact that to capture *Amazon* he would need as many men as he could muster, combined with the crew of *Otter*. It was therefore reasonable to assume that he would leave his guns unmanned while the boarding action took place, or at least with only a skeleton crew to man the gun deck.

As he came to this conclusion an idea started to develop in his head, helped along by their previous close call with some men from the *Otter*. If he was wrong he would likely be flogged and disrated, but then if he was wrong he would most likely be dead anyway.

'Men!' he shouted. 'Cease fire!'

The crews stopped their efforts to reload and turned to face him.

'I intend to board *Bedford* through their gun ports and attack them from within.'

He felt relief now that he had committed himself to the decision, and was pleased to see the men's faces showed no evidence of fear or surprise. They would do their duty whatever he asked of them, and the knowledge gave him confidence.

He walked over to Clark, the burly seaman who had recently saved his life. Judging by the way Clark was stooping under the deck beams, he was well over six feet tall, with a frame to match. His black hair was slightly receding at the front and tied back into a tight ponytail, which, along with his tattooed forearms, instantly identified him as the prime seaman he was.

'Pick twenty men, Clark, steady men who know how to swing a cutlass. Bring them over to the arms chest.'

'Aye aye, sir,' Clark replied, turning away and shouting out names as he walked.

Fury walked over to the arms chest himself and swapped his dirk for a cutlass while he waited for the group of men to join him, led by Clark.

'Take a cutlass each, lads, but no pistols – I want to surprise them if possible.'

He walked back over to the remaining crew members and picked out one of the quarter gun captains, Stollings, a steady and reliable man if his memory served him correctly.

'Stollings, you will be in command until further notice. Keep the deck secure from attack by boarders. If any orders come down from the captain in my absence, you will have to carry them out as best you can.'

'Aye aye, sir,' Stollings replied, knuckling his forehead. 'Good luck, sir.'

'Thank you,' Fury said as he turned to the group of men armed with cutlasses now gathered up behind him.

'Follow me, lads,' he ordered, beckoning with his cutlass as he walked to one of the aft gun ports.

It was a simple matter to lean forward and put his head through the *Amazon*'s port and into one of *Bedford*'s open ports, the ships touching as they were. There was a short gap between the ports due to the tumblehome of the ship's sides, but nothing that could not be bridged by stretching a little. He twisted his head once it was through *Bedford*'s open port and looked forward along her deck: dead bodies strewn here and there but no sign of a living soul! So far so good. He placed his hands on the *Bedford*'s lower port sill and heaved himself through with a low grunt, landing on her deck on his hands and feet. Still crouching, he moved inboard a little way to let the other men through after him one by one.

Finally they were all through, with little sound other than the occasional thud or grunt – certainly nothing which could be heard above the continual sounds of shouting and clashing steel as the boarders attacked. Slowly his group of men followed him as he moved forward. He paused. More shouting, but there was something strange about it this time. It took him some moments to realise that it was coming from down below, not up on deck. He turned to Clark, who stood beside him.

'Do you hear that?'

'Aye, sir,' Clark replied in a whisper.

'What d'you make of it?'

'Well, sir . . . it could be the old crew of the *Bedford*.'

'My own thoughts exactly,' Fury replied. He paused. 'Very well, we'll take a look,' he decided swiftly, swallowing hard and leading his men over to the aft hatchway where a steep ladder led into the darkness below.

'You five!' He pointed to the first five men at the front of the group, one of whom was Clark. 'Follow me. The rest of you stay here and take cover. We'll be back shortly.'

He turned towards the hatchway again, but turned back as Clark touched his elbow.

'Beggin' yer pardon, sir, but *Amazon's* yer first ship, ain't it, sir?'

'Well – yes,' he replied, wondering what on earth this had to do with the present situation.

'Maybe it's best if I lead the way, sir. It'll be pitch-black down there an' I'll know me way around a bit better, beggin' yer pardon agin, sir.'

Fury thought for a moment and quickly realised that Clark was right.

'Very well then, carry on.'

The thought of wandering blindly in the dark round an unfamiliar ship was not pleasant, and he was slightly upset he had not thought of that himself. He followed Clark down the ladder, feeling with his feet where the last step was as the darkness swallowed him up. He heard the other four men reach the deck behind him, bumping into each other in the darkness.

'We'll wait a few seconds,' Fury whispered, 'to let our eyes get accustomed to the dark. Then we'll be off.'

They all waited in silence until gradually the blackness seemed to soften slightly, enough so that a man nearby could be made out as a darker shape against the gloom.

'Very well, Clark, carry on.'

Clark started making his way forward, Fury realising as they were going how utterly lost he would have been. He could not make out which way they were going, only that they went down one more steep ladder, the shouting getting gradually nearer before suddenly it seemed to be right underneath them. The huge bulk of Clark loomed up in the gloom to whisper into Fury's ear.

'Whoever they are, sir, they're in the hold underneath us – this is the hatch leading down there,' he hissed, lightly kicking the hatch coaming.

Fury knelt down and could see the hatch had been battened down to prevent anyone below from pushing it open. He cupped his hands to his mouth and shouted in as loud a whisper as he dared.

'Ahoy down there!'

The shouting and murmuring below continued uninterrupted, so he tried again, this time raising his voice slightly. In response, the noise down below ebbed away and Fury could make out a single muffled voice.

'Avast there – someone's up top.'

The man must have made his way over to the closed hatch because his next sentence was much clearer.

'Who are you?' he asked.

'I am Midshipman Fury of His Majesty's frigate *Amazon*,' Fury replied. 'Who are you?'

'Thank God! I'm second mate of the *Bedford*, formerly of the East India Company's service. We was taken three days back on our way to Bombay.'

Fury would have liked to ask him more questions, but knew that time was short. He had considered the possibility that the man was not who he said he was, but dismissed the thought. Even if he wasn't, the fact that they were battened down in the hold suggested they were on the same side.

'Very well, we'll have you up in a moment. Stand back.' He turned to Clark. 'Clark, let's have that hatch up, if you please.'

'Aye aye, sir.'

Fury heard the sounds of banging and then tearing wood before Clark stood up once more and reported the hatch was up. Almost immediately he saw a shadowy head poking through the hatchway, looking around cautiously before climbing out.

'I'm Hoskins,' the man said, finding Fury somehow, 'I'm much obliged to you, young sir.'

Fury bit his tongue – he did not appreciate being spoken to like a child.

'We'll make the introductions later,' he replied brusquely. 'How many men have you down there?'

'About twenty-five,' Hoskins replied, moving to allow more space for the men as they began to emerge from the hold.

'Good. I hope they can all use a cutlass. *Amazon* has been boarded.' He moved over to find Clark and to cut off any further conversation. He was well aware that time was of the essence. 'Very well, Clark, lead the way out, if you please.'

The journey back to the main deck seemed to take only a fraction of the time of the initial one down to the hold. Clark stepped aside at the foot of the ladder leading to the main deck and Fury started to climb, pausing at the top as he slowly surveyed the deck. It looked empty so he climbed out, beckoning the men behind him to follow. As he turned back round, the rest of his men appeared as if from nowhere.

'Any trouble?' he asked the leader, a thickset man with remarkably short legs and a barrel chest, named Harris.

'No, sir – no sign of a soul.'

'Good. We've some of the former crew of *Bedford* with us. They need weapons – see to it, if you please.'

'Aye aye, sir,' Harris replied, waddling away like a penguin.

Fury turned to the hatchway to find almost all the men now up on deck.

'Listen, men, we'll go up and take the quarterdeck first – there shouldn't be too many manning it. After that we'll board *Amazon* and help our lads out. Any questions?'

He looked around at the men but no one said a word.

'Very well then, follow me.'

He turned away as Harris reappeared with his arms laden with cutlasses, causing a short delay as these were handed out. Once they were ready, Fury made his way further forward towards the waist and paused to glance upwards before moving over to the ladder leading up to the quarterdeck. He turned to Harris.

'Harris, take ten men and secure the fo'c'sle.'

He paused with one foot on the first step of the ladder, watching while Harris and his men reached the ladder leading to the fo'c'sle. It would be best if they went up together to maintain the element of surprise. A nod, and they both started to climb, Fury pausing as his eyes reached the level of the deck. How many men? He could only see seven or eight. Three were by the – damn. Shouting from forward told him Harris and his men were storming the fo'c'sle, the men on the quarterdeck swinging round in surprise.

Fury sprang up on deck, still clutching his cutlass in his right hand, and charged forward, silently mouthing invective at Harris's impatience as he went. He caught the first man by complete surprise, half turning towards him as the blade slashed across his side and stomach, dropping the man to the deck instantly.

His shipmate managed to draw his cutlass and the two circled each other, Fury vaguely aware that the rest of his men had now arrived on the quarterdeck and were overwhelming their opponents. The man came forward, cutting down with his cutlass, only to meet Fury's raised blade in parry. Again he swung, again Fury's raised cutlass deflected the blow, the force of it this time sending Fury staggering backwards, his arm feeling slightly heavier from the strain of blocking the man's strike. The third swing came, Fury knowing he didn't have the strength to block it this time. He stepped to the left and angled his blade so that the man's cutlass ran down it, deflecting off the hilt and sending him off balance. Fury seized the chance and lunged, the point of his blade entering the man's lower back and exiting from his stomach, before Fury withdrew it with a savage grimace on his face. He quickly turned round to watch for any further attack and was surprised to see the fight was over, the last of the enemy raising his hands in surrender just too late to stop the cutlass thrust at his stomach. He looked across at the fo'c'sle to see that Harris and his men had control there also.

'Clark!' he shouted.

'Yes, sir?'

Clark hurried up to him, blood on his shirt.

'Run down the colours please, Clark.'

'Aye aye, sir,' he replied with a grin.

Fury looked across at the *Amazon*'s quarterdeck, a mass of heaving men fighting for their lives. It was unsurprising none of the boarders from *Bedford* or *Otter* had seen the events on board *Bedford*, busy as they were. Here was Clark again at his side.

'Colours run down, sir.'

'Very good, Clark.'

It would have been nice if they could have run their own colours up, but there was no time to go searching for the ensign now. They had to get across to the *Amazon*. Fury looked across to where the *Amazon*'s men were facing him, engaging what must have been the entire crew of the *Bedford*, their backs to him as they tried to fight their way forward across the *Amazon*'s quarterdeck. They were gradually pushing the frigate's crew back by sheer weight of numbers.

'Right, men, over we go. Shout as loudly as you can!'

His group, now numbering some fifty men including those on the fo'c'sle, sent up a loud roar. Fury ran over to the rail, his voice already hoarse from shouting and screaming like a madman. He was conscious of Clark by his side, reassuring with his bulk and quiet confidence.

Luckily the deck of the *Bedford* was much the same height as the *Amazon*, so it took little effort to climb over the *Bedford*'s rail and bridge the narrow gap to the *Amazon*'s, caused by the tumblehome of the two ships' sides. Not waiting to see if the rest of his men were following, Fury jumped forward into the melee, just managing to keep his feet as he landed on the deck. The boarders from *Bedford* were beginning to turn in alarm at the sound of screaming and cheering behind them.

Slashing wildly, Fury leapt forward, catching one man across the chest before instinctively parrying left to catch a swinging cutlass. He was hemmed in tight now as his group of men came up at his side, stabbing and thrusting at the enemy in front, men slipping as they lost their footing on the blood-soaked deck. Here was Clark at his side still, blocking a fierce cutlass swing meant for Fury's head, but not quite quick enough to beat Fury's lunge into the man's chest, the point of his cutlass deflecting downwards off the man's ribcage and tearing into his stomach. Attacked on both sides like this the boarders stood no chance, Fury's men fighting their way through until the man in front of him looked vaguely familiar.

'Avast there – *Amazon*s!' he screamed, stopping the man just in time from thrusting his sword at him.

He saw the blood lust and fighting madness in the man's eyes gradually subside as he recognised Fury. Fury turned away, realising suddenly that he was sick of fighting. Two men came staggering past him, still locked in a fierce struggle. He saw immediately that one of the men was Mr Douglas, the *Amazon*'s first lieutenant, trying to hold off his opponent's sword arm at the wrist while the man had his other hand round Douglas's neck. Every man on deck watching the struggle seemed to be frozen. Douglas finally went down, his opponent freeing his sword arm and raising it to deliver the killer blow.

Fury darted towards him at once, swinging his own cutlass as the man's sword was beginning its downward arc. He caught the man's arm just above the wrist, the sword seemingly jerked from his hand and clattering to the deck. There was a momentary pause while the man looked at his bloodied arm, and then to Fury's astonishment he came charging at him, empty-handed. Instinctively Fury swung his cutlass, his other arm coming up to protect his face. He did not see where he caught his assailant, only felt the sensation of his blade slicing through something soft, followed by a deflection off something harder. By the time Fury had lowered his arm from his face, the man lay in a heap at his feet, blood spreading across the deck from under him. Lieutenant Douglas was on his feet now, cutlass in hand once again

'Thank you, Mr Fury' was all he said as he moved away.

Fury looked around, realising that men were putting down their weapons now, hands raised in surrender. He looked round for the captain, and seeing him over by the taffrail began to walk over to him. Captain Barber was in the process of accepting the sword of one of the officers, a small, suave-looking man with an air of arrogance about him. Lieutenant Douglas beckoned over a marine corporal and instructed him to convey the officer down to the cable tier and put him under guard.

'Sir, sir – I am a French officer. Yo-you cannot lock me up. I have given my *p . . . parole!*' the man stammered, clearly struggling to express himself in a foreign tongue.

'Take him below!' snapped Captain Barber suddenly, his patience finally exhausted.

The corporal grabbed the officer by the arm and led him forward, the man submitting sulkily as he realised there was nothing he could do.

'Sir?' said Fury. 'May I offer you my congratulations on your victory, sir.'

'Thank you, Mr Fury,' Barber replied wearily, turning to the first lieutenant. 'Mr Douglas, please see that all the prisoners are confined below and guarded. The men can have a bite to eat and a rest once that is done and the prizes have been secured, but not before.'

'Aye aye, sir,' Douglas replied, turning away and bellowing orders to the ship's petty officers.

'Mr Fury,' the captain said, turning back to him. 'Please inform the carpenter and the surgeon that I would like a report immediately. They can make it verbally for the present.'

'Aye aye, sir.'

Fury walked over to the taffrail and looked out over the wide expanse of sea. His head was hurting like the very devil now that the action was over. He reached for his favourite pocket watch to find out the time, but it was no longer there. He regretted the loss; it had been a present from his mother on his leaving home to join *Amazon*.

He gripped the rail to stop his hands shaking slightly. What was it – fear? No, more relief – relief that he had done his duty when the stakes were at their highest, that he hadn't been found a coward. As he stood there in silence he suddenly realised he was exhausted, not just physically but mentally as well. Lieutenant Scott had been right, he thought: he was sick of battle already. One final deep breath, and he turned back to face the quarterdeck – and his duty.

Chapter Six

Midshipman Fury walked into the captain's great cabin in HMS *Amazon* as the sentry at the door announced his arrival. Captain Barber was sitting at his desk as he entered, head down, engrossed in the mountain of paperwork that was needed merely to keep *Amazon* in commission.

Fury could see the calm blue waters of the Indian Ocean sparkling in the sun through the long stern windows behind the captain's desk. It crossed his mind that his uncle would become a wealthy man if he could get the prizes safely back to Bombay, far more wealthy than any member of his family had ever been before. The thought of his own small share of the prize money brought a smile to Fury's lips as he stood there in silence. After a moment Barber put his quill pen down.

'Mr Fury,' the captain began, looking at him coldly, 'as far as I can recollect, your station was on the upper deck commanding the guns, was it not?'

'Well – yes, sir,' Fury replied, his smile vanishing and a feeling of apprehension flooding over him.

'Perhaps you could enlighten me then, sir, as to how you came to be on the quarterdeck of the *Bedford*?'

'I, er – well . . .'

'Damn it, Mr Fury, when we are in action I need to know that I can trust my officers – that they will not disobey my orders!' Barber shouted.

What seemed like a long pause followed.

'Yes, sir, I understand. I'm sorry, sir.'

The captain sighed, leaning back in his chair as if too weary to carry on with his tirade.

'You were lucky yesterday, John,' he said at length. Fury realised that he was speaking to him now as an uncle, not as his commanding officer. 'Your gamble paid off. It may not always be the case. The service needs steady men who can obey orders, John, trustworthy and responsible, not hotheads who go off on their own at the first opportunity.'

Another long silence ensued while Fury digested this, standing there stooped over to avoid the deck beams above, trying desperately to look dignified.

'Very well, Mr Fury,' Barber said at last, apparently satisfied that he had got his point across. 'You are dismissed.'

Fury turned on his heel and walked out of the cabin, past the marine sentry and up to the companion ladder, pausing to let the master, Mr Hoggarth, pass before ascending the ladder to the quarterdeck.

The decks of the *Amazon* were still bustling with men carrying out repairs after the previous day's battle. Was it only yesterday? Fury had had little sleep since then, along with the majority of the *Amazon*'s officers – just an hour's nap during the night after he had changed out of his blood-soaked shirt and breeches.

One of the seamen nearby knuckled his forehead respectfully as Fury caught his eye. He could sense a change in the crew's attitude towards him since the battle. Had he finally won them over?

He looked up at the sky; the deepest blue with only the very lightest of white clouds over to the nor'west. They had been lucky in that the weather had remained calm since the battle, so that the *Amazon*'s carpenter and his crew had been able to go round the ship and her two prizes, *Bedford* and *Otter*, plugging shot holes and repairing damage to ensure they would be seaworthy once they got under way. The *Bedford* had received the worst of the damage. Her rudder had been shot away, which was evidently the reason why she had made no attempt to turn and avoid the *Amazon* as she crossed her wake and raked her. Only after a jury rudder had been rigged had she been able to come up alongside *Amazon* and board her. The *Amazon*'s carpenter had already fashioned a more permanent replacement which should see them safely back to Bombay, and had now shifted his attentions to plugging the shot holes in her hull.

Luckily none of the masts and spars on any of the ships had received major damage, the only repairs aloft being to the running or standing rigging where ropes had been parted by flying shot, and the occasional hole made in the sails. The captain had sent a party of seamen to each ship to assist in resplicing these, while the sail-maker and his crew had been busy patching up or replacing the damaged sails.

Immediately after the battle the dead had been sewn up in their hammocks and slid over the side after a brief service read by the captain. Fury had been present on the quarter-deck when the surgeon, Pike, had come up and made his report. The butchers' bill had been thirty-six dead and fifty-two wounded, fourteen of whom he did not expect to live.

With two new prizes that would mean they would be very short-handed. It had been fortunate that many of the former crew of *Bedford* and *Otter* had been immured in their respective holds, although many of them were now probably wishing they had remained there after Captain Barber had pressed every man into the navy except the masters and their mates.

From the gossip he had overheard, *Bedford* was fully laden with cotton, although it still was not clear how she came to be taken, nor was it known how the *Otter*, which had sailed from Bombay a month before, along with the East India Company's flagship, the twenty-four-gun *Mornington*, had come to be captured. Fury looked across to where the two ships lay, obvious signs of battle showing along both their sides where his own guns had crashed into them.

'Mr Fury!'

He turned to see the first lieutenant, Mr Douglas, looking at him. He walked across to him, the deck underfoot now gleaming once more after the men's efforts with sand and holystone.

'Sir?'

'You look dreadful, Mr Fury. It is up to us to set an example to the men. I suggest you go and get washed up and snatch a couple of hours' sleep.'

That Scottish drawl of his had a pleasant tone.

'Aye aye, sir,' Fury replied, turning back towards the ladder and climbing down to the upper deck below.

He paused at the top of the next ladder to let Pike up from the lower deck.

'How are you today, Mr Fury?' Pike asked as he completed his climb.

'Well, thank you, sir.'

Fury still had a faint headache from the fall he had suffered as the first broadsides had thundered out, but he would
not bother Pike with such trivialities; he had enough on his
plate caring for the wounded, some of whom had suffered
terribly.

'You don't look it, if you don't mind me saying so. I suggest
you get some rest, Mr Fury.'

'I am on my way now, sir.'

'Excellent. I have no wish to see you in my sick bay with
exhaustion. Now, if you will excuse me, I have my report to
make to the captain.'

Fury nodded and watched as Pike walked aft towards
Barber's cabins, before quickly descending the ladder to the
deck below. A minute later and he was in the midshipman's
berth, dully lit by lanterns and stifling in the heat, the
awnings and wind funnels which had been set up on deck
seemingly having no effect down here.

He perched himself on his sea chest and waited while one
of the servants brought him a bowl of water. As he splashed
his face, a dull sting reminded him of the wound he had
received on his chin, probably caused by a flying splinter,
although he could not be sure.

His memory of the battle, after the shock of the initial
broadside, was patchy. The only thing he was sure about
now was the thin thread by which life hung; he could picture
little Marsden dying from a splinter wound, holding his own
intestines in his hands, while Fury – standing only inches
from him – was untouched. He shook off the depression
which was hovering over him, got up and somehow
managed to drag himself to his hammock, falling into it face

first. He was asleep almost instantly, not even stirring when, five minutes later, the servant came in and quietly removed his boots.

Captain Barber was sitting on the long bench in his day cabin which ran right the way across the stern of HMS *Amazon*. The glass of wine in his hand was warm and sweet, and did nothing to cool him in the early evening humidity. He looked out of the stern windows at the low orange orb to the westward which was continuing its downward arc until, at last, it would disappear below the horizon, perhaps showing itself slightly one last time as the *Amazon* rose to the swell, before vanishing once more to usher in the dusk.

He looked at his pocket watch. Seven o'clock – halfway through the second dog watch. Another hour or so and it would be time to pipe down hammocks, when the watch below would turn in for a few hours' sleep until called again at midnight for the changing of the watch. He was trying to rearrange his thoughts, clear his head for what would be his last task that day before climbing wearily into his cot, slung next door in the sleeping cabin.

'Pass the word for the first lieutenant!' he shouted, finally deciding that it could wait no longer.

He heard the marine sentry outside his cabin echo the order, followed by others around the ship until finally it would reach Mr Douglas. He sat and waited quietly until at last he heard the marine sentry's shout signalling Douglas's arrival. Just enough time had elapsed since he had passed the word for the first lieutenant for Douglas to quickly wash and change, evidenced by the clean yet slightly creased uniform he came in wearing. From the look on his face he had obviously been sleeping when he was called. Well, it would do the man no harm to lose a little sleep, Barber thought.

'Ah, Mr Douglas – there you are.'

'Sir,' Douglas replied, touching his hat in salute.

'Mr Douglas,' Barber began, 'please be so good as to have the French officer we captured yesterday escorted to my cabin for a glass of wine with us.'

'Aye aye, sir,' Douglas replied. He scrutinised Barber's face suspiciously for as long as he dared, knowing full well his captain's dislike for Frenchmen. Seeing nothing, he turned and left the cabin to arrange for a marine escort for the prisoner.

It was a full ten minutes before he arrived back at the captain's cabin, this time with the little French lieutenant behind him looking somewhat dishevelled, protesting volubly at his treatment as he was prodded along by the tip of the marine corporal's musket. Again the sentry tapped his musket on the deck in salute and announced their arrival.

'Thank you, corporal, you may wait outside,' Captain Barber said quietly to the marine escort as they entered the cabin. 'Sir,' he turned to the Frenchman. 'I am Captain Barber of His Britannic Majesty's frigate *Amazon*.'

'And I, sir,' the Frenchman replied, 'am Lieutenant Bedeau, commander of the *Otter*. I must protest at my treatment!' He was almost tripping over his words, so eager was he to voice his protests. He stopped abruptly as Captain Barber held up his hands to request silence.

'All in good time, sir. Now please, gentlemen, be seated.'

Barber proferred a couple of chairs which Bedeau and Douglas both sank down into with apparent relief. He walked over to the decanter on the sideboard.

'Wine with you, sir?' he asked, turning to the Frenchman.

'*Oui*, thank you, *capitaine*,' Bedeau replied, pacified for the time being at his pleasant reception and gratefully accepting the glass as it was passed to him.

Captain Barber sank back into the chair behind his mahogany desk, remaining silent for several seconds as he studied his glass.

'Tell me, lieutenant – that flag you were flying under – it is unfamiliar to me.'

'Ah yes, *capitaine*,' Bedeau explained, 'we sail under the flag of the Sultan of Mysore.'

That explained many things. The Sultan of Mysore was, as his father before him, engaged in a fierce and long-running war with the East India Company. Strange, however, since the Sultan's kingdom was not on the coast. Presumably he must have had assistance from neighbouring rulers. It would take a good deal of gold to hire a French ship of some force, as he assumed her to be, having taken both *Otter* and *Bedford*.

'You fought *Otter* magnificently.'

The man was obviously self important and it would do no harm to pander to him for the time being.

'Thank you, *capitaine*, I had a good teacher.'

'How did you come to capture the *Otter* and *Bedford*, sir?' Barber persisted.

'We intercepted *Bedford* three days back; she tried to outrun us but, heavily laden as she is, she could not. The *Otter* we encountered a day later. I believe she mistook us both for merchantmen at first. By the time she realised her error it was, of course, too late.'

'More wine, sir?' Barber enquired, not waiting for an answer as he took Bedeau's glass and refilled it from the decanter before sitting down again.

It was significant that both his and Lieutenant Douglas's glasses were both still full, neither man having touched a drop.

'Tell me, lieutenant, what ship are you from?'

The question was sudden and seemed out of context with the previous gentle conversation, but Bedeau did not seem to notice. Seated in a comfortable chair and with his second glass of wine half finished, he seemed perfectly willing to answer. A typical Frenchman, Barber thought.

'She is a *frégate*, *capitaine*, the *Magicienne*, Capitaine Comte Dubriec in command.'

'I see.'

The fact that her captain was a count explained much. With the storming of the Bastille three years earlier and the subsequent Revolution, many noblemen had fled France to avoid the guillotine. The count had probably been pleased to be given a detached command such as this. He could hire out his ship, making himself rich and, with any luck, by the time he returned home, the fervour of the Revolution would have subsided.

'Tell me about her, lieutenant,' Barber asked quietly.

'She is a beautiful vessel. Very fast!' Bedeau stated proudly.

'And her armament?' Barber almost whispered the question.

'She has thirty-six guns, *capitaine*. Alas, your vessel would be no match for her with your popguns. She would pound you into a wreck with her eighteen-pounders.'

'Indeed?' Barber replied. 'And where is she now?'

'I do not know for sure, *capitaine*. The last I saw of her was two days ago – she sighted a strange sail and left us to give chase.'

'But she has a regular cruising ground, no?'

'Why, of course, *cap*—' Bedeau broke off suddenly, realising he had said far too much already. 'I will say no more, *capitaine*,' he said defiantly.

Captain Barber sat back in his chair with a loud sigh, as if he had been hoping to avoid his next task. He opened one of the drawers in his desk and reached in to pull out the pistol he had placed there earlier, a lovely piece of craftsmanship, perfectly balanced. Bedeau's eyes widened in alarm as he saw what Captain Barber was holding.

'Yo – you are a gentleman, *capitaine* – you would not—' He broke off as Barber stood up and walked round his desk to stand over the now visibly cowering Frenchman.

'I can assure you, lieutenant, that I can and will. Tell me where the *Magicienne* will be cruising.'

A deafening silence engulfed the room. Barber cocked the pistol, the click as the hammer went back sounding as loud as one of the main-deck guns in the silence. He raised his arm and rested the muzzle of the weapon against Bedeau's sweating forehead.

'I will count to three, lieutenant – there will not be a four. One . . . two . . . thr—'

'Very well, I will tell you!' Bedeau burst out, almost in a panic, '– but please put that pistol away!' He was shaking in his chair.

'Very well,' Barber relented, uncocking the pistol and placing it back on his desk. 'You were saying?'

'The *Magicienne* will be cruising between latitudes eight and ten degrees north, longitude seventy-two degrees.'

Barber knew the French were still persisting in measuring longitude from Paris instead of Greenwich. If he remembered correctly, Paris was approximately two degrees east of

Greenwich, therefore the lieutenant's estimated longitude would become seventy-four degrees according to his calculations.

'Thank you, lieutenant,' he replied quietly. 'Now, if you have finished your wine, I will say good night to you.' He turned to Lieutenant Douglas. 'Mr Douglas, please escort Mr Bedeau back to his quarters.'

'Aye aye, sir,' Douglas replied, possibly the first words he had uttered since arriving back in the captain's cabin.

Lieutenant Bedeau made no further protests as he was led back to the hold. He was perhaps merely thankful he was still alive. Barber moved over to the bench once more as his guests left. He had much to think about – not least the presence of a thirty-six-gun eighteen-pound frigate in the area.

He knew the East India Company had sent a ship round to inform the senior officer on the India station, Commodore Cornwallis, of the attacks on their shipping. Even so, it would be at least another month before one of Cornwallis's ships could be expected, having to come round the southern tip of India from their base in Calcutta or Madras. With the *Amazon* in her current state and his crew short-handed after putting prize crews into *Otter* and *Bedford*, she would indeed be outgunned and outmanned by the *Magicienne*. If they were to meet . . .

Midshipman Fury tossed back the glass of blackstrap which the servant had just handed to him, his face screwing up with displeasure as the cheap wine slid down. Wine was an acquired taste, or so he had been told, and he had had little opportunity to drink it so far. His uncle seemed overconcerned that he, at barely seventeen years old, should not join the ranks of the many drunkards who served in the navy.

His mother never touched a drop either. 'I will not put a thief in my mouth to steal my brain!' she used to say. He felt he needed a stiff drink today, however, having just come off the morning watch. He was desperately tired, and hoped the wine would help him relax a little.

The gunroom steward came in carrying his breakfast of oatmeal gruel, or skilligalee as it was also called. Fury looked at the unappetising bowl, filled with finely ground oatmeal boiled in fatty water, with a little salt. He wished he had been able to afford some private provisions when they had docked at Bombay, suddenly finding it completely unfair that midshipmen did not get paid. Any small allowance his uncle did grant him – and it was small – had disappeared immediately on his uniforms and small stash of books – Falconer, Norie, Clark; every manual a young gentleman could possibly need to become a good seaman and officer.

He looked around the empty mess; there were normally one or two midshipmen down here skylarking or reading. It felt eerily quiet, and even on a cramped ship of more than two hundred men he felt a sudden pang of loneliness. He had hardly seen the others since the battle; little Marsden was dead, young Howard was injured, and the others had been kept extremely busy trying to get the three vessels manned and ready to sail.

All the necessary work had finally been completed at about six bells in the morning watch – seven o'clock – as he had been on deck. They would be making sail shortly, heading back for Bombay no doubt to deliver the prizes.

Still, he thought, swiftly spooning the thick gruel into his mouth, he could afford to be unconcerned by such things – the responsibility was not his. He would finish his breakfast and then try to get an hour's sleep before his lesson in navigation with Mr Hoggarth at half past nine. Nothing on earth disturbed the sacred routine of life on board a King's ship.

He finished the last of the gruel and pushed the empty bowl away, his appetite satisfied. Getting up wearily from the table, he turned to go to his hammock, nearly bumping into Midshipman Pascoe as he did so.

'Hullo, William. Should you not be on deck?' Fury asked, slightly curious as to why he was down in the gunroom when he was supposed to be on watch.

'Aye, I am, John,' Pascoe replied, 'but the captain sent me down. He would like to see you in his cabin as soon as it is convenient.'

'Very well.'

Fury adjusted his uniform with a sigh and looked round to try and find his tricorn hat. When a captain asked to see a midshipman 'at his earliest convenience', it was a polite way of saying 'now', and it would be unwise for any ambitious midshipman to treat it any differently.

He pushed all thoughts of sleep to the back of his mind as he strode forward and up the ladder, emerging on the upper deck just abaft the main mast. Turning aft, he made his way towards the captain's suite of cabins covering the whole breadth of the ship, wondering what on earth Barber wanted with him now. As he approached, the marine sentry outside the cabin saluted and bellowed his arrival to the captain.

'Mr Midshipman Fury, sah!'

Fury strode past and walked through the captain's dining cabin into his spacious day cabin, which overlooked the sea through the stern windows.

G.S. Beard

'Sir?' he enquired. 'You wished to see me?'

Captain Barber was, as ever, bent over his desk, sorting through the paperwork that lay around him. He looked up.

'Ah, yes – Mr Fury,' he said, leaning back as if with relief at the interruption and waving Fury to one of the chairs opposite his desk.

Fury sat thankfully. He disliked having to stoop, especially when he was speaking to the captain; he found it difficult to think in such a posture.

'There is little time, Mr Fury, so I will get straight to the point,' Barber started, Fury beginning to wonder what he could possibly have done wrong now. 'I intend to be under way within the next two hours with our prizes,' he continued. 'If this weather holds we shall hopefully make Bombay in a week or so. As you know, the new second lieutenant, Mr Carlisle, is still in the sick bay recovering from his fever. The surgeon tells me he should be fit again imminently.'

'Yes, sir,' Fury replied, wondering now what all this had to do with him.

'In the meantime, because of the lamentable death of Lieutenant Scott, I am extremely short of officers. I am therefore placing you in temporary command of the *Bedford*. You will transfer any belongings you may need over to her immediately.' He paused to gauge Fury's reaction. 'Well? Have you anything to say?'

Fury was shocked.

'We— I – d . . .' It was true – he did not know what to say.

The captain saved him from further stuttering by continuing.

'The prize crew is already aboard awaiting you. I have allowed you a crew of forty men – a mixture of *Amazon*s and ex-*Bedford*s. All prime seamen mind, so look after 'em. We can't afford to lose prime seamen. There are also four marine privates on board under Corporal Davis. It has only been a short time since the ex-*Bedford*s were pressed, and I want the marines there as a deterrent if they get any silly ideas.'

'Aye aye, sir,' Fury replied, only just finding his voice again after the initial shock.

'*Amazon* will be taking up station as the conditions dictate, so you do not have to worry about station keeping. Just keep her on course with a firm press of sail – as *Bedford* is the slowest vessel, it will be up to *Otter* and ourselves to shorten sail as required. See my clerk on the way out for a copy of the signal book. Then see the master; he will inform you of the course we will be setting.' He paused for a moment to allow Fury a chance to digest all this information, before continuing. 'As soon as Mr Carlisle is fit to resume duty he will take command, with you as his second. Any questions?'

'No, sir,' Fury replied.

'Very well then. Good luck, Mr Fury. Carry on.'

Fury rose out of the chair, saluted and walked out, stopping off at the clerk's little office outside the captain's cabins where he was given a slim volume containing the necessary signals. He stopped off at the midshipmen's quarters next to pick up a few pieces of clothing, including his pea jacket in case of heavy weather, before making his way to the quarterdeck to see the master. Mr Hoggarth was by the binnacle, silently supervising the men as they coiled down the braces, lifts, topsail halliards, tacks and sheets on deck, clear for running when the time came to make sail. He walked over to him.

'Mr Hoggarth, sir, I will be transferring over to *Bedford* shortly. The captain desired me to see you and obtain our course.'

'Ah, yes,' Hoggarth replied, 'I've been expecting you, Mr Fury.'

He reached into his pocket and brought out a scrap of paper with the course roughly written on it. He handed it to Fury, wished him luck and turned back to his work.

Fury stood for a moment in indecision – he had been expecting something more from the master. A few words of advice perhaps, or at the very least a little more excitement from him at Fury's step up.

What next? He could think of nothing else he needed to do other than to get over to the *Bedford*. He caught sight of Mr Douglas as he turned away from the master, the problem of how to get across to the *Bedford* suddenly solved. He walked over to him.

'Excuse me, sir,' he interrupted Douglas tentatively. The first lieutenant was notoriously short-tempered when under pressure. 'May I have a boat to take me across to the *Bedford*?'

'Ah, yes, Mr Fury – your new command. Congratulations.'

Fury was surprised at the pleasant reception.

'Thank you, sir.'

'Of course you may have a boat,' Douglas continued. 'I believe the cutter is already hoisted out.' He turned away to shout at one of the bosun's mates, Jessop. 'Muster the cutter's crew here immediately!'

'Aye aye, sir,' Jessop replied, turning away to bawl out further orders.

Within two minutes the boat's crew had been mustered and were climbing down into the cutter. Fury took his leave of the first lieutenant and walked over to the starboard entry port, handing his small bundle of belongings down into the boat before turning his back and beginning the climb down the side battens into the boat below. Fortunately the sea was still quite calm, the freshening breeze yet to kick up more waves, so it was an easy task to wait for the gentle swell to lift the cutter up towards him before jumping into it, making his way past the silent men to sit in the stern sheets alongside the captain's coxswain, Gibbins.

'Shove off!' ordered Gibbins. 'Give way all!'

He put the tiller over towards the *Amazon* so the bow of the cutter would immediately swing outwards as the men started to pull. Fury sat there in silence studying the *Bedford* as the cutter approached. Her hull was scarred and battered but she was still seaworthy, and by the looks of her rigging it had not been touched in the recent battle – two days past now. Hardly surprising really, since he himself had ordered the gun crews to aim low for the hull.

'Pull round her, if you please, Gibbins,' he said, Gibbins immediately putting the tiller over with a nod so the cutter could row round the *Bedford*.

It would be useful if he could have a good look at her before going on board, to get an idea of how she was trimmed and whether she would gripe or not. Fortunately she was one of the smaller of the East India Company's merchantmen, about five hundred tons with scantlings about the same size as the *Amazon*, but with bluff bows. The largest East Indiamen were about twelve hundred tons, with scantlings based on a sixty-four. It would have been impossible to handle a ship of that size with a prize crew of forty.

The cutter finally completed its lap, Fury subconsciously noting that she was down slightly by the head and may therefore require a touch of weather helm. The cutter was soon hooked on and so Fury dragged his mind away from her trim for a short time to concentrate on getting safely on board. He clambered over the oarsmen and reached for the battens of the entry ladder, pulling himself up. He reached the entry port and stepped on deck to be met by the familiar face of Clark, the burly seaman who had saved his life as they had struggled to repel the *Otter*'s boarders swarming in through *Amazon*'s gun ports. Strange that the sight of Clark should settle his nerves and give him a little more confidence.

Fury looked around the deck – his deck – his first command at only seventeen, albeit a temporary one until Lieutenant Carlisle should recover from his fever. She was much the same as the *Amazon*, the long quarterdeck reaching up to the mainmast, then open air down to the waist, with gangways on either side to link the quarterdeck with the fo'c'sle.

He was beginning to experience a vastly different feeling from when he had been thrust into command of the *Amazon*'s gun deck after the death of Lieutenant Scott. There he had only to fire at what was put in front of him and reload as quickly as possible, having no control over the movements of the ship. Now he would be solely responsible for the safety of every man aboard. If he handled her badly or wrecked her due to his incompetence or inexperience he would probably never find employment in the navy again, assuming he survived, of course.

Clark was speaking to him now, dragging his mind away from its wanderings and back into reality.

'Welcome aboard, sir.'

'Thank you, Clark,' he replied. 'We shall be sailing in the next two hours.'

'Aye aye, sir,' Clark replied, knuckling his forehead.

Fury looked aloft, where the fore topsail had been backed

to counterbalance the thrust of the main topsail, keeping her more or less stationary in the water.

'Is the cargo secure?' he asked.

'Aye, sir,' Clark replied, 'I had a couple o' men check it this morning. Nothing except cotton, sir.'

'Very well.'

The cotton would likely be stowed on all decks save for the upper deck just below him, where the men would also have slung their hammocks. Just enough space would be saved in the hold to store provisions, spare spars and sails, powder and shot. The rest of the space in the ship, including the lower deck just below the gun deck, must be entirely taken up with cotton.

Fury continued to look around the deck. All along the side of it the men were coiling down all the ropes that would be needed when setting sail, ensuring that they were all free to run without fouling on anything. He moved over to the side of the ship, looking down and checking one or two of the scupper flaps to ensure they moved freely. Those flaps stopped water coming in through the holes, but allowed any water which had come on deck to run out.

'Has the well been sounded?' he asked Clark, still at his side as he moved around the deck. It was a logical question to ask after checking the scuppers, and Clark was ready with the answer.

'Aye, sir, this morning. Four inches o' water in the well.'

'Very good.'

It was a reasonable amount, especially after being in battle where there was a chance of shot hitting betwixt wind and water. Fury doubted whether there was a ship afloat that was completely dry. Water tended to find its way in by a thousand different routes, and the best carpenter in the world would not stop it.

He looked around trying to think what else he could check. As usual when he was concentrating too hard on not missing anything important, he had a nagging feeling there was something obvious he was forgetting. He tried to remember what Falconer had to say on the subject, suddenly wishing he had brought his copy with him. Ah yes!

'Have the wheel put from hard a-starboard to hard a-port, please, Clark.'

'Aye aye, sir.'

That would ensure the tiller ropes ran freely for steering.

'And have a man check the rudder pendants and ready the relieving tackles and spare tiller,' he continued, the confidence beginning to grow inside him as his memory began to function.

The relieving tackles would ensure the ship could be steered if anything happened to the wheel, while the spare tiller was always handy in case of damage to the current tiller.

'When that is done, I would be obliged if you would join me in the master's cabin. I will need to draw up a general station, watch and quarter bill – you know the men's abilities better than I.'

'Aye aye, sir,' Clark replied.

He watched as Clark walked forward to carry out his orders. Strange that a man ten years his senior and with vastly more experience should carry out his orders with no sign of contempt or condescension, Fury mused, as he picked up his spare clothes and walked towards the ladder leading down to the upper deck. It would be interesting to see what his new quarters would be like . . .

Chapter Seven

The wind had freshened steadily since dawn and was now blowing briskly from the sou'west, kicking up small white caps on the crests of each wave. After two days of back-breaking work, the small, makeshift squadron was now ready to sail. Captain Barber, standing on his quarterdeck, finally gave the order. The men hauled on the braces to bring the main topsail yard round, the sail flapping and then filling as the wind caught it, instead of being thrust back on to its mast as before. A quick order to the quartermaster at the helm brought the ship's head round on a course to pass closely alongside her prizes, *Otter* and *Bedford*.

Fury was standing on the quarterdeck of the *Bedford* and could see *Amazon* slowly approaching, Captain Barber visible by the larboard main chains with speaking trumpet ready in hand. He hurried over to the starboard side, remembering to pick up the speaking trumpet he had found in the late master's cabin.

'Mr Fury!' bellowed the captain through his speaking trumpet, his words being carried by the wind. 'You may make sail now, and steer the course given you by the master!'

'Aye aye, sir!' Fury shouted back, unsure as to whether his

voice would carry against the wind. No matter, the captain would be able to guess at his reply.

He turned inboard, where his crew were at their allotted stations awaiting his commands. He felt a rush of nerves at this, his first experience of handling a large ship on his own, fearful lest a wrong command might cause confusion or worse. He could feel the sweat dampening his palms, so he rubbed them against his breeches, cursing himself for his weakness and hoping that none of his men had seen the movement and had guessed at his nervousness. One gulp, one steeling of his resolve, and he was ready.

He raised the speaking trumpet to his lips – the men would probably be able to hear him without but he wanted no errors or misunderstandings.

'Hands to the fore topsail braces!' he shouted.

The men hauled on the braces to swing the fore topsail yard round, the sail flapping as it came through the eye of the wind before finally billowing out as the wind caught it. Gradually *Bedford* started moving through the water. Fury fumbled around in his pocket and brought out the crumpled piece of paper with the master's course scribbled on it. One glance and he turned to the helmsman.

'Steer nor'-nor'west a half north.'

'Aye aye, sir,' the helmsman replied, turning the spokes through his hands as he looked at the compass housed in the binnacle.

The *Bedford* came slowly round as the rudder got more bite in the water, until at last the wind was slightly forward of her larboard quarter.

'Nor'-nor'west a half north, sir,' the helmsman reported.

'Very good,' Fury replied, 'keep her at that.'

Another shouted order from Fury to the men at the braces had the topsail yards trimmed round slightly to catch the wind fuller. It had been lucky that the wind had picked up in the last few hours – it would speed their progress to Bombay.

Fury glanced round to see where their consorts were. *Otter* was out ahead about one and a half cables away, two points off the starboard bow. *Amazon* was about a cable's length distant now on their larboard quarter, obviously intending to keep well up to windward to enable her to swoop down and protect either *Otter* or *Bedford* should an enemy appear over the horizon.

He looked up at the topsails which were drawing well, and decided with the wind fair he would see how much sail she could carry. Captain Barber would not be happy unless he clapped on all the sail he could manage – understandable with a thirty-six-gun eighteen-pounder enemy frigate cruising in these waters. He raised the speaking trumpet to his lips once more.

'Hands aloft to loose courses!' he shouted, watching closely as the men scrambled like monkeys up the rigging, laying out on the yards and untying the gaskets which held the sails in place against the yard.

'Man the tack and sheet! Let go clew garnets, buntlines and leech lines!'

A small pause while he made sure everyone was ready.

'Let fall!' he shouted, the men on the yards releasing the sails and sending them dropping down in great folds.

'Get the tack aboard! Haul aft the sheet!' he bellowed, the men hauling away on the tack to bring the weather lower corner of the sails down and secured forward, while the sheets were hauled to bring the lee corner of the sails down and sheeted home aft. The sails flapped noisily as the wind caught them and escaped, until the corners of the sails were at last secured, the canvas now billowing taut as the wind was captured and harnessed.

From his position on the starboard side of the quarterdeck, Fury could see that the fore course on the starboard side was not catching the wind very well, being blanketed somewhat by the larboard side of the main course.

'Men!' he shouted. 'Haul up the weather clew of the main course!'

He watched while the lower corner of the main course was raised to the yard, clearing the way for the wind to strike the fore course fully. The fore course was a more useful sail than the main course and would have a lifting effect on the *Bedford*'s bow, reducing the amount of weather helm she would have to carry. He turned to the helmsman once again.

'How does she handle?'

'Well enough, sir, she's carrying maybe a touch of weather helm.'

That was good. It was helpful to carry a little weather helm: it would enable *Bedford*'s bow to swing into the wind that much more easily when she was tacking.

Fury looked about him, where everything seemed to be solid, the *Bedford* picking up speed now she had set her courses. The bow was rising and pitching into the swell, sending up a shower of spray which seemingly hung there suspended for a moment, before being whipped aft by the wind. He could feel the salt on his lips now, carried by the wind and spray as he stood swaying on the quarterdeck to the movement of the deck, the steady sou'westerly wind warm as it buffeted him. It felt glorious after those two days spent heaved to, with little or no wind to cool the skin. He could feel his spirits and confidence soaring with each breath of wind, the invigorating feeling increasing his boldness and prompting him to make the decision to increase sail.

'Lay aloft and loose topgallants! Clear away the jib!' he shouted through the speaking trumpet.

The men went scampering back up the rigging, hanging out and backwards as they negotiated the futtock shrouds to reach the fighting tops, then up further past the topsail yards until finally they reached the topgallant yards and lay out along them. Fury could see another group of men were already stationed forward to hoist the large jib when he ordered it.

'Man topgallant halliards and sheets, jib halliards, weather topgallant braces!'

He could see the men were already prepared for it.

'Let go topgallant clew lines, lee braces, jib downhaul! Haul taut! Sheet home! Hoist away topgallants and jib!'

The string of orders were obeyed instantly, the men on the fo'c'sle now hauling the jib up the stay while the men on the topgallant halliards were raising the fore and main topgallant yards to their cap, the sails billowing as the yards rose, the clews already having been loosed by the yardmen and sheeted home to the topsail yards below them. Fury looked up, satisfied. She was heeling over more now, as could be expected with a greater press of canvas aloft, but she was not heeling so much that it would affect her grip on the water. He turned to go back below to the master's cabin, calling over to Clark as he made his way forward to the ladder.

'Yes, sir?' Clark replied, hurrying over to him.

'I am going below to the master's cabin for the time being. I will leave you in charge of the deck. Call me if the wind changes or if *Amazon* signals.'

'Aye aye, sir,' Clark replied, 'you can rely on me.'

'And send down Corporal Davis to see me in half an hour,' Fury finished, descending the ladder. Corporal Davis was in charge of the small marine detachment that Captain Barber had given him.

He reached the master's cabin and sat down at the desk, satisfied with the way things had gone during the morning. The men had taken a lot longer to make sail than he was used to in the *Amazon*, but that was to be expected with only a skeleton crew. It was lucky the captain had let him have the four marines on board also. As dumb as sheep they might be, but shove a rope in their hands and they could pull and haul as well as any man.

He reached into the desk drawer and pulled out the copy of the signal book, thumbing through the pages to familiarise himself once more with the signals. He had already served a time as the *Amazon*'s signal midshipman, the captain insisting all his 'young gentlemen' should get experience in each duty before they became lieutenants. He realised his memory of it was more than a little rusty as he pored over the pages, unsurprising considering he had not looked at the signal book for some months.

Fury looked up startled as the marine Corporal Davis entered the cabin and came to attention. Had thirty minutes passed by already? He sat back and studied the man, surprised by the fact that his scarlet tunic matched his face almost perfectly; whether he was merely flushed at this time or whether his face was permanently red he could not be sure, even after fifteen months on board the *Amazon* with him. He could not see a spark of intelligence in Davis's eyes as he scrutinised his face; as with most of the lower ranks he had probably been drilled so hard he had ceased to think for himself. Fury shook that thought out of his mind – he disliked judging people solely on appearances – he would wait until he had got to know him more. Davis removed his hat and placed it under his arm, showing off a wispy mop of fair hair, some plastered to his forehead with sweat.

'You wished to see me, sah!' he asked, more of a shout than a question, and obviously necessitated by the silence with which he had been greeted.

'Yes, I did,' Fury replied. 'Until we reach Bombay you will split your men into two watches along with the seamen. The captain expressed concern over the mood of the ex-*Bedford*s, so I would like two of your men on duty at all times, fully dressed and equipped. Is that understood?'

'Yes, sah,' Davis replied.

'You will also understand that, short-handed as we are, it may be necessary for your men to assist in the working of the ship at times. Nothing skilled, merely hauling on a rope along with the seamen.'

'Yes, sah,' he replied again, obviously a man of limited vocabulary.

'Good. That will be all, thank you.'

Davis saluted and walked out, leaving Fury alone once more in the cabin to continue his studying of the signal book.

The *Bedford*, *Amazon* and *Otter* thrashed along under full sail for two days, the wind constant on the larboard quarter and fair for Bombay. Not a single ship was sighted as they made their way northwards under the blue sky, now dotted with thick bushy white clouds.

Fury had marvelled at the beauty of the oceans, the vast expanse of deep blue flecked with white as the brisk wind whipped at the wave tops, a wind so warm it felt as if it had come straight from the cook's copper oven underneath the fo'c'sle. There was no log line to be found on the *Bedford*, so it was not possible to measure her speed, but Fury estimated it to be around six knots judging by the way she enthusiastically thrust her bow into each successive wave, sending a shower of spray over the men on the fo'c'sle before rising in time to plunge into the next one.

Standing at the taffrail looking aft, her creamy wake seemed to stretch for miles, gradually diminishing more and more until finally disappearing, swallowed up by the waves to erase all trace of their passing. Fury was glad he had not had much to do in the past couple of days – the *Bedford* had pretty much sailed herself. He had needed only to make sure the sails were drawing well and the course was correct.

He had taken in the topgallants at night to be cautious, of course, as any prudent mariner would, especially with only a small crew. It would be easier to handle the ship in the dark with no topgallants set in the event of something unexpected happening. Nothing did, however, and each day the approach of dawn had seen the men scampering aloft once more to raise them.

'Sir!'

He swung round, interrupted from his reverie. It was Clark, whom he had temporarily rated master's mate so that he could stand a watch, no other officer being available.

'*Amazon*'s signalling, sir!'

He was obviously repeating something he had already said, so engrossed had Fury been in his thoughts. He hurried over to the binnacle and took the telescope from its becket before going over to the larboard side and training it on *Amazon*. She had indeed hoisted a signal, although it was difficult to make out with the wind blowing straight towards them. He flicked through the signal book after he had convinced himself which flags she had hoisted.

'Clark!' he shouted, unnecessarily, as the man was standing right next to him. 'Heave to, if you please.'

'Aye aye, sir,' Clark replied, turning away and bellowing the orders which sent the men running to their stations to furl the topgallants, jib and courses.

Fury watched the men as they worked. Naturally it would take longer than usual to reduce sail and bring her to, due to the fact that they could not be furled all at once. He did not have enough men for that. But the crew looked cheerful and willing enough, going about their tasks with the minimum of fuss or noise. Even the ex-*Bedford*s, who might originally have resented being pressed against their will into the navy, seemed to be settling down well. Fury looked aloft as the men finished their work.

'Back the fore topsail!' he shouted, before turning to the man at the wheel and giving the order which would bring the *Bedford*'s head round until the wind was abeam.

Gradually she swung as the helmsman moved the spokes of the wheel through his hands. The men at the braces were hauling the fore topsail yard round, the sail flapping as the yard came through the eye of the wind until finally the wind caught the sail from forward, throwing it back against the mast. Her way slowly diminished as the forward thrust of the main topsail was counteracted by the backward thrust of the fore topsail.

Fury looked across to where the *Amazon* was ploughing down towards them, the momentary doubt in his mind as to whether he had read her signal correctly being dismissed as he saw her courses disappear before she came up into the wind, half a cable to windward with her main topsail aback. He raised his telescope to his eye once more and studied her, watching as she lowered her cutter into the water before the boat's crew scrambled down into her, followed by what looked like Lieutenant Carlisle. A wave of disappointment flooded over Fury at the thought of being superseded.

The boat, dancing around amid the waves, crept closer as the men bent to their oars. A wait of what seemed like hours followed, with Fury pacing impatiently about the quarterdeck. She finally hooked on and a moment later Fury was standing at the entry port looking into the slightly gaunt features of the *Amazon*'s second lieutenant, Mr Carlisle.

His uniform jacket looked ill fitting due to his loss of weight, and some of his blond hair was plastered to his forehead with salt spray, giving him a somewhat dishevelled appearance as he looked around the deck.

'Welcome aboard, sir,' Fury greeted him, touching his hat.

'Thank you, Mr Fury,' Carlisle replied, reaching up to brush the hair away from his forehead. 'Old sawbones has given me the all clear at last, thank God, and Captain Barber ordered me over to take command. You may resume our course now. I shall be down below in the master's cabin and I would be obliged if you would join me once we are under way again.'

'Aye aye, sir,' Fury replied, quickly turning and shouting the commands to get *Bedford* under way once more, while Carlisle made his way below.

Still a little shaky on his feet, Fury thought, as he watched him go. Understandable, really, for a man who had spent ten days in the sick bay with a dangerous fever. It had been an unfortunate time for him to be struck down, with the subsequent unexpected battle taking place. It had been his section of guns that Fury had taken command of during the battle with the *Bedford* and *Otter*, before the death of Lieutenant Scott had required him to take command of the whole deck.

Fury wondered if he had been aware of the battle taking place above him. Probably not: any officer who was not unconscious or insensible with fever would have made every effort to resume his duties, knowing the ship was going into action, no matter what his condition. He looked above at the sails now drawing once more, with courses and topgallants reset. He had been daydreaming again, he admonished himself, turning to go below.

'You have the deck, Clark,' he said as he passed the acting master's mate, no doubt shortly to be reduced back to able seaman now that Carlisle had arrived on board.

'Aye aye, sir,' Clark replied, watching as Fury made his way below.

Fury did not hear his acknowledgement. He was busy mentally preparing the verbal report which Lieutenant Carlisle would no doubt ask for.

The weather slowly started to worsen during the first night of Lieutenant Carlisle's command of the *Bedford*. Morning saw her wallowing along uneasily over the oily swell of the Indian Ocean, the water now a pale greyish colour in stark contrast to its previous brilliant turquoise.

Fury could see as he came up on deck that she was riding along under reefed topsails and courses, the topgallants having been furled the previous night, and the jib replaced with the fore topmast staysail. The wind felt stronger than it did when he had left the deck earlier, each gust buffeting him as he carefully crossed the deck. He was still feeling heavy eyed after only a fitful sleep since he had finished his last watch at four o'clock, and the wind was helping to strip away the drowsiness.

He had been right about Clark: Lieutenant Carlisle had reduced him to able seaman once more, meaning that Fury and Carlisle had to stand watch and watch about, four hours on and four hours off, day and night. It was not easy, but it could be done for the one week it would take to reach Bombay. Anything longer and their lack of sleep might endanger the ship because of a wrong decision being made, a wrong order given.

He reached Carlisle over by the wheel, shocked to see how haggard he looked, standing there hatless with his blond hair streaming in the wind.

'Good morning, Mr Fury!' Carlisle greeted him, the brightness in his eyes suggesting his mental fitness was far better than his physical.

'Good morning, sir,' Fury replied, raising his voice just slightly so it would be heard over the noise of the wind.

'Nasty weather,' Carlisle continued. 'It will get worse before it gets better, mark me. Do you think you can handle her?'

'Aye, sir,' he replied, with a confidence he did not entirely feel.

'Very well then, I will catch some rest. It will be good training for you, I suppose. Call me if you need to.'

'Aye aye, sir,' he replied again, as the lieutenant began to turn away.

'Oh, and Mr Fury!' Carlisle said, swinging back. 'Let's see how much you have learned on board the *Amazon*. Please be so good as to prepare the ship for stormy weather. You should have had enough practice at that on the way out here!'

That was true enough. *Amazon* had encountered several periods of dirty weather on her voyage out from Portsmouth.

'I shall inspect your preparations when I return on deck at the end of your watch,' Carlisle finished.

Four hours did not give him long to make the necessary preparations, especially short-handed as they were, Fury mused, as Carlisle finally turned to go below.

'Clark!' he shouted, the seaman coming over almost at once. He seemed to be nearby whenever he was needed, leaving Fury beginning to wonder if the man ever slept.

'Aye, sir?' he enquired.

'I will be inspecting the *Bedford* to make sure she is ready in the event of the weather worsening. I shall need your help.'

'Aye aye, sir,' he replied simply, waiting for Fury's orders.

'I want you to check the wheel ropes, ensure the relieving tackles are hooked on to the tiller, and ready the spare tiller and rudder chocks.'

The rudder chocks would be needed to wedge into the rudder port, either side of the rudder head, to steady the rudder if the tiller broke, until the spare tiller could be shipped. That was a very distinct possibility with the replacement rudder that they currently had, which had been fitted by the *Amazon*'s carpenter. That was only intended to be a temporary measure until they reached Bombay, and was certainly not sufficient to endure prolonged heavy weather.

'Report to me once that is done. I will be inspecting the guns.'

'Aye aye, sir,' Clark said again, turning away and going below.

Fury turned to the men at the wheel, two of them now that the weather was worsening.

'I will be down below inspecting the guns. Call me if you need anything.'

The man on the weather side of the wheel nodded his acknowledgement as Fury turned to go below.

By the time he reached the companion ladder leading down to the upper deck, Fury was quietly talking to himself, a habit he had adopted to ensure he did not forget anything. He arrived in the gloom of the upper deck and walked aft, moving over to the starboard side to check the guns one by one. He checked the breechings and tackles and made sure the muzzles were lashed securely to the clamps above the gun ports just under the deck beams. He took his time, acutely aware that he had never done it before. He wished the *Amazon*'s gunner was on board; it would be his responsibility then – and a large one, because if one of those guns came loose in a heavy sea it would likely smash right through *Bedford*'s side. He was nearing the end of his inspection when Clark came up and reported.

'All ready, sir. And I've told a couple of men to man the tiller if the wheel ropes part.'

'Very good,' Fury replied. The man thought of everything.

'I will be finished here shortly. In the meantime I want to make sure the anchors are secure. Check to see that the ring and shank painters are taut and secure, and have preventer painters rigged.'

'Aye aye, sir.'

The ring and shank painters were the lashings which kept the anchors secure to the ship's side, and would need to be checked to ensure nothing would part as the ship's movement worsened.

Finally finishing his inspection of the guns, Fury looked along the length of the deck where all the guns were lashed up, their muzzles at forty-five degrees to the ship's side. Satisfied, he made his way back up to the quarterdeck, stumbling once on his way as a rogue wave caught the *Bedford* unawares, unexpectedly altering her roll. He reached the deck still talking quietly to himself, going through what else remained to be done before he would be confident that *Bedford* was well prepared.

'Evans!' he shouted, recognising one of the *Amazon*'s men.

Evans came hurrying over, his face showing slight concern.

'Yessir?'

Fury looked at him, pausing a moment to get his thoughts clear in his head.

'I want those hammocks stowed below,' he ordered, pointing to the hammocks lashed in their nettings along the bulwarks. 'Once that is done, find some spare line from somewhere and rig lifelines along the weather deck. Understood?'

'Yessir,' Evans replied, knuckling his forehead and moving away just as Clark came up.

'Anchors secure, sir,' Clark reported.

'Very well,' Fury replied. 'Pick out some reliable men and clear away any excess gear in the tops. Send down the topgallant masts and yards – I want them properly lashed down on deck. Studdingsail booms down off the yards and the stunsails and royals out of the rigging. Spanker boom and gaff – down and well lashed below the bulwarks. Then rig preventer braces on the weather side. Do you think you can manage all that?'

'Aye aye, sir,' Clark replied, Fury's heart warming, not for the first time, to his cheerfulness and confidence.

'Very well then – carry on.'

Fury moved over towards the boats stowed on the booms above the waist. The covers were already on to prevent water from getting in, so it only remained for him to check that the lashings holding the boats in place were secure. That did not take long, and he moved back to the larboard side of the quarterdeck, getting clear in his mind what was left to do.

He looked up at the sky, now a sweeping grey and seemingly much lower than the clear blue skies of before. Fury felt distinctly trapped, as if hemmed in from above, able only to watch and wait as nature decided his fate. He must have been looking up at the sky longer than he realised, because here was Evans again, knuckling his forehead and trying to get his attention.

'Hammocks all stowed, sir, an' I've set a couple o' men at rigging the lifelines.'

'Good,' Fury replied, 'see that the hatches are battened down below, and then see if you can find any storm canvas lying about.'

'Storm canvas, aye aye, sir,' Evans repeated, turning away once more.

It was as well to get the hatches battened down early. The sea was already picking up, with the *Bedford*'s bow throwing more water back with each pitch. Battening down the hatches would stop any water getting below, especially important if the cargo was to remain undamaged. Fury walked over to the wheel where the two helmsmen were, keeping her on course at nor'-nor'west a half north.

'Can you handle her?' he asked the weather helmsman, the senior of the two.

'Aye, sir, for th'moment.'

'Let me know if it gets too much and I will station another two men to assist.'

'Aye aye, sir, thank you, sir,' the man replied, as Fury turned away.

There was nothing more he could do now but wait while the preparations were completed. He stood by the mizzen chains, one arm hooked through the foremost shroud to steady himself against the ship's movement as he scanned the horizon with his telescope. He could see no ships on the horizon other than *Amazon* and *Otter*, both now further off, striving for more sea room in the event the weather deteriorated further.

Six bells rang out – an hour to go before the end of his watch. Evans came up and made his report. All hatches were now battened down and the men had finished rigging the lifelines along the deck – Fury could see that for himself. He had been through the entire ship, however, and could find no storm canvas; indeed he could find no sign of any spare canvas whatsoever. Any spare which had been carried when she left England had probably been taken off when she had been captured.

That was unsurprising really: every ship, especially one on a long voyage, would want the security of lots of spare canvas on board in the event of accident. This Frenchman, *Magicienne*, had obviously been in need of it. Fury could only hope that in the coming weather the sails remained undamaged, at least to the extent so that they could maintain steerage way and make good their course for Bombay.

Seven bells rang out signalling only half an hour to go before the end of his watch. Here was Clark hovering nearby at last, ready to report.

'All secure aloft, sir. Preventer braces rigged. T'gallants have been got down and all spare booms and spars have been taken down from the rigging and secured on deck.'

'Very good, Clark,' Fury said, pausing to decide whether there was anything else he wanted doing.

Nothing urgent perhaps, but it would be best to keep the men on deck busy, and it would be as well to make sure . . .

'Set the men to work for the rest of the watch at checking the rigging for signs of chafe. Examine the shrouds, check the deadeyes and lanyards are secure. You know the type of thing.'

'Aye aye, sir,' Clark replied, as always it seemed.

Fury had the distinct impression that if he ordered Clark to attack and board a first rate with just a cutter and a crew of twenty, all he would get in reply was 'aye aye, sir'. He turned to hide the half-smile which the thought had provoked, looking up at the rigging set against the menacing sky. Everything looked well secure, but only time would tell.

He turned back just in time to see Carlisle appear on deck, ready for his watch.

'You may make your report, Mr Fury.'

Fury took him through all the preparations he had made during his watch, confident that he had omitted nothing. Carlisle listened, nodding his head in agreement as Fury went through it all.

'What about the pumps, Mr Fury? Have those been rigged and made ready in the event that we take on water?'

'No, sir,' Fury stammered, embarrassed that such an obvious step had been forgotten.

'No matter, I will see to that, and we had better put some hands to work sharpening the axes in case we have to cut any rigging away.'

'Yes, sir,' Fury replied, inwardly fuming at his own incompetence.

'You may go below and get some rest now, Mr Fury,' Carlisle continued, 'I have the deck.'

Fury touched his hat, now planted firmly on his head to keep it from being whipped away by the wind, and made his way below to his hammock slung in one of the master's mate's cabins. He climbed in to rest his eyes for a moment, and it was not long before a sound sleep ambushed him.

Chapter Eight

The weather continued to worsen during the course of the day, the thick clouds covering the horizon lower than ever and now a darker grey than before. The wind came up, steadily freshening as the hours passed and in turn kicking up the sea into a boiling mass of foam and spray, the size of the swell gradually increasing.

The galley fire had been extinguished since morning, so the small crew had to make do with hard tack and a generous issue of grog to warm them. Lieutenant Carlisle had ordered sail to be shortened about six bells in the afternoon watch in response to a signal from *Amazon* to 'make all sail conformable with weather and to run before the wind', effectively abandoning their desired course until the weather eased.

As a result *Bedford* was now scudding along under reefed fore course, reefed main topsail and fore topmast staysail. In the event of the sea rising even higher, the main topsail would ensure that *Bedford* did not lose the wind in the trough of a wave, thereby ensuring she would not slow enough to allow the following wave to catch her up and 'poop' her – crash down on to her quarterdeck and sweep it clear. With no thick storm canvas on board there was a good chance that the sails would blow out if the wind kept steadily increasing, but, other than running under bare poles, that was a chance they would have to take.

The sunset came earlier than usual that day, about six o'clock, so that when Fury came on deck at eight o'clock for the start of his watch it was completely dark. He wrapped his coat closer around him as he reached the quarterdeck, holding on to one of the lifelines to keep his balance in this heavy sea. He made his way aft to relieve Lieutenant Carlisle.

'Course north, Mr Fury. We are running before the wind under main topsail, fore course and fore topmast staysail. We lost sight of *Amazon* and *Otter* as the sun set. Keep a lookout for any lights showing. You have the deck!' Carlisle's report was shouted into Fury's ear over the buffeting of wind and sea.

'Aye aye, sir,' Fury replied, absorbing the information as Carlisle staggered along the lifeline to go below for some rest.

The wind must have backed during the last dog watch, Fury thought, because when he had turned over the deck at the end of the first dog watch it had still been at sou'west. Luckily their current course was only a slight variation from their original course so they still had no problem in reaching Bombay, assuming of course the weather eased in time, allowing them to set a more easterly course.

His eyes were becoming more accustomed to the dark now and he looked around the deck. Darker shapes against the ship's side showed where the men on watch were huddled together, down under the bulwark in an attempt to shelter from the wind and spray. The unfortunate men whose duty as lookouts required them to stand up were hanging on to the bulwarks to stay on their feet – one on either side of the bow, one at each side by the main chains and one on each quarter. The lookouts aloft had been brought down at sunset as the darkness closed in. With visibility as it was now, Fury wondered if the lookouts on deck would be able to see a thing, especially the two men on each quarter, facing partially into the wind and spray.

Despite the blackness, as he looked around he was sure he could sense an air of dejection settling over the deck like a blanket. Every man on deck seemed completely forlorn. The usual cheerfulness and confidence of the jolly jack tar seemed to be missing, as if evaporated in the sodden atmosphere. Strange, that; the men had been through storms before and he had never seen them like this. Maybe it was just the ex-*Bedford*s, he thought, or maybe it was just his own bad mood and exhaustion playing tricks on him.

Dismissing the thought from his mind, he looked out over the transom. He could see the large waves following them by the phosphorescence of the foam as the peaks of the waves overhung, before finally tumbling down heavily into the trough. The strength of the wind, probably around fifty knots, was blowing the foam in dense white streaks along its course, hitting the *Bedford* and her decks and stinging skin and eyes.

Fury turned forward, his cheeks aching after being screwed up against the wind and spray. There were now four men at the wheel to keep *Bedford* steady as she plunged her way through the churning seas, and from the looks of them they were not having too much trouble handling her. There was nothing else to do now but keep her before the wind and wait, hoping for the wind to ease.

Fury was partially glad for the spray flying about and stinging his face as it kept him from falling asleep as he stood there, exhausted, clutching the lifeline by the wheel and waiting for his watch to end.

Fury woke up sharply, a momentary confusion shrouding him as his befuddled brain gradually worked out where he was. His immediate feeling was one of shock – his hammock was swinging around at an alarming rate, the deck suddenly coming up as if to meet him on one side, before quickly falling away and appearing over the other side as the ship pitched and rolled. He was surprised that he had not been woken earlier by the motion; he must be more tired than he had realised.

Swinging his legs over the side and carefully watching the movement of the deck he managed to get himself out of his hammock in one piece, clutching at anything solid to stay on his feet. He felt lucky now that he had dropped into his hammock fully clothed after his last watch. It would be next to impossible to get dressed with the ship pitching as she was. It was hard enough to struggle into his coat, wedging himself into a corner to keep from toppling over.

He could hear the howling of the wind and the creaking of the *Bedford*'s timbers as she worked. That was a good sign – she was being pliable, not rigid and brittle. He realised he had heard the fierce wind from the moment he awoke, but his mind had not registered it until now, being occupied as it was by the ship's movement.

He began to make his way towards the quarterdeck, covering the journey bit by bit as he waited for the right moment to scramble to the next available handhold to cling on to before the deck dropped steeply away from his feet once more, leaving his stomach momentarily in his mouth until her bows rose again, allowing him to catch it.

It was still completely dark as he reached the top of the companion ladder leading to the quarterdeck after what seemed an age, clinging to every rung to avoid being flung into the air and overboard like a rag doll, never to be seen again. Clutching the bulwark and trying to keep his feet on the deck as water rushed past and out of the scuppers, he looked aft along the quarterdeck.

He was already soaked through, his eyes stinging sharply, so that it was a moment before he grasped what he could see. His sharp intake of breath was purely instinctive as he stood in terror, looking as the following wave rose up behind *Bedford*'s stern like a wall of water. This was not like facing battle; he had not been this terrified by far, knowing that his fate depended to some extent on his own abilities, and with some small comfort in the knowledge that he was doing his duty. This was death of a useless kind, where its victims were helpless against the ferocity of nature, as if being punished for some of mankind's mistakes.

Fury braced himself for the inevitable as the wave towered above, seemingly set to crash down on top of them all, sweeping the deck clear. But was she – ? Yes, she was! The *Bedford*'s stern was slowly rising and rising, until it seemed to Fury that the deck was vertical as the wave swept under them, the stern now dropping as the *Bedford* passed down the after side of the wave.

He shook himself free of his terror, inching along the bulwark and looking across at Carlisle who was clinging to one of the lifelines rigged along the deck, within hailing distance of the four men who were now fighting the wheel, trying to keep the *Bedford* stern on to the waves so they could run before them to avoid being pooped. If she were allowed to yaw, presenting her quarter to the following waves, then she would broach to, the wave pushing her bow round so she would be broadside on to the waves, before being rolled on to her beam ends and sunk. Please God the men at the wheel stayed alert.

He looked aloft to see that the masts and yards were bare. They were running along under bare poles, the wind too fierce for even a small scrap of canvas to be set. He could make out a man huddled in the foretop; probably one of the cathead lookouts, sent aloft there so he wouldn't be swept overboard at the bows. That was the only man aloft as far as Fury could see. Unsurprising, since it was still a couple of hours away from daylight.

He looked back towards Carlisle. His eye caught sight of something aft, and he looked again. Yes, there it was! A hawser, leading out of one of the aft gun ports on the larboard side with what looked like a spar lashed to the end of it. Carlisle must have ordered that to help the men at the wheel: the hawser would prevent *Bedford*'s stern from coming round into the wind and broaching to.

He began to make his way slowly towards Carlisle, having to use every ounce of his nerve to release his grip on the bulwark and stagger over to the lifeline, clutching desperately at it until his hands gratefully reached it and he clung on as the next wave came along. Gradually pulling himself along it, he finally reached Lieutenant Carlisle near the wheel.

It took Fury a few moments to catch his breath, exhausted as he was after the efforts of clinging on and hauling himself up the steep deck. Carlisle was shouting something next to him, but the howling of the wind was whipping his words away before they could even reach the short distance to him. The blank look on Fury's face obviously told Carlisle that he hadn't heard him, and he edged closer till he was shouting at the top of his voice into Fury's ear. One word only, but that word invoked more terror than the sight of a thousand enemy line-of-battle ships.

'Cyclone!'

Fury looked at him in disbelief for a moment before nodding as he realised that Carlisle was right. This was not merely a heavy storm: it was what every seamen feared most, what few seamen ever experienced and what even fewer ever survived. They were called different things in different parts of the world – hurricanes in the Caribbean and north-east Pacific, typhoons in the north-west Pacific, and cyclones in the Arabian Sea and Indian Ocean. He realised now why the men had looked dejected during his last watch – they had known from experience that this was more than just a storm.

He had heard stories of them; winds and seas that flung the largest two-thousand-ton ship about like a cork until her masts went by the board, unable to stand the tremendous strain, and she was dragged round – her masts and rigging acting as a sea anchor – broadside on to the huge rolling waves. Then the decks would be washed clear of men, guns, the wheel, capstan, everything, before she would finally fill and sink. Her only hope would be that the wreckage could be cut away before she was filled, giving her a chance to right herself.

It was still not clear whether the *Bedford* and her consorts were passing close to the eye of the cyclone or whether this was more towards the edge of it. Judging by the size of the sea, Fury had to believe it was the former – it was impossible to contemplate waves any larger than these.

He tried to shake such thoughts out of his mind. If they were going to survive, he would need as clear a head as possible. He slowly edged over to the binnacle, peering down into the compass to see what course they were heading. Nor'west. The wind had backed even more. This course was taking them gradually away from the mainland of India and their destination of Bombay, although they were still heading north.

Unfortunately they had no choice. There was no question in this weather of doing anything other than running before the wind. Fury tried to look on the bright side – at least they had ample sea room. If the wind had veered to a more easterly heading, they would be flying along towards the coast of India and possible shipwreck.

He turned forward towards Lieutenant Carlisle and braced himself against the buffeting. It was difficult to face into the wind such was its strength, and even more difficult to talk into it, the task not made any easier by the blinding spray, stinging the eyes and invading the throat. Leaning over towards Carlisle's ear he shouted as loudly as he could.

'Any sign of *Amazon* or *Otter*, sir?'

It was a stupid question; Fury realised that as soon as it was uttered. In this visibility and with only one lookout aloft in the foretop, it was next to impossible that they would be in sight, even if they were carrying lights.

'No!' Carlisle shouted in reply.

In this weather and with these seas it was highly likely they would be scattered far and wide, so that *Bedford* would have to make her way to Bombay on her own. If any of them survived, that is.

'Sir!' He leaned forward to shout into Carlisle's ear once more. 'It's my watch, sir, get some sleep below!'

'No!' Carlisle bellowed back, 'I'll stay on deck – it can't last like this for much longer!'

There seemed to be a general feeling on deck, borne from experience maybe, that this was it. If they could survive this then the weather would ease afterwards. Or maybe it was hope: men at the end of their endurance merely unwilling to believe the conditions could possibly get any worse. He could not be certain. He could be sure, though, that he could not take much more himself.

After what seemed hours to Fury the darkness all around started to turn into a softer grey as dawn approached, the men about the deck becoming more distinguishable instead of merely darker shapes against the blackness. It came slowly, as if reluctant to light up the terrible scene.

Huge waves dwarfed the tiny *Bedford* as she was thrown about, pitching and rising almost vertically as the waves passed under her with such force that it was a miracle her masts did not go by the board. The howling wind was like nothing Fury had ever experienced before; indeed, nor had many of the experienced seamen. It was impossible to breathe facing into it, and the strength of it was such that men were forced to cling on to anything solid with all their seeping strength to avoid being lifted off their feet and plucked from the deck of the *Bedford* and into oblivion.

The air was completely filled with foam and spray, seriously affecting visibility and making it difficult to keep eyes open for long.

Fury clung to the lifeline and peered at the compass housed in the binnacle once more to judge the *Bedford*'s course – still nor'west. The four men at the wheel had just been replaced after their spell, staggering below exhausted after fighting the rudder for two hours. Relieving the men at the wheel was always the most dangerous time for a ship running before a storm, not merely because of the changeover itself, but also because the new men would have to get a feel for the ship's movements. One wrong step and they could lay her broadside on to the waves. Fury had been reassured to see that Clark was one of the new weather helmsmen. He could not quite put his finger on the reason, but it eased the strain slightly knowing that Clark was responsible for keeping *Bedford* on course.

Here was Lieutenant Carlisle turning towards him once again, trying to get his attention.

'Send four men down to relieve the men at the pumps!' he bellowed, Fury nodding his understanding.

Pumping out the water which seeped into the hull via a thousand different routes was a hard and thankless task, but it was necessary, especially in conditions like these. The pumps had been at work since the increasing wind had first kicked up the seas, initially for fifteen minutes in every hour and then for thirty minutes, as the deteriorating conditions caused more water to pour in. It was a disheartening task in which it was an effort merely to keep the water levels from gaining, otherwise the *Bedford* would gradually fill up so much that she would sink.

Fury hauled himself along the lifeline, his feet slipping on the sloping deck as he edged forward towards the mainmast on his way to where a group of men were huddled underneath the bulwark to shelter from the wind and spray. He recognised the stocky frame of Evans among them and managed to hurl himself across to the ship's side, clinging on to the bulwark and crouching next to the man so that he could hear him. The howling wind was much less audible down here, sheltered as it was, so it was not necessary to lean over to Evans's ear to shout.

'Evans, take three men with you and go and relieve the hands at the pump!'

'Aye aye, sir!' Evans shouted back, somewhat reluctantly it appeared to Fury.

The hardship of working the pumps was partially countered by the fact that down below they would be out of the wind and spray altogether. Even so, the men's faces as Evans swiftly called out three names told Fury they would rather stay where they were.

He stood up once again to make his way back towards the wheel, shocked at how powerful the buffeting of the wind was, even after only a few seconds down in the shelter of the bulwarks. His arms were aching now as he pulled himself along, the water streaming down his face and neck underneath his coat, making him shiver in spite of his exertions.

He was about to make the perilous journey from the bulwark to the lifeline next to the wheel alongside Lieutenant Carlisle again, when he heard something. What was it? A sharp crack or whipping sound, so loud as to make itself heard above the din of the cyclone. He reached the lifeline next to Carlisle in a frantic dash.

'Did you hear that, sir?'

Another stupid question, judging by the look on Carlisle's face and his anxious glances aloft to try and spot any parted rigging. Here came Cooper, one of the seamen stationed forward on the fo'c'sle, hurrying aft far too quickly for safety.

'Sir!' he shouted, reaching them eventually and reporting to Carlisle. 'The lower foremast stay has parted!'

A moment's silence passed while Fury and Carlisle digested this disastrous news, before Carlisle responded.

'Get all hands on deck except those men at the pumps. Every man is to be issued with an axe in the event one of the masts goes by the board and we have to cut it loose. See to it, if you please, Mr Fury!'

'Aye aye, sir!' Fury shouted, turning back to Cooper. 'Pass the word along – every man is to equip himself with an axe. If we lose anything, we must cut it away as soon as possible. And get that man out of the foretop!'

Cooper nodded and began to make his way back along the lifeline, beckoning to the seamen huddled along the deck as he passed. Fury began to make his way forward as well to ensure every available hand was on deck.

The lower foremast stay supported the foremast forward, and was made fast to the end of the bowsprit. There was a lower preventer stay rigged to share the strain equally with the lower foremast stay, but with one now gone all the weight would be on the preventer stay. Fury would be surprised if that managed to hold on its own. If they both went, there was a good chance the foremast would go by the board, and that might have a domino effect on the main and mizzen, most of the forward stays being supported against the mast in front as they were.

He finally reached the forward part of the quarterdeck and was making ready to transfer himself to the bulwark, waiting for the right moment in the ship's movement, when there was another cracking sound. He looked forward, his first thought being that the preventer stay had parted, but he could see nothing unusual there through the driving spray.

The *Bedford*'s stern was reaching higher up into the air now as another huge wave began to pass under her, Fury still clinging to the lifeline and awaiting his moment. Finally she reached the crest and started her downward slide, down the after part of the wave with her bows now reaching to the sky.

Crash! Fury looked forward, startled by the loudness of the noise and the unmistakable sound of splintering timber. The foremast had snapped about two feet from the deck, hanging backwards in a tangle of rigging for a moment against the mainmast before deflecting off it and over the starboard side, trailing along in the water by the rigging. A moment later another crash sounded, not as loud this time as only the main topmast snapped off, sagging backwards against the rigging of the mizzen mast. The twanging of parting ropes echoed out as the strain proved too much for the mizzen stays, and almost immediately another splintering crash sounded as the mizzen topmast, now without its stays, snapped off just above the mizzen mast cap, falling backwards to trail over the *Bedford*'s transom in the sea, still attached by its rigging.

Fury stood still for a second, looking in terror at the foremast completely gone and trailing over the side, the main topmast hanging down by its rigging, and the mizzen topmast trailing astern of the *Bedford* by its rigging. He shook himself into action, shouting orders to the men on deck as he jumped over to the bulwark and started to make his way forward along the gangway to the fo'c'sle.

It was useless – there was no chance of the men hearing him in this wind. Luckily they all knew as well as he did what needed to be done first and he could already see men through the driving spray converging on the fo'c'sle, axes in hand, to begin the urgent task of cutting away the foremast. It was already proving to be too late, however, as the foremast, dragging along the starboard side, began to act as a sea anchor, slowly pulling the *Bedford*'s bows round. They would soon be broadside on to the monstrous waves if the trailing rigging could not be cut away immediately. Fury grabbed an axe from somewhere and, still clinging to the bulwark, hauled himself along to where the rigging of the foremast was hanging over the side. What had previously been shrouds, halliards, braces and lifts was now a tangle of useless rope, endangering the safety of the ship every second.

He started to swing the axe wildly, still using one hand to keep himself up. He could feel rope parting under his blade as the axe crashed into the top of the bulwark. He was swinging again and again as quickly as possible, the other men doing the same so that with each blow the mast was that much closer to being released. Then it was gone in a flash, no more rigging left to be cut and the *Bedford* finally free of the mast's drag effect.

Fury looked up, seeing the next wave tearing down upon them and realising in a panic that, in the time it had taken them to cut away the mast, the *Bedford* had been swinging round all the while and was now lying broadside on, awaiting the next wave. She was slowly starting to turn back now, the hawser and spar laid out of the larboard quarter gradually bringing her stern round again, but it was going to be too late, even Fury could see that – the wave would reach them long before she had been pulled round fully.

'Hold on, men!' he shouted as the wave came upon them, an unnecessary order as the men had themselves been looking on in mute terror.

Clinging on to the bulwark, Fury put his head down and waited for death to come. He could feel a torrent of water hitting him, before he lost his footing on the deck as the wave thrust *Bedford* over on to her beam ends. A splintering crash sounded above the rush of water as something else snapped under the strain. Please God the hatches were battened down well; that was their only chance. If water got into the hold they would sink like a rock.

Fury tentatively raised his head as he momentarily regained his footing on the deck. The *Bedford* had reached the crest of the wave, and now began quickly sliding down the aft side, with Fury holding on for dear life once again as he looked over to larboard. Those crashes must have been the main and mizzen masts going by the board as the ship was laid over and the wave hit her. They were now hanging over the larboard side, helping steady the *Bedford*'s deck as she was swept down the aft side of the wave.

'Cut those masts away, lads!' Fury shouted, scrambling across the deck as *Bedford* reached the trough of the wave, miraculously still afloat and now back upright for a few precious seconds.

The drag of the main and mizzen masts over the side was acting just as the foremast had done, only the main and mizzen were hanging over the larboard side, not the starboard, and so the drag was bringing the *Bedford*'s stern round back towards the waves. Fury experienced a flash of hope as he realised this – there was still a chance!

He reached the larboard bulwark after slipping and sliding across the deck, the solid oak reassuring as he grasped it with both hands. He started to make his way aft to where the mainmast rigging was hanging over the side, still attached to the mainmast itself, which was being dragged along beside them.

Looking aft he could see men on the quarterdeck hurrying over to cut away the mizzen mast as he finally reached the tangled mass of rigging draped over the bulwark. He started hacking away with the axe, which was somehow still in his hand, the other men joining him in an instant.

He clung on for dear life with one arm as the next wave was upon them, the *Bedford*, incredibly, now stern on to the waves once again, the effect of the main and mizzen masts having dragged her back round. Up she rose, stern high into the air, the men's feet slipping on the canting deck as they continued to hack away at the rigging.

Then the crest of the wave was upon them, the *Bedford*'s deck horizontal for only a second before she began sliding down the back of the wave, bow now reaching upwards. There was something not quite right, though, about the angle of the deck – Fury could feel it, and he sensed the men could too. The *Bedford* was no longer stern on to the waves as she slid down the back of this one; the masts alongside had continued to drag her round so that she was now showing her larboard quarter to the next wave. In another few seconds she would be broadside on to the waves once more, only this time the larboard broadside, not the starboard.

Fury continued hacking away frantically at the rigging, all these possibilities flashing through his mind as he worked, head down on his chest to reduce the water coming into his mouth and stinging his eyes. A last swing by one of the men saw the final rope parted, the mainmast drifting away. Fury looked aft once more to where the men on the quarterdeck were still hacking away, the last rope being severed as he watched. Over to his right he could see the next wave coming to meet them. He could see the floating spar, lashed to the hawser from one of *Bedford*'s larboard gun ports, floating up the side of the wave as it approached, the spar now abeam of the *Bedford* instead of astern.

'Hold on, men!' he shouted once again as the *Bedford*'s deck canted and she was swept up by the wave, the deck once more falling from under his feet so that he had to hold himself up by the bulwark as the torrents of water cascaded over him, gushing into his eyes and throat and making him cough and retch.

He was beginning to give up the struggle, his grip weakening on the bulwark and the last grains of strength seeping from his arms. The deck appeared again under his feet just in time as the crest of the wave passed under them, before the *Bedford* began sliding inexorably down the other side.

How many waves they went through, Fury could not guess, only knowing that each time, as he was about to give up hope that the *Bedford* would right herself, the crest of the wave would appear and the *Bedford*'s ballast help to right her hull, allowing his feet to touch the deck once more and giving his burning arms a brief respite before the next wave arrived.

Somehow throughout it all the hatches remained intact, and gradually the *Bedford*'s stern began to swing back round towards the following waves, the trailing hawser and spar led out of one of the larboard gun ports slowly acting to straighten her up. Once she was straight again her motion was much like before – hard to think that she now had no masts, Fury thought, coughing up sea water by the bulwark as he clung on still.

The men who had been with him cutting away at the foremast and mainmast rigging were still there next to him, having survived the recent pummelling. Fury turned to the nearest seaman.

'Go down and check the men at the pumps!' he shouted, the wind still howling continuously around them. 'Then report back to me how much water we've taken on board!'

The *Bedford* did not feel too sluggish to Fury but it was as well to make sure. The seaman nodded, making a reply that Fury didn't hear before scrambling off.

Fury turned aft and started to make his way back to the quarterdeck, noting as he passed along the gangway that the boats, which had been stored on the booms amidships along with the spare spars, had been swept overboard.

As he reached the quarterdeck he transferred himself to the lifeline, seeing with surprise that the wheel was still there, along with the helmsmen, although the binnacle had vanished. Fury could only guess at how they had managed to survive during the recent broaching. He was glad to see Lieutenant Carlisle standing by the wheel.

'Sir!' he shouted. 'I've sent a man down to check the wells and report back!'

'Very good!' Carlisle bellowed in reply. 'Organise a muster of the men too!'

'Aye aye, sir!'

'Glad to see you're still with us, Mr Fury – a close run thing!'

'Aye, sir!' Fury replied, well aware of just how close it had been.

'It's damn lucky the guns were all secured well – it doesn't look like we lost one!' Carlisle continued, Fury suddenly remembering that he had personally checked the storm lashings on each gun before the cyclone hit. There was some satisfaction in the knowledge.

Chapter Nine

The two officers stood on the *Bedford*'s quarterdeck, clinging on to the lifeline in silence, each one reliving those terrible moments when they thought they would die as the ship had rolled over on to her beam ends. It had been a miracle that they had survived.

When the seaman returned from seeing the men at the pumps with the report that they would have the water in the wells back down to their previous levels within half an hour, Carlisle and Fury had looked at each other in astonishment. Some good news at last! They certainly needed it, with no masts, spars or sails left on board, not to mention the loss of all the ship's boats. It would be up to the whim of nature where they were finally swept by the force of the wind on the ship's hull, and what little effect the rudder would have.

The muster of the men which had been carried out at first light showed that four were missing. A miraculous escape, considering what they had been through. Fury was certain one of the men must have been the lookout perched in the foretop, lost when the mast went by the board. The other three had probably been swept overboard when the *Bedford* was rolled on to her beam ends. That left them with a ship's company of thirty-one seamen, four marine privates, one marine corporal, one midshipman and one lieutenant.

For the moment both officers were just glad to be alive, the *Bedford* now meeting each wave squarely on her stern, thanks to the steadying effect of the hawser laid out behind, and the helmsmen keeping the rudder square.

Up, up, the stern rose as the next wave swept under her, followed by the stomach-churning downward sweep with the bows now pointing high into the sky and the rain still lashing down, combining with the driving spray to keep everything and everyone soaked to the skin.

It seemed that Fury held on there for hours; indeed it probably was, the sun beginning to set when at last Carlisle broke the silence.

'You may as well go below and take a rest, Mr Fury. I think we've seen the worst of it. You can relieve me in three hours.'

'Sir,' Fury protested, 'you've been on deck all day. You should get some rest. I can take the next watch.'

'Thank you, Mr Fury, but I am perfectly fit. Now go below and get some sleep. That's an order.'

'Aye aye, sir,' Fury shouted back reluctantly, noting as he did so that the sounds of wind and wave were diminishing.

At the mention of rest, he suddenly realised how tired he was, both physically and mentally. He hauled himself wearily forward towards the companion ladder in an effort to get below.

When he finally reached his tiny cabin, it took only a moment to collapse into his hammock and let sleep envelop him.

Fury arrived back on deck in complete darkness. The wind had eased considerably in the three hours or so he had been below. It was no longer howling constantly in his ears – in fact it felt little more than a breeze, although Fury knew that it only seemed light in contrast to the cyclone winds they had been experiencing for the past two days. It would still be gale-force, he estimated.

He looked overboard: the seas were still running high, although not quite as high as before. It would be some hours after the wind subsided before the seas would calm significantly. He suddenly realised how cold he was and wished he had had the sense to change into dry clothes when he had gone below. The clothes he wore were still very damp and the wind felt as if it was cutting right through him. Well, at least the rain has stopped, he thought, shifting himself over to the lifeline to make his way to the wheel and relieve Carlisle, wincing as his hands touched the rope. Many hours of hanging on to wet rope had chafed the palms of his hands, which were now red-raw. It would be the same for everybody, he thought, gritting his teeth and making his way aft.

'Reporting for duty, sir,' he said to Lieutenant Carlisle, grateful that it was no longer necessary to shout at the top of his voice to make himself heard.

Even in the darkness he was shocked at how Carlisle looked as he turned towards him. His face was gaunt and drawn, his eyes no more than large black holes above his cheekbones. He had doubtless looked that way for some time, Fury not noticing it before because of his own exhaustion.

'Very well, Mr Fury, you have the deck. Keep her before the wind until the sea eases,' Carlisle croaked. The man had probably not touched a drop of fresh water in over a day, the salt from the spray drying out his mouth and throat. He started to make his way wearily below without waiting for Fury's reply.

Fury looked out over the transom at the following waves, noticeably smaller now, so much so that it was not necessary to crane his neck back in an effort to see the crests as they approached. Looking up at the darkness above he could see one or two stars dotted about the sky, evidence that the thick storm clouds were breaking up. Nevertheless, he knew they were still in a dire situation. They would have a better idea when the weather cleared and they could take a noon sight to try and fix their current position.

Until then, he attempted to go through the possibilities in his head as he stood his watch. Looking along the battered deck it was clear that they had no masts, no spars and, as far as he knew, there were no spare sails or cloth down below. They could perhaps use the capstan bars as makeshift spars, but even if they managed that they would have no sails to hoist on them. That pretty much ruled out any hope of them reaching Bombay in the *Bedford*. She would merely drift along wherever the wind and waves took her.

After that there was an unlimited number of possible scenarios. It was useless to think any further than that until they knew exactly what they faced. The binnacle was gone, and with it the compass, but that was no major problem – there would be a spare compass below which could be readily bolted to the deck.

What else? The fact that they had no boats was a concern; if they did manage to reach land, how would they get ashore? He was pretty sure the majority of men on the *Bedford* could not swim. Then there was the question of getting provisions ashore so that they could survive until rescued.

On top of all that, *Bedford* was carrying a valuable cargo of cotton. The East India Company would not be impressed to learn that, after retaking *Bedford*, they had subsequently wrecked her. That was besides the wrath of Captain Barber who would stand to lose a small fortune in prize money.

Was there anything else he had forgotten? Probably, but he could bring nothing else to mind at that moment. He looked up at the stars overhead as if for inspiration, but none came. It left him beginning to wish he had never started thinking about it.

Throughout the rest of that night the wind continued to ease, and by morning it was little more than a fresh breeze from out of the sou'west, with broken white clouds overhead interspersed with blue sky, the first glimpse of blue they had seen in more than two days. The heavy swell of the sea had gradually receded during the night, until at last it resumed its former calm, turning as it did so back into the familiar clear turquoise of the Indian Ocean.

As the dawn broke, Fury was on deck, telescope in hand, anxiously scanning the horizon for any sign of the *Amazon* or *Otter*. Nothing. Perhaps they had not survived? He consoled himself with the thought that the visible horizon from the *Bedford*'s deck was only about two miles. The horizon from the top of the *Bedford*'s mainmast would have been about twelve miles, and would possibly have revealed the other ships, but of course the mast was no longer there. Three splintered stumps were all that remained of the masts, each one standing only two or three feet high.

As the sun slowly rose in the sky and began to filter through the dispersing cloud, it brought steam rising from the *Bedford*'s deck as it dried up the planking. Fury could feel the heat of it on his back as he stubbornly continued his search for their consorts. Finally, after more than an hour, he gave up and made his way below.

He spent the rest of the morning down below inspecting their cargo of cotton. He was glad of the work to keep his mind from dwelling on their predicament. They had got away lightly by the looks of it, with only a small amount of the cargo suffering excessively from water damage.

At noon he had rejoined Lieutenant Carlisle on the *Bedford*'s deck, standing there with quadrant in hand to 'shoot the sun' in order to fix their latitude. Down below, a hurried calculation revealed their latitude to be about fourteen degrees six minutes north. About five hundred miles south of Bombay – but how far west had they been blown? It was impossible to tell without either an accurate chronometer or a set of lunar distance tables, neither of which they had on board. If only they could set a scrap of sail and make their way eastwards, they would eventually arrive on the west coast of India, which they could then just follow north until they reached Bombay.

Fury and Carlisle must have spent nearly an hour sitting in the small master's cabin trying to figure out a way to set up some kind of jury rig, but to no avail.

They were finally interrupted by the arrival of Clark, informing them that dinner was now ready. It was slightly later than the normal noontime meal, but that could be forgiven considering what they had all been through in the past few days.

Fury could still not believe that, with everything going on around him the previous night, Carlisle had still remembered to order a man to put some beef in water to steep overnight. With the weather as bad as it had been, today was the first day they would be able to light the galley fire.

So this morning when he had arrived on deck, Fury had set a couple of the men to boiling the beef, along with some of the vegetables they had taken on board from the *Amazon*. A hot meal for them now would be important, even if the beef had not been steeping for the normal twenty-four hours – a little more salt in the beef than usual would not kill them. Along with a good measure of grog, it should help pick the men's spirits up, not to mention their energy.

He and Carlisle sat there in silence eating the tough beef, every bite like chewing on a block of wood. The look on Carlisle's face as he struggled with the meat suggested he was not entirely enjoying the meal. It was perhaps as a result of his recent illness, but Fury also wondered how long it had been since Carlisle had eaten men's ration food. It would do him no harm, he thought, with a sly grin.

Finishing his own plate and draining his grog, Fury excused himself and went back up on deck to continue scanning the horizon with his telescope.

For the next two days *Bedford* was driven to the north-east by the steady sou'westerly wind, the reel of the log line showing they were making a slow one and a half knots. What little cloud that remained in the sky after the cyclone had passed did not last long, and the morning after working out their latitude it was cloudless. The ocean stretched away as far as the eye could see, the deepest blue Fury could ever imagine.

It was broken only by the harsh glare of the sun, melting the pitch in the deck seams and making the men on deck cower for shelter from its intensity.

With no masts there was no way of rigging awnings on the deck to protect against its glare, and many men suffered terrible burns, the skin blistering up and turning purple. Fury himself, his face already well tanned from the outward voyage, was turning a deep mahogany underneath his dark brown hair.

More than once the men spotted dolphins alongside as they crept by, arcing out of the water majestically before surging ahead, seemingly mocking the *Bedford* with their speed. The *Bedford* herself had to be content with drifting along helplessly, only the pressure of the wind on her hull driving her through the water.

Over the past two days Fury and Carlisle had spent hours talking, trying to find a way that they could reach Bombay. As things stood they were quite satisfied with their progress, fate seemingly taking pity on them after their recent hardships. If the wind kept steady at sou'west, they would eventually reach the north-westernmost coast of India, in the Arabian Sea. It should be possible then to find some way of making the journey south to Bombay. Assuming, of course, that they could reach the shore safely.

'Land ho!'

The shout from one of the lookouts stationed at the bows reached Fury on the quarterdeck as he stood engrossed in thought. Six lookouts had been posted permanently round the ship – one on either side of the bow, one on each side of *Bedford* amidships, and one on each quarter. With no masts left standing, they were the best replacements available for the usual masthead lookouts.

Fury hurried forward along the gangway that joined the quarterdeck with the fo'c'sle and reached the bow, where the man stationed on the larboard side was standing looking forward through the telescope.

'Where away, Wilkin?' he asked as he approached him. Wilkin was the lookout in question, a Scotsman with a terrible pockmarked face which gave evidence of his victory over the smallpox at some time in the past.

'Pretty much dead ahead sir,' Wilkin replied, turning to him and handing him the telescope, pointing in the direction to which Fury should look.

Fury placed the glass to his eye, swinging round slightly to catch more of the horizon. Nothing – no, wait! He brought the glass back slightly and found it once again. A low grey smudge on the horizon.

'I see it,' he muttered as he stared at it, adjusting the focus of the glass to sharpen the image.

Wilkin had done well to spot it – it must be close to three miles away. He turned to find Carlisle, who was already hurrying along the gangway to the fo'c'sle. He had obviously heard the shout from down below.

'What have we, Mr Fury?' he asked as he approached, accepting the proffered telescope eagerly.

'What looks like an island, sir, dead ahead,' Fury replied. He used the word 'island' deliberately, knowing full well that they were miles away from the mainland of India. He had spent a long time studying the charts of this area, below in the master's cabin along with Carlisle, and they were both well aware that the chart did not show any trace of an island in this vicinity.

'Well,' said Carlisle, after himself studying it for a moment and handing the telescope back to the lookout. 'If the wind stays like it is, we'll be blown right into its lap.'

'Aye, sir.' Fury had already reached the same conclusion himself.

'Call me when we get within half a mile, or at the first sign of any reefs,' Carlisle ordered, turning to go back below, his face impassive.

Fury knew he was worried. Unsurprising, really, considering the *Bedford* was drifting down on to an island in the middle of the Indian Ocean with no way of avoiding it if the wind kept steady from the sou'west. If they did survive the actual shipwreck – and that was doubtful – they would be stranded on an uncharted island with no chance of reaching Bombay, and with diminishing provisions.

Fury turned away to return to the quarterdeck; it would be a while yet at their current speed before they were within half a mile of the island, and there was nothing he could do in the meantime. Reaching the quarterdeck, he began pacing with his head down, seventeen paces to the taffrail, turn, and seventeen more paces to the rail overlooking the waist. Back and forth, back and forth, the thoughts tumbling through his head. He was so engrossed, he did not hear the lookout hailing once again a couple of hours later.

'Sir,' interrupted the man at the helm.

'Eh? What's that?'

He looked up, startled.

'Forward lookout's reporting, sir,' the helmsman said.

'Ah! Thank you,' Fury replied, striding forward once again.

'We'll be about half a mile off in a minute or two, sir,' reported the lookout as he approached, holding out the telescope which Fury took without a word.

The island leapt into focus as he trained the telescope forward, showing a white sandy beach on the western side, stretching away to the north and closely backed on to by rainforest. He swung the telescope round to the south of the island, where the beach ended and rocky outcrops began, sweeping round the southern end. It was quite a low island by the looks of it, and from what he could see was probably about seven miles long from north to south, assuming, of course, that was the northernmost part he could see, and not some false headland.

He lowered the telescope slightly, bringing the water into view. The blue of the ocean turned into an emerald green about fifty yards off from the shore, where it shoaled up to the beach. Not much surf showing up either – that was a good sign. He moved the glass back out further from the beach, something catching his eye as he scanned. Where was it? Ah, yes – there it was – a line of foam about one hundred yards out from the beach, generated by the small waves breaking on hidden reefs that must be lurking just beneath the surface of the water. They ran in line about half a mile wide, directly in front of the *Bedford*. Bad, but it might be worse, far worse. The speed *Bedford* was making through the water made it highly unlikely that she would hit the reef with enough force to make her sink when she drove on to it. Their main problem then would be how to transfer men and provisions from the *Bedford*, which would be about one hundred yards out, to the safety of the beach.

Fury whispered a silent thanks to whichever force had ensured they were heading for the beach and not for the rocky part of the shoreline, where the reefs would likely be much more jagged.

He turned aft and made his way down the companion ladder, knocking on the door to the master's cabin before entering to make his report to Lieutenant Carlisle.

'We are now about half a mile away from the island, sir, wind steady at sou'west.'

'Are we going to hit her?' Carlisle asked.

'Yes, sir. There is shallow water leading up to a beach, little surf, but with hidden reefs about one hundred yards out.'

'Very well, Mr Fury. I will come up and take a look,' he said, scraping his chair back and rising from behind the desk.

'Aye aye, sir.'

Fury led the way out of the cabin and up to the fo'c'sle, handing Carlisle his telescope without another word. Carlisle studied the island for what seemed like hours before finally turning away and handing back the glass.

'Very well, Mr Fury. Have the men go through the ship, bringing anything up on deck that will float. If they can't find anything, they can start breaking up the bulwarks. We need enough for all the men in the event we have to make a hurried departure when she strikes.'

'Aye aye, sir.'

Fury turned and relayed the order to Clark, who was standing nearby. Clark gathered a small number of the crew and led them below.

'Well, Mr Fury,' Carlisle continued, 'there is nothing to do now but wait. We shall soon see if the gods are smiling on us.'

'Aye, sir,' Fury replied, staring silently forward as the island gradually grew larger. He had wanted to argue with Carlisle, to insist that there must be something they could do to change course, but the roots of navy discipline had been deeply engrained in him and so he merely looked forward, feeling strangely impotent as their fate bore down on them.

He turned frequently as sounds from aft told of Clark and his men dumping items on the deck which would float if thrown overboard. Soon after he heard the familiar splintering crash of axes tearing into wood, and he looked round to see Clark and another man at work destroying part of the bulwark. A short time later Clark, apparently satisfied with their efforts, made his way forward to the fo'c'sle and reported.

'I think we have enough now, sir. We've brought most of the bulkheads up on deck, along with all the capstan bars. They should float well enough. We had to go to work on the bulwark to get the rest of it.'

'Very good, Clark,' Fury acknowledged, turning to Carlisle. 'All ready, sir.'

Carlisle gave a silent nod to indicate his satisfaction, but did not take his eyes from the island ahead, growing gradually larger as they neared.

The *Bedford* was easing her way through the water almost imperceptibly, the only evidence of any forward movement being a small parting of water at her cutwater as her bow sliced through the calm swell.

All around the deck the men were still, watching as they approached the island. Some were muttering quietly to their shipmates and pointing, no doubt excited about the whole thing and not giving a second thought as to the consequences of being marooned there. Like children, Fury thought pompously, forgetting that he was still little more than a child himself.

The excited chatter began to die away now as the breakers which marked the position of the hidden reefs grew steadily closer. Fifty yards . . . thirty yards . . . fifteen yards . . . five yards. They must be on them now, Fury thought. A slow scraping noise sounded as the *Bedford*'s keel came into contact with the reef, her speed dropping away until finally her bow rose slightly as she lodged herself on the final reef and came to a standstill, so gently that it was hard to believe they had grounded.

'Clark!' Fury beckoned to the burly seaman who had been standing nearby waiting. 'Get below and check on the damage.'

'Aye aye, sir,' Clark replied, wasting no time in hurrying below to see if they were shipping water.

'Well, Mr Fury,' Carlisle swung round, 'it looks as if we have arrived at our new home. We must begin to make preparations for disembarking.'

'Aye aye, sir,' Fury replied, unable to see how they could disembark without boats.

'Lads!' Carlisle shouted. 'We will need to make rafts to get ashore. Two should be sufficient. Starboard watch will make one and the larboard watch will make the other. There is plenty of wood and rope aboard. Grab the axes and gather together suitable pieces of planking – use the bulwarks and the upper deck. We shall secure them to a couple of empty casks. I want them ready by first light tomorrow. Carry on!'

The men dispersed, grabbing every available axe and setting to work getting together suitable planks of wood under the supervision of Fury and Carlisle. By the time Clark returned to report that *Bedford* was rapidly taking on water from a large gash in her keel, the work was well under way. Even with the water coming in, *Bedford* was perfectly safe from sinking, perched on top of the reef as she was, so it was not necessary to divert any of the men's energies away from putting together the makeshift rafts.

In the cool of the evening the men worked enthusiastically, the sound of chopping wood to be heard long after the sun had sunk in the west and the first stars had appeared overhead.

Chapter Ten

By first light the following morning the men were standing around the deck, waiting for the off. Much of the *Bedford*'s quarterdeck bulwark had been torn down to provide planking for the rafts, making Fury feel curiously exposed as he waited for Carlisle to begin proceedings.

The two rafts had both been finished at about midnight, and Lieutenant Carlisle had allowed the men to choose whether they would like to sleep below in their hammocks or on deck underneath the stars. Without exception they chose the latter. They had already been given ship's biscuit for their breakfast and were waiting silently as Carlisle finally joined Fury.

'Ready, Mr Fury?'

'Ready, sir.'

The two officers, dressed only in breeches and open shirts, commenced their examination of the two rafts.

They were both almost identical and consisted of planking – mainly from the bulwarks – lashed to two empty casks brought up from the hold, one on each side. A number of oars had been fashioned by taking some capstan bars and fixing short pieces of planking to one end. They would not be particularly effective, but did not need to be with the sea calm and only one hundred yards to the beach. Each raft could probably take fifteen men safely, so three trips would be needed before they could start taking off provisions.

'Right, lads!' Carlisle shouted after he had finished the examination. 'Over the side with them!'

Some of the crew tailed on to the ropes which were secured to each raft, while others hauled them over to where there were now large gaps in the bulwark, heaving them through as the men on the ropes took up the strain. The rafts, now hanging vertically, were lowered away smartly, and a moment later loud splashes could be heard as they hit the water. The ropes were then tightly secured to the Bedford so that they would not drift away.

Fury looked down over the side at the two rafts; they were sitting very high in the water, to be expected with two empty casks for buoyancy, but they looked to be safe enough.

'Right, lads!' Carlisle shouted again, the excited chatter which had arisen from the men dying down. 'I want six seamen in the first raft, along with the marines. Mr Fury,' he turned, lowering his voice again, 'you will go in the first raft. Keep the men in order and once you reach the shore, don't let them wander off! The marines are to provide cover in case we meet any hostile inhabitants. Understood?'

'Yes, sir,' Fury replied, saluting and walking over to Corporal Davis. 'Mr Davis, when we reach the beach, you will station your men to provide cover for the landings.'

'Yes, sah!' Davis replied, coming stiffly to attention.

Fury casually acknowledged the salute and walked over to the bulwark, or what had once been the bulwark, where one of the rafts was moored. He shouted out six names, all

*Amazon*s and all men he knew could be relied upon. They came forward grinning.

'Right, lads,' he said, 'your new vessel awaits. Handsomely now!'

The men piled down on to the raft, sitting down on the planking wherever there was room, followed by the clumsy marines with pipe clays and muskets. The raft sank slightly in the water with each man on board, but, with only Fury remaining to get on, it was still well above the glassy surface. Looking at the water and feeling the sweat beginning to soak his shirt as the sun grew stronger, Fury was tempted to dive in and swim ashore. He was a fair swimmer, certainly much better than most men in the Royal Navy. He thrust the temptation away, watching as two of the makeshift oars were passed down to the seamen on board the raft, one kneeling at each side, before he started climbing down the *Bedford*'s side himself. He felt his feet touch the raft and he tried to sit down on the planking as quickly as possible – it felt very unsteady even with the present smooth sea.

The rope was cast off and the raft floated away from the *Bedford*, Fury looking up to see the faces of the men left on board as they looked down at their progress. Slowly the raft drifted closer towards the beach, the slow current helping them along so that it was hardly necessary to use the oars, just the occasional stroke to keep the raft on course and to keep Fury and the marines facing the beach.

Fury looked down at the water, clear as crystal now as the depth decreased as they approached the beach. He jumped off the raft as soon as he considered it shallow enough. The water, coming up to his knees, was warm yet refreshing. He grabbed the raft, nodding to Corporal Davis who shouted an order which sent his men immediately splashing down into the water.

Careful to keep their muskets dry, the marines waded on to the beach, fanning out and facing the trees backing on to the beach with muskets ready and bayonets fixed. The rest of the seamen slid off the raft, the casks floating higher and higher as they disembarked so that the job of hauling it the last few yards up on to the sand was not so tiresome.

Fury turned to the *Bedford* for the first time. He was shocked by his first sight of her. She looked strange, her bow up slightly on the reef and with no masts and battered bulwarks. He waved his handkerchief in the air, and could see the small shape of Carlisle waving back. Men were pouring down into the second raft now, shoving off and drifting in towards the beach.

It took fifteen minutes for them to arrive; Fury had not realised it had taken that long. Once they had all disembarked and gathered on to the beach, he turned to face them.

'Which of you can swim, lads?' he asked.

Out of the thirty or so men standing there, only four could swim. He called them over. 'Now, lads, two each in the two rafts – paddle back out to the *Bedford* and pick up the rest of the men. Lieutenant Carlisle should also have some supplies to bring back. Carry on!'

The seamen walked over to the rafts, clambered on, and the rest of the men pushed them back out into the water. Fury watched as they slowly made their way back out to the *Bedford*. Although only a weak tide, it was apparently tough work for the men to paddle against it, especially with their makeshift oars.

Finally, after what seemed like hours, they clawed their

way out to *Bedford* and ropes were thrown down to fasten the rafts; it had taken forty minutes. Fury could see items being passed down on to the rafts, before the rest of the *Bedford*'s meagre crew climbed down on to them and they pushed off.

Fifteen minutes later the rafts were on the beach once more, with Lieutenant Carlisle, breeches dripping, walking over to Fury.

'We've enough over today to keep us going. We'll bring whatever else we can when we've had a chance to take a look around, set up a camp and make sure we are safe.'

'Aye aye, sir,' Fury replied, looking over to where the men were unloading the raft.

There was the compass, which Carlisle had obviously had removed from the deck where it had been fixed, the men's hammocks with their belongings rolled in them, and some items of food: ship's bread and cheese, along with some flasks of water taken from the ship's casks. With luck, that would be sufficient until they could sort out something more permanent. Several men were now lifting a large chest off one of the rafts, and by the look of exertion on their faces, it was very heavy. It took a few seconds for Fury to realise that it contained all the small arms on board – cutlasses, muskets, pistols and tomahawks.

'Mr Fury,' Carlisle was saying once again, 'our first priority is to find a supply of fresh water, because it will be impossible to get the water casks stowed from *Bedford* over here. I will take some men and have a look around. I will leave you in command here until I return.'

'With all due respect, sir . . .' Fury paused, wondering if it was sensible to disagree with a superior officer.

'Well, come on, man, spit it out!' Carlisle responded impatiently.

'Well, sir, it may be hard going tramping around the forest in this sun, sir, and what with your recent fever . . .' He left the rest unsaid; Carlisle's imagination would persuade him more than any words from Fury.

'Very well, Mr Fury,' Carlisle relented. 'You can lead the search party. Take six men and arm them with cutlasses and pistols. But don't get lost!'

'Aye aye, sir,' Fury said, trying hard to keep the delight out of his voice for fear of changing Carlisle's mind.

The thought of sitting on the beach doing nothing appalled him, and he felt slightly guilty about having to use Carlisle's recent illness to avoid it. He moved over towards the men.

'Clark, Evans, Johnson, Prichard, Sewell, Barnes – follow me!'

The six men moved away from their companions and followed him over to where the supplies were sitting on the beach. Fury turned to face them.

'We're going to take a look around – see if we can find fresh water and somewhere to set up camp. Arm yourselves with pistols and cutlasses just in case. Clark – take one of those flasks of water as well; no one to touch a drop unless I say so.'

'Aye aye, sir,' Clark replied, slinging the flask over one shoulder.

Fury stooped and picked up two pistols, which he shoved into his waistband, and a cutlass. Lieutenant Carlisle was beside him once again.

'All ready, Mr Fury?'

'Aye, sir, all ready. I think we'll start off along the beach first, sir, see if we can find any openings in the forest.'

'Good idea, Mr Fury, carry on.'

Fury turned to his men again.

'Follow me, lads!'

He started walking northwards along the beach, keeping close in to the trees at the back of the beach where there was at least some shade afforded from the relentless sun. They had hardly gone fifty feet before every man was soaked in sweat. It was proving hard work to walk on land again after so many months at sea, especially on the soft sand, but there was no avoiding it with the thick undergrowth inland.

The men behind him were talking quietly among themselves, and Fury did not have the energy to order them into silence. Instead, he tried to block their words out, concentrating hard on the thick foliage to their right, hoping that they would see an opening soon before they had gone too much further.

'Ssshhhh!'

The men's voices subsided and Fury instinctively held up his hand as a signal to them to stop. They had only gone about three hundred yards, and the men they had left behind could still be clearly seen back along the beach. He was sure he could hear something, a faint noise to his right. He motioned the men to stay quiet and they all stood there, heads strained forward slightly as if that would help them hear. Fury was surprised he could hear anything above the heavy beating of his heart, but there it was, in the distance – a kind of hissing sound, possibly rushing water.

'Right, lads, we'll go in here.'

There had been no sign of the trees thinning out as they had trudged along, so here was as good a place as any. Fury drew his cutlass from its scabbard. The trees themselves were not that tightly packed together, it was the undergrowth between them – the vines and branches – which made it look impenetrable. He slashed down with his cutlass, the vines parting as his blade sliced through them. He continued slashing as he worked his way slowly forward, the men behind doing the same at each side to make the path wider.

It was slow going. Occasionally a stubborn vine would require him to stop and hack at it two or three times before it parted, but as they moved inland the sound they had just heard grew louder. It took perhaps half an hour to move fifty yards inland before they came across the stream, about ten feet wide. The sound had been caused by the water rushing over a number of rocks strewn across its width to form a kind of mini-waterfall.

Fury bent down at the water's edge and cupped his hand into the flowing water, bringing it quickly up to his mouth. Fresh water! Not merely fresh, but cool and clear as well. After living for months on stagnant water from the ship's casks with algae and fungus growing in it, this was delightful. The men behind him were now at the water's edge on their knees, trying to drink eagerly from their cupped hands. Fury turned to Clark.

'Empty the water from that flask, Clark, and fill it from this stream.'

'Aye aye, sir,' Clark replied, not needing to be told twice.

He emptied the contents of the flask on to the ground and plunged it into the water. Fury allowed the men to drink their fill from the flask, before ordering Clark to refill it one last time so that they could move on.

The opposite side of the stream looked to be nothing but mangrove swamp, the trees as tall as any Fury had seen backing on to the beach, although not as tightly packed together. The ground in the swamp looked predominantly dry, betraying the lack of rainfall, and Fury made a mental note that it might be worth exploring at some time in the future for possible sources of food.

For now, though, having found fresh water he was not inclined to leave it. As the stream evidently ran from north to south along the length of the island, there was little point in going north, which would take them further away from the rest of their men, so he set off southwards along the bank. Their progress now was much quicker, due in part to the men being much refreshed after their drink, but mainly because the undergrowth along the banks of the stream was thin.

They followed the stream as it began to move inland slightly, away from the beach. After what Fury judged to be three hundred yards he stopped and listened hard, but he could hear nothing of the *Amazon*'s men on the beach.

'Are we going back on to the beach, sir?'

That was Evans asking the question.

'No,' he decided, 'we'll carry on a while longer – see where it takes us.'

There was some truth in the benefits of finding out where the stream led, but that was not the main reason why Fury had decided to move on. He had no wish to be shot by one of the *Amazon*'s marines as he came hacking his way out of the trees; they would undoubtedly still be covering that area.

He moved on along the bank in silence. After another fifteen minutes the stream turned sharply inland and another fifty yards or so brought them to a clearing. Fury stopped in surprise, the men behind him bumping into each other. The dry swampland continued on the other bank of the stream as it led inland to the east, but on this side there was nothing but grass – a clearing about two hundred yards wide and which stretched eastwards for what looked to be about a mile, the other three sides surrounded by the trees and thick undergrowth.

Out of the trees on the far side a low peak could be seen rising above the tree tops, possibly the highest point on the island, Fury guessed. Not big enough to be described as a mountain, but a little too big for a hill. This was perfect! They would have an unlimited supply of fresh water and would be hidden and protected by the trees, so anyone wishing to attack through the forest would have to make a lot of noise cutting their way through first. Additionally, assuming they could get someone to the top of that peak with a glass, they should have a good view of the sea all around the island.

'Right, lads, I think we've seen enough. Let's get back to the beach.'

He turned and made his way back into the trees, cutlass in hand. Slashing and hacking away once again, it took Fury nearly an hour and a half to reach the beach. He had cut his way through three hundred yards of undergrowth, on more than one occasion wishing he had brought the compass to make sure of his direction.

Finally he emerged on to the sand, the sharp glare of the sun making him squint after the deep shade of the trees. He looked to the right where he could see the small figures of the rest of the men, about half a mile away back along the beach. He started to make his way back to them, his men following behind him. He made sure he was walking in the middle of the beach, refusing the shade offered by the trees backing on to the sand. The *Amazon*s would be expecting them from the other direction, and he wanted to be clearly identified on his approach to avoid any confusion. Carlisle must have recognised him through his telescope, because he came walking fifty yards to meet him.

'Thought you'd got lost, Mr Fury!' he said as he approached.

'No, sir,' Fury replied breathlessly, grinning in spite of his tiredness.

'Well – make your report.'

Fury took a deep breath, and told Carlisle everything they had seen.

The men were kept extremely busy for the next three days. During the first afternoon, Lieutenant Carlisle had set the men to clearing a path through the trees and undergrowth using axes and cutlasses. The stream and the clearing could now be reached from their landing spot on the beach in twenty minutes of walking. It had taken much longer to transfer everything they had taken off the *Bedford* to their new home, particularly the chest containing the small arms.

They had spent the first night ashore sleeping in the clearing on the ground, using their rolled-up hammocks as pillows and trying to fight off the swarms of mosquitoes and flies which suddenly appeared out of the trees at sunset.

The following day Carlisle had all the men at work, chopping any suitable wood they found, and collecting bracken and leaves for some sort of shelter. He had agreed wholeheartedly when Fury had suggested collecting lots of loose undergrowth and leaves and using it to hide their pathway through the trees from anyone looking from the beach.

The rough shelters were completed by the third night. It was amazing to see how the men had adapted from knotting and splicing rope to extracting and using twine taken from the forests. Branches had been fastened together to form the skeletal structure, and the large, thick, green leaves which were in abundance in the forest were laid on to form a waterproof roof, one end of which was fixed into the ground, the other end being held up at forty-five degrees by stouter branches stood vertically. The ground had then been laid with thick layers of bracken and foliage to provide a comfortable mattress. There were eleven of these in all; one for Carlisle and Fury, and the others for the men themselves.

It was little wonder the men were in high spirits, Fury mused, sitting under the shelter as dusk was beginning to settle at the end of the third day. They had an unlimited supply of fresh, clear water, their sleeping arrangements were vastly more comfortable than they were used to on a man o' war, and the work they had to do was not as physical as on board ship. On top of all that, with the exception of those men whose turn it was to stand sentry duty around the camp with muskets ready, they each had a chance of an uninterrupted night's sleep, mosquitoes permitting. Still, it was important they were kept busy. Idleness would result in petty quarrels among the men, especially since there was still a decided split between the former *Bedford*s and the *Amazon*s.

Lieutenant Carlisle came walking up after seeing the sentries were posted and sank down beside Fury, swatting away a fly as he did so.

'Now we have the camp set up, Mr Fury, you can take two

men first thing tomorrow morning up to the top of that peak. Take a look around and report back. The men will stay there until they are relieved in two days' time. Make sure they have the necessary provisions and equipment.'

'Aye aye, sir,' Fury replied, pausing before asking the next question. 'May I ask what you have planned for the rest of the men, sir?'

'I think tomorrow we will take a trip back to the *Bedford* and strip her of everything we can, including her cargo. That should keep the men busy for a few days. When we have everything off her, we'll have to destroy her. I also thought that Corporal Davis could begin drilling the men in the use of small arms. God knows the ex-*Bedford*s will need it.'

Fury nodded his agreement, before tentatively putting forward his next suggestion. It was unwise of an officer to make too many suggestions to a superior.

'I have also seen several hogs roaming around this part of the island, sir. May I suggest a hunting party? It would do the men good to have fresh meat to eat after salt beef and pork held in casks for months.'

'Indeed it would, but we do not have an officer available to lead the party,' Carlisle replied.

'Clark, sir,' Fury suggested, 'he is a reliable man – he stood a watch on *Bedford* as my second before your arrival, sir. I'm sure he could be trusted.'

'Very well, I will think it over, Mr Fury. Now get some sleep – we all have a busy day ahead of us tomorrow.'

'Aye aye, sir,' Fury said, lying back on his mattress and closing his eyes to the world.

Chapter Eleven

The whole camp was awake before dawn the next morning, Fury taking a quick duck in the stream after breakfast to freshen himself up. Some of the men gave him amused glances as he splashed around in the cold water. They thought it strange that a man should wash every day when given the opportunity, and even more strange that anyone could find enjoyment at being in the water.

Fury pulled himself on to the bank, grabbing the towel and vigorously rubbing his body to stop himself from shivering. He pulled on his shirt and breeches, struggled into his boots, and went to choose the two men who would man the lookout spot for the next two days.

He decided to pick one *Amazon* and one ex-*Bedford*: it was about time the two sets of men started mixing. He saw Crouder sitting cross-legged, finishing off his breakfast. With his fair hair tied back in a pigtail and his rugged, weather-beaten face, he looked every inch the seaman he was. He was in Fury's division on board *Amazon* and Fury knew him to be a reliable, level-headed man. He looked around at the rest of the men to choose Crouder's companion, subconsciously splitting them between *Amazon*s and *Bedford*s. A large man with flame-red hair caught his eye; Fury could vaguely recollect him clinging beside him hacking away at the main-mast rigging as they had attempted to free it during the cyclone. He beckoned him over.

'What's your name?'

'Drinkall, sir,' the man replied somewhat nervously, obviously worrying about what was in store for him. The navy's reputation for discipline and cruelty was well known by merchant seamen, which was partly the reason why they were so reluctant to join the service in the first place.

'Wait here a moment, Drinkall,' Fury said, turning to Crouder, who was just getting to his feet. 'Crouder! A moment, if you please.'

Crouder walked over to him with that casual gait typical of seamen.

'Sir?' he enquired, matter-of-factly.

'D'you see that peak over there?' Fury asked, pointing behind them both to where it could be seen rising from out of the trees at the far end of the clearing.

The two men looked at it before turning back to him.

'Yes, sir,' they replied, almost in unison.

'We are going to use that peak as a lookout post. We should be able to see all round the island from up there. You two men will take the first watch. You will be relieved in two days. If you see anything, one of you will have to come down and report while the other keeps lookout, but I want it manned at all times. Is that understood?'

'Aye aye, sir,' they muttered.

'Good. Now I'm afraid it'll have to be nothing but ship's biscuit while you're up there, so go and see Clark and he'll provide that, along with a flask each of water. Take it easy with the water – remember you'll be there for two days. Apart from provisions, you can have a telescope each, along with a cutlass and pistols each just in case. Any questions?'

'No, sir,' they replied.

'Very well. I'll see you each receive an extra tot of grog when you return. We'll leave as soon as you have your equipment. Carry on.'

They turned away to collect their rations for the next two days while Fury went to pick a cutlass out for himself, along with two pistols, which he pushed into the waistband of his breeches. He then collected a flask and filled it from the stream – it would be a tiring day making their way to the top of the peak, especially once the sun had strengthened.

He returned to the rendezvous and was joined by Crouder and Drinkall after only a few minutes. He walked over to Lieutenant Carlisle and reported that he was ready, and after a brief good luck from him was soon back with his men and setting out along the left-hand side of the clearing.

From what Fury could see, the stream ran along the entire length of this side of the clearing, before disappearing into the trees at the far side, just to the left of where the ground started sloping up towards the peak. By keeping along the side of the stream they could drink freely until they reached the far side of the clearing, when they would then have to refill their flasks before turning right and starting up the slope.

The ground along here was flat and grassy, making walking easy, and it could not have been more than twenty minutes before they covered the mile or so to the trees at the far end.

After stopping for a short rest and refilling their now empty flasks, they turned away from the stream and headed for the foot of the slope. The going was tough now as they began cutting through the undergrowth and trees, hardly realising they were on the side of the peak, so gradual was the slope at first. A burning at the top of his legs told Fury how difficult progress was up the slope, as the incline grew steeper and the trees started to thin out.

Suddenly they broke through the trees, like drowning men bursting the surface of the water, Fury turning to take in the view around them over the tops of the trees. There was the large clearing, with small figures in the distance showing where the rest of the party were. He looked up. There was about another seventy feet to go, with mostly loose mud and rock covering the ground, from what he could see.

Following a short rest and a drink for the men from his flask, they set out to complete the final leg, Fury warning the men to watch their footing. More than once, they found themselves slipping on the loose dirt and stones as they continued to climb, and by the time they finally reached the top all three had cuts or scrapes on their filthy hands from the small, sharp rocks as they put their hands down to stop themselves slipping.

Fury was surprised at the size of the peak – big, quite flat all around and probably about thirty feet to the opposite edge, with several large boulders lying on the ground. God alone knew how they'd got there, Fury thought, looking up at the beating sun high in the clear blue sky. With luck the boulders would provide some relief from the sun in the heat of the day.

He walked over to one of them, rested a telescope on its top, and started to scan the horizon. All around the sea was completely clear of shipping. The south side of the island was a mere half-mile from where they stood and Fury could see a beautiful sweeping cove with rocky outcrops at each end. Maybe the rocks to his right were those he had seen on the *Bedford*'s approach to the island? He could not be sure. All along the western and eastern coastlines were sandy beaches and rocky outcrops. He scanned north; the sea was visible near the horizon but he could not get a good view of the coastline, unsurprising considering the northernmost part of the island was a good five miles away. He passed the telescope back to Crouder, resting while the other two men studied the horizon with their telescopes.

'Right, lads,' he announced, after he had recovered his breath, 'I had better be getting back to report. I will see you in two days. Good luck!'

'Thankee, sir,' they said, watching him as he made his way to the edge and started to scramble down, moving sideways on to the slope and using his hands to aid his descent.

Thankfully the journey down proved a lot quicker than going up, but, even so, Fury found himself envying Crouder and Drinkall the chance to rest up there. It was not until he reached the foot of the slope, out of breath again, and emerged through the trees back into the clearing, that he realised how lucky he was. With the hot sun up there beating down on them, and the boredom of two days just watching the horizon, it would be very uncomfortable for the men. Most likely they were envying him the chance to get straight back down again into the shade of the trees and with an unlimited supply of water.

Water! The thought of it reminded him how thirsty he was and he quickly made his way over to the stream. He dropped straight down on to his knees as he reached it, plunging his head into the cool current to refresh himself before filling his flask once more and holding it to his lips, head thrown back with the torrents gushing into his mouth and down his cheeks and chest. A pause to regain his breath, and he set out on the last leg of the return journey across the clearing and back to camp.

Fury splashed into the gentle surf and climbed on to the raft, along with Clark and the two seamen who were paddling. Up and down the small raft bobbed as it inched off shore over the low surf, edging ever closer to the *Bedford*, now little more than an empty hulk.

For three days since Fury had returned to camp after setting up the lookouts, the men had been working constantly. Corporal Davis had spent hours drilling the men in the use of cutlass, pistol and musket, while others had been out under either himself or Clark on hunting expeditions. The latter had resulted in fresh-cooked meat for all for the last two days. The remaining men had been employed rowing back and forth, taking everything off the *Bedford* that they could manage. That included spending considerable time unloading the tons of cotton on board, bit by bit, and transferring it to their camp.

'It may be a waste of time, but it'll keep the men busy,' Carlisle had confided to Fury the first day.

It was true; there was little they could do with most of the items taken off *Bedford*, such as the cotton and paint. Still, if there was some way they could get the cargo to Bombay, it would be valuable, so it was worth a try. Now all that remained aboard along with her timbers was her armament. Powder down in the magazine, shot in the lockers, and her nine-pounder guns which were far too heavy to take off the

Bedford, especially with no masts or yards to rig tackles and slings with which to hoist them out.

It was obvious merely by looking at her that the *Bedford* was too badly damaged to be made seaworthy again. The large tear in her keel caused by striking the reef would necessitate a whole new bottom being fitted, in addition to the task of setting up new masts, spars and rigging, while the water which had swamped the cable tiers would make warping her off and towing her to port impossible.

There was a small enough risk of an enemy encountering the *Bedford* and using her guns, but it was a risk just the same. To Carlisle, Fury and the men, though, she was useless, merely a broken shell.

It was all these considerations which had finally led Lieutenant Carlisle to order *Bedford*'s destruction. Not an easy decision for someone who had been given command and safeguard of her by his captain; even Fury could appreciate that after only two days in command. Nevertheless it was the right decision. Now it was up to him to make a good job of it.

He looked up to see they had almost reached the *Bedford*. The men paddling were clearly out of breath, their tongues hanging out as if they were dogs, the sweat pouring down their faces. It was hard going against the current in a makeshift raft, but Fury had no idea how long it had taken to reach *Bedford*. He reached out and grabbed the rope that had been left hanging overboard from one of *Bedford*'s bulwarks, fastening the raft to it. Standing up tentatively and grabbing the side ropes, he hauled himself up and planted his feet on the battens which served as a ladder.

It took only a moment to reach the deck, now completely empty apart from a wheel with no wheel ropes (they had been used in making their camp) and three jagged stumps which had once been masts. By now Clark was beside him, the two seamen remaining in the raft ready to set off back as ordered – they would not want to stay around too long once the charges had been set. He turned to Clark.

'Have you got the matches, Clark?'

'Aye, sir,' the man replied, holding up two reels, one of quick match and one of slow match.

Fury took the reel of quick match off him and walked over to the bulwark, pulling out a belaying pin which was still sitting there.

'Wait here,' he instructed Clark, as he began to make his way below towards the powder magazine.

The deserted ship seemed extremely eerie down below as he climbed down the hatchway from the gun deck to the lower deck, turning aft. It was very dark here in contrast with the blazing sunlight above and Fury had to feel his way along the deck until his eyes became accustomed to the gloom.

His outstretched hand touched a serge curtain – the entrance to the magazine. Brushing this aside he stepped slowly through. The men down here would ordinarily have worn list slippers to reduce the risk of a spark from their shoes igniting the powder, but he had no such luxury. Slowly he advanced, coming to the door which led to the powder room itself; there was a small rectangle of glass in the middle of it through which the light from a hanging lantern outside would have illuminated the powder room where the gunner was at work. He reached into his pocket and fumbled for the key to the door which Lieutenant Carlisle had taken from the master's desk when they had first abandoned ship. A turn of the handle and the door creaked open. Fury could see nothing inside – it was completely dark.

He entered carefully, knowing that a single spark from his boots and the whole magazine would explode. Although effectively blind, he knew roughly what he would find inside the room. He reached out cautiously, his fingers touching a cartridge, one of many probably sitting on shelves around the walls, serge cylinders already filled by the gunner and ready to be taken to the guns by the powder monkeys. He lowered his outstretched hand, feeling for the casks of powder that he knew would be there. Good, he could feel them now. He reached again for the shelf, grabbing a cartridge and placing it carefully on the floor. Another cartridge then another came off the shelf until there were six, sitting there in the dark with Fury kneeling down over them.

He pulled out the knife he had borrowed from Clark, thrusting it carefully into the pile of cartridges. He lifted one up, feeling its weight reduce and hearing a steady streaming as the powder ran out of it and on to the floor. He gently touched the pile of gunpowder now sitting on the deck. That should be enough to provide a firm covering for the quick match when he thrust it in.

He next unwound a length of the match from the reel and withdrew the belaying pin from his breeches, tying the end of the quick match round the bottom of the pin. He thrust the pin into the heap of gunpowder, carefully making sure it was completely covered. Gripping the reel with one hand, he slowly rose to his feet and withdrew backwards, the reel of quick match slowly unwinding as he made his way out of the magazine, careful lest a sudden movement should jerk the belaying pin out of the powder. He moved slowly, up to the main deck and then finally back up to the quarterdeck, where the brilliance of the sunshine made him blink and squint for several seconds.

Once he had rejoined Clark, Fury carefully put the reel down on to the deck, withdrawing the knife again from his waistband and cutting off the quick match. He was unsure how much of the quick match he had unravelled, but it did not matter – once the fuse had been lit it would take less than a second for it to reach the magazine. He handed the unused quick match to Clark, accepting the reel of slow match in return.

Because of the importance of accuracy when using slow match, Fury knew it had been well tested by the Ordnance Board, and so he could be sure that it would burn true. He remembered what Carlisle had said before he left: it will burn in still air at exactly thirty inches per hour. It had been agreed that twenty minutes was sufficient time to quit the *Bedford* and get back safely on shore before the explosion. Ten inches they would require, then, plus a little extra to take into account the amount needed to bind together with the quick match. He unreeled a part of the slow match, carefully judging the length. Satisfied it was sufficient, he cut it off and proceeded to tie it on to the end of the quick match, taking care that the bind was close together.

He stood up, happy at last. A quick nod to Clark, standing there with flint and steel ready, gave him the signal to light the fuse. Fury went over to the side and lowered the reels down to the raft, where the men waited, looking somewhat apprehensive. It was not easy sitting calmly next to a ship which could explode at any moment due to any number of errors on Fury's part. He turned round to see Clark coming towards him.

'Fuse is lit, sir,' he said, beginning to climb down into the raft straight away.

Fury took a couple of paces closer to the fuse to ensure it was burning well before turning back and following Clark down into the raft. He undid the mooring rope and the men at the paddles started pulling with a will, the raft surging away from the *Bedford*, helped along by the current.

It took what must have been only ten minutes to reach the beach – a record. It was amazing what men could achieve when given the right incentive, Fury mused, as he waded up to the beach, helping to pull the raft up after him. Assuming he had cut the right length of fuse, they still had a good ten minutes to wait before the whole thing went up. Carlisle came hurrying up to him.

'Well?'

'All set, sir,' he replied, 'shouldn't be long now.'

They moved back towards the trees lining the back of the beach in case they needed cover, and waited. Silently the minutes wore on, Fury becoming more and more edgy. Had something gone wrong? Had he accidentally pulled the belaying pin out of the powder as he made his way back to the quarterdeck? He was still going through the possible mistakes when the *Bedford* blew.

An ear-splitting explosion rent the air, followed almost immediately by fire and black smoke, wood flying high and wide into the sky and raining down splashing into the sea. One large chunk of blackened wood even reached the beach, dropping with a thud on to the sand fifteen yards from where they crouched. A couple of smaller explosions followed, a thick pall of smoke rising high into the air now as what remained of the *Bedford* burned, slowly falling apart and into the sea.

Twenty minutes later, all that was left of her was a thousand floating pieces of timber, slowly rising and falling on the gentle swell.

Chapter Twelve

Lunge, parry, and lunge again. Fury's grip on the cutlass was beginning to slip as his palms grew more sweaty with the effort of striking and deflecting his opponent's blade.

'Very good, sah,' Corporal Davis announced as they both relaxed, signalling the end of their informal practice.

They both walked the short distance over to the stream and plunged their hands and faces into the running water. A week had passed since the destruction of the *Bedford*; a week in which Fury and Carlisle had tried desperately to keep the men busy with endless drills and hunting parties. Even so, the excitement that had surrounded their initial shipwreck had now worn off, and Fury could see signs of restlessness among the men. No amount of freshly killed meat could take that away. They wanted to be back on board their ship, reefing and furling sail, exercising the guns – a world they were used to. He sat on the bank, trying to get his breath back.

Lieutenant Carlisle had led a party of men out more than an hour earlier on a hunting expedition. He had heard a couple of musket shots not long after they had left, but nothing since, so they were obviously not having much luck.

Hearing the stamping of feet behind him, he turned to see one of the men, Carroll, half running and half dragging his feet towards him. He looked to be struggling, sweat dripping off his forehead and nose and his face crimson. He stopped in front of Fury, obviously trying to say something as he stood there, gasping for breath.

'What the devil—' Fury began, cutting himself off short as it suddenly dawned on him that Carroll was supposed to be on lookout duty along with Pritchard up on the peak.

'Sir,' Carroll began, still breathing heavily. 'There's a ship standing in towards the island. She looks like the *Mornington* to me, sir, but it's too far to make out the flags!'

It took a moment for Fury to register the last statement. The *Mornington* was the flagship of the East India Company, and the last time she had been seen was leaving Bombay in company with *Otter* for a cruise. Carroll, being an ex-*Bedford* man, would know her well.

'How far off is she?' he demanded.

Carroll thought for a moment. 'About three miles away, sir, when I left. It looked like she was standing in for that cove on the south side of the island.'

'Very well,' Fury replied, 'you had better get some rest.'

He looked around. The men had clearly been listening in, but this was no time for reprimands.

'Cooke!' he shouted, at which the man in question came running over to him, his blond hair bobbing up and down as he did so. 'Get up and join Pritchard as soon as possible. If the *Mornington* is flying the flag of the East India Company, fire your muskets in the air – anything to try and attract her attention. If she looks as if she has been taken, Pritchard is to report to either Lieutenant Carlisle or myself as soon as you have ascertained where they are heading. Is that understood?'

'Aye, sir!' the man replied, turning away to grab a flask of water before starting the long journey up to the lookout point.

Over the next two hours Fury forced himself to act calmly in front of the men, as if nothing unusual were occurring. It was made easier by the knowledge that all they could do was wait for the time being until they received a further report from one of the lookouts. Six months earlier, even three, he would have rushed to the lookout point himself, but he was beginning to realise that sometimes command meant just sitting and waiting in apparent calm, even if your stomach was churning and your impatience made you feel as if you would explode.

If the strange sail was the *Mornington*, and she had been taken by the *Magicienne*, then all they would have to do would be to keep out of sight of her. If, on the other hand, she was still under the flag of the East India Company, they would have to find some way of making her aware of their presence so they could be taken to Bombay to rejoin the *Amazon*.

Lieutenant Carlisle returned empty-handed from the hunting trip about one hour after Carroll had first broken the news. His face had brightened perceptibly when Fury had told him of the sighting, and he had agreed that they should wait for the next report from the lookout.

Thus the afternoon wore on under an invisible blanket of tension and expectancy, with Fury trying to relax beside the stream. It was not until approximately four hours after the original report that a short 'Pritchard is coming, sir!' from Clark startled Fury into life, prompting him to stand up and walk over to join Carlisle, eager not to miss the report when it came.

They waited side by side as Pritchard approached, the sweat pouring down his face and neck and soaking through his shirt.

'A flask of water for Pritchard there!' Fury shouted to one of the men by the stream, who came hurrying over to hand Pritchard the flask as he stopped and saluted Fury and Carlisle.

It was perfectly obvious that he was in no fit state to talk, so Carlisle ordered him to catch his breath for a couple of minutes and take on some water. To Fury, standing there impatiently, it seemed like hours while Pritchard slaked his thirst before finally attempting to speak.

'Sir, the strange sail is definitely the *Mornington*, and it looks as if she's flying colours over the East India Company's flag. It could be the same colours as worn by *Otter* and *Bedford*, but I can't be sure, sir.'

Fury could have guessed that much himself – if they had identified her as friendly they would have fired their muskets as ordered. The next question came from Carlisle.

'Where is she now?'

'She anchored in the cove on the south of the island about an hour ago, sir. Her fore topgallant mast has gone.'

'Very good,' replied Carlisle, 'that will be all.'

Once they were out of earshot of the rest of the men, he turned to Fury.

'Well, Mr Fury. What do you make of it?'

Fury paused to think for a moment.

'Well, sir . . . ,' he began, 'she may be stopping here for repairs, or maybe they have stopped to water and provision.

Either way, it seems too much of a coincidence that she has merely stumbled upon this island. I would think they already knew it was here.'

'Exactly, Mr Fury. And it's a good bet that no matter what they are doing here, they'll be here for a couple of days.' He paused to let Fury digest this last statement before continuing. 'That will give us enough time to take a closer look.'

Fury looked up sharply. Carlisle had sounded as if he was going to attempt something, a thought that had not even crossed Fury's mind. They would probably be completely outnumbered, not to mention the fact that to cut out the *Mornington* they would need boats.

'But, sir—' he began, attempting to put his thoughts into words.

'Surprise!' interrupted Carlisle, pausing as if to let that one word sink in. 'Surprise, Mr Fury, is half the battle. Surely you have heard of that?'

'Yes, sir.'

'Good. Pick six men to go to the south of the island and look around. Since you have been to that side of the island already, you had better lead them. Be quick, though; you will need to arrive before it gets dark.'

'Aye aye, sir.'

Fury walked over to where Clark was standing by the stream, thankful that for him at least the waiting was over.

'Clark! I'm taking a small party over to have a look at the *Mornington*. Pick five men who know how to move quietly. Each man is to have a cutlass and two pistols. If any man's pistol goes off accidentally, I'll have him flogged tomorrow!'

'Aye aye, sir,' Clark replied with a grin, moving away to pick the men. If any man's pistol did go off, it was doubtful whether any of them would be alive tomorrow, and Fury knew it. Not to mention the fact that they had no cat o' nine tails with which to perform any such flogging.

Fury watched Clark go with complete confidence. It was better to leave the selection to him – he would know the men's backgrounds better than Fury. Most ship's companies included at least some who were former poachers or burglars, and so would appreciate the importance of silence.

He went over to the chest and picked himself out a cutlass and two pistols, making sure the pistols were not cocked before tucking them into his waistband. He then collected his telescope along with some paper and a pencil, and waited for Clark and his men to appear.

'Ready, sir,' Fury reported to Carlisle once his small party was assembled.

'Good luck, Mr Fury.'

Fury acknowledged this with a nod and led his men over to the stream to begin the long walk to the other side of the clearing, his mind going through what route they would take as he walked.

He had seen the cove in question from the top of the peak, but had not actually been there. It was located about half a mile south of the peak, so when they reached the other side of the clearing they would have to turn right and go along the trees on that side, passing the lookout point high to their left, until they reached the other corner. At that point they would have to find a way through the trees between the clearing and the cove, with luck coming out at the back of the beach.

The men walked in silence, stopping for water once they had reached the far side of the clearing before taking their

designated route. To Fury's relief, the trees blocking their way
to the cove did not look as thick as those they had cut through
when they had first searched for water. Even so, the going
was slow, Fury picking his steps carefully so he didn't make
too much noise. When a cutlass was needed to hack away a
protruding branch it was done carefully, piece by painstaking
piece.

Gradually the gentle sound of breaking surf grew as they
approached the beach. Judging by the gloom within the trees,
the sun must be low on the horizon. They had arrived at the
right time, Fury marvelled, putting it down to luck rather than
judgement. He held up his hand as a signal to the men following to stop. Then, crouching down low, he moved forward
on his hands and knees, pushing aside leaves and branches.

Suddenly there was sand in front of him and he looked
up to see that he had reached the back of the beach. He
retreated slightly and lowered himself on to his stomach,
pulling his telescope out. He looked up and down the beach
– not a soul in sight. He could see they were on the right-
hand side of the cove as they looked seaward. Not far away
to his right the beach swept away, with more trees, until
beach turned to rock and the trees disappeared, forming the
westernmost headland. Away to his left, the beach stretched
for maybe half a mile before sweeping around on the other
side to meet the other headland.

Anchored about one hundred yards out in between the
two headlands was the *Mornington*, her bow pointing
seaward. Lights were beginning to appear about her decks
as the sun finally dipped below the horizon and dusk settled.
Fury raised his telescope to get a clearer view. Her fore topgallant mast had certainly gone, and Fury could see water

pumping over the side. Had they a leak? He scanned the deck; nothing – not even a small watch to guard against attack. They were obviously confident, Fury mused, hardly surprising given their current location.

He scanned forward and saw her anchor cable leading out of the starboard hawsehole, the cable continuing forward and to the right. He could see she was snubbing against the anchor cable, so presumably there was a current running from right to left as he looked. He scanned lower – two boats bobbed on the gentle swell, nudging themselves against the side of the ship as they tugged at their fastenings.

The gentle murmuring of the ship's company reached them across the water as the crew below decks conversed with each other. Perhaps they were drinking, Fury thought hopefully. A mental picture suddenly formed of a crew of drunkards down below as the *Amazon*s swept on board unseen and attacked. He pushed that thought aside quickly – they could not even reach the ship at the moment with no boats at hand. He fumbled for the paper and pencil which were tucked away in his pocket, flattening the paper out as best he could on the ground. He began sketching a picture of the cove and the exact position of the *Mornington*, glancing up frequently to ensure he had left no detail out.

It was almost completely dark by the time he was satisfied with his sketch. He looked out at the *Mornington* once again, now no more than a dark shape against the horizon, the light from the moon reflecting on the water around her, making it seem as if she was floating on a sea of diamonds.

Well, he thought, putting away his paper, there is nothing more that can be done now. If the *Mornington* had developed a leak, as he suspected, then they would more than likely

still be here the following night. That would give them all
tomorrow to make the preparations for any attack.

He stopped himself again, wondering why his subcon-
scious persisted in the idea of an attack when they could not
even reach their enemy. Half turning, still on his stomach,
he whispered to Clark to pass the word along that they were
making their way back. A yard or two from the beach and
they were all on their feet again, retracing their steps through
the trees back to the clearing.

They reached it in spite of the darkness in the trees and
started out towards the stream on the far side. They found
the path which led through the trees up to the lookout point;
it towered up on their right-hand side, Fury suddenly realising that it was only manned by one seaman now that
Pritchard had come down and made his report.

'Thomas,' he said, looking over to the young cockney who
wore what seemed to Fury like a permanent smile on his
face underneath a mop of brown hair. 'Can you read a watch?'

'Yes, sir.'

'Good.' Fury fumbled in his pocket for his watch and
handed it to Thomas. 'Here is mine. Make your way up to
join Cooke on lookout duty. You are to remain up there all
day tomorrow out of sight until half past six o'clock, when
you will both make your way back to camp. Is that clear?'

Thomas digested it for a moment to make sure he understood before nodding.

'Aye aye, sir.'

'Very well then, carry on,' Fury replied, watching Thomas
disappear into the shadows of the trees before beckoning the
rest of the men to continue, thoughts tumbling through his
head as he walked.

He was glad he had remembered to recall the lookouts. There would be little point in having any lookouts tomorrow night if they were to attack the *Mornington* as he expected. He had accepted now that they would attack, no matter what the obstacles. The ability of the British seaman to overcome the insurmountable was legendary, and he had full confidence in Carlisle as a leader. Even so, they would need every man they had to carry a cutlass.

According to the last muster they had at their disposal thirty-three officers and seamen, along with four marines and their corporal. Thirty-eight men in total against – how many? It was impossible to guess. If she was manned as well as *Bedford* and *Otter* had been, then ninety men would be a conservative estimate. About two men at least for every *Amazon*, then. Enough to go around, anyway, he thought grimly.

A sudden thought struck him; part of the crew of both the *Bedford* and *Otter* had been imprisoned below in the hold, the rest presumably being taken on board the *Magicienne*. What if some of the crew of *Mornington* were held down below as well? If they could get down to them, it would even up the odds slightly.

They had reached the stream on the far side of the clearing now, the men pausing to drink before they continued on the last leg of the journey. Away to the west, nothing could be seen of the camp through the darkness. Carlisle had presumably ordered no fires to be lit lest they should betray their presence to the enemy. A wise precaution, Fury thought, as he made his way along the bank of the stream back towards them.

He turned his mind to the thought of how they could possibly reach the *Mornington* without boats, but the answer continued to elude him. It would be very difficult to transfer the rafts round to the cove. Even if they got them there, they were hardly suitable for sneaking up on a ship unseen. It had taken half an hour at least to reach the *Bedford* each time against the current; if they were seen, they would be sitting ducks.

They were close to the camp now with no sight ahead of their men, only darker shadows against the trees which betrayed the presence of the men's shelters, invisible to anyone who was not looking for them. Fury thought more about the rafts, but finally dismissed the idea when he realised that, even fully loaded, there would not be enough room on the two rafts to carry all the men over to the *Mornington*, even if they didn't have to face the incoming current.

He pictured the *Mornington*, sitting there in the darkness with her boats alongside bumping her side as the current pushed them into her. An idea came to him, suddenly, unexpectedly. A crazy idea perhaps, and a long shot, but if it came off it would give them a chance! He could only hope they would still have their boats over – he broke off sharply as a slight clicking noise startled him, the subsequent challenge crisp and clear in the darkness.

'Who goes there?'

He stopped instinctively, surprised even though he had been expecting it. His reply of '*Amazons!*' came quickly enough.

'Advance and be recognised.'

He stepped forward several paces, a dark shadow rising on his left as the marine sentry came towards him with cocked musket at the ready, immediately recognising Fury in the moonlight as he got closer.

'Sorry, sir, carry on,' he said, slipping away into the darkness once again as Fury and his men continued on, soon arriving back in the middle of the camp where the rest of the men were talking in low whispers among themselves.

Fury dismissed his men and made his way over to the officers' shelter, where Lieutenant Carlisle was sitting up in the dark.

'Make your report, Mr Fury,' he said curtly.

'She's there all right, sir,' Fury confirmed. 'Anchored between the two headlands of a cove on the south of the island. Her fore topgallant mast's gone, and they were pumping water over the side, so they may have sprung a leak. No watch of any kind on deck when the sun went down, sir. I think we're safe enough here for tonight.' He groped in his pocket, pulling out the crumpled sketch and handing it to Carlisle. 'I made a detailed sketch of her position. And I also sent Thomas up to join Cooke on lookout, sir, with orders that they were both to come down tomorrow at half past six o'clock.'

'Very well,' Carlisle replied, slipping the paper into his pocket, 'I've doubled the sentries around the camp. Other than that there's not much more we can do tonight, so we'll wait until tomorrow.'

'Yes, sir,' Fury replied, collapsing on to his bedding as he suddenly realised how tired he was.

Chapter Thirteen

The sun rose early the next morning to reveal another cloudless blue sky stretching across the horizon. Lieutenant Carlisle had been sitting studying the sketch of the cove for some time, concentrating so hard that Fury had decided against disturbing him with his absurd plan to board the *Mornington*. The chances were that Carlisle would come up with a plan which was much more simple and effective. Finally Carlisle looked across at him.

'Well, Mr Fury. Have you any suggestions?'

Fury sat in silence for a moment, unsure, before finally thrusting his doubts aside and taking the plunge.

'I had an idea last night, sir – but it's a long shot.'

Carlisle looked at him eagerly

'Well, we've nothing better at the moment so let's hear it!'

'I could explain better with the sketch, sir.'

Carlisle reached into his pocket and pulled out the folded paper, which he opened out on to the floor, flattening the creases with his hand.

'Well, sir, from what I could see last night, there's a current running on to the beach from a bit of an angle, west to east,' Fury explained, indicating with his finger on the sketch which direction it ran, before continuing. 'If it's anything like the current on our beach it'll be pretty strong – remember how long it took the men to paddle out to the *Bedford* against it?'

'Yes, yes,' Carlisle replied, somewhat testily, a subtle reminder to Fury to get to the point.

'The *Mornington* is anchored about one hundred yards off from this headland here, sir,' he pointed to the western headland on the sketch, 'and last night she had two boats lowered and secured by painters. If I could get to the end of this headland and swim out to her, I'll be able to unfasten the boats. The current will then drift them down on to the beach. If the boats are spotted, they'll just think they weren't fastened properly.'

Carlisle sat for a moment in thought. 'Could you swim that far?' he asked eventually.

'Yes, sir, I think so – if I get to the end of the headland, I'll only have to swim across the current part of the way. Once I get to the right spot, the current will take me right down on to her.'

'And if you did manage to get the boats loose – what then?'

Fury had already thought about that. 'I could get in one and lie down while it drifted to the beach. If the boats were spotted, I'd have to take my chances – I doubt if they would see me in the dark if I kept my head down. And if they aren't seen, we can man the boats once they reach the beach and cut her out.'

It was a risky plan, and Fury knew it, but it was the only one they had. He sat nervously awaiting Carlisle's response. There was a long silence while Carlisle thought it over.

'Very well,' he said at last, 'if no other opportunity arises, we'll give it a try. Muster the men, if you please, Mr Fury.'

'Aye aye, sir,' he replied, getting stiffly to his feet and walking the short distance to the middle of the camp. 'Fall in men!'

The men's murmurings subsided as they all crowded eagerly round the middle of the campsite, waiting to hear what was in store for them. Fury returned to where Carlisle was sitting, only now beginning to fold the paper up and place it back in his pocket as he got to his feet.

'All mustered, sir,' Fury reported.

'Thank you,' Carlisle replied tersely, moving over to the front of the crowd of men. 'Lads!' he shouted. 'As you all know, the *Mornington* is over yonder with a prize crew!' He pointed towards the south of the island, prompting several heads to turn in that direction. 'I intend to take her tonight!'

He paused a little to let his words sink in. An excited chatter arose among the men. After two weeks of relative inactivity they were eager for action, even if they would be outnumbered two or three to one. The odds didn't matter to them – in their eyes, one Englishman was equal to two Frenchmen any day of the week. Carlisle continued.

'I want all our stores except the weapons and five tins of paint to be taken into the trees near the beach and covered. The cotton can be left where it is. There is no time to move it today. The shelters can be left up this afternoon, but before we leave tonight I want them all flattened, so they cannot be seen from a distance. Very well, carry on.'

He turned away as the men dispersed, while Fury tried to make sense of the orders he had given. If things went wrong tonight and they had to remain on the island, it would not take two minutes to re-erect all the shelters again. If they did succeed, then they could pick up at their leisure the stores that they had hidden. Naturally, they would need the weapons left out so they could arm themselves before attacking, but he could not understand why Carlisle had ordered the paint to be left out. His thoughts were interrupted by Carlisle himself.

'Mr Fury, send Cooper over to the cove to make sure they still have their boats lowered.'

'Aye aye, sir.'

'Have a man check all the cutlasses, pikes and tomahawks for sharpness too, and make sure there is enough biscuit and grog for the men's dinner and supper. We can't expect the men to die on an empty stomach!'

'Yes, sir,' Fury replied, walking away to find Cooper as the men began hauling their stores back from the clearing into the trees towards the beach. There was much to move, including the food they had taken off *Bedford*, largely untouched recently thanks to the regular supply of fresh meat on the island.

It took the men all morning to haul the supplies over to the spot Carlisle had designated, just back from the beach, and cover them with loose undergrowth, vines and branches which they had collected; a morning of constant work, broken only by a short half-hour lunch of hard biscuit and grog at midday. Finally, by early afternoon, all that remained of the campsite were the men's crude shelters, spanning out in a semi-circle from the stream with the arms chest and five tins of paint sitting isolated in the middle. The cargo of cotton remained lined against the trees.

'Right, lads!' Carlisle shouted to them once they had gathered back around him. 'We shall be leaving at about six o'clock.' That should ensure they met Thomas and Cooke returning from lookout duty. 'I suggest you get some rest for the remainder of the day. It may be a while before any of us gets some sleep again. Dismissed!'

The men broke up while Carlisle and Fury returned to their shelter and sat down.

'Well, Mr Fury, let's just hope they still have their boats lowered.'

'Yes, sir,' Fury replied – he had been thinking the same thing himself.

Cooper returned from the cove in the early afternoon with the welcome report that the *Mornington*'s boats were indeed still lowered, much to Fury and Carlisle's relief. The rest of the afternoon wore on, the sun beating down relentlessly as it slowly passed westwards.

The men spent their time resting, some catching naps, others swapping tales with their shipmates while cooling by the stream. Fury and Carlisle themselves spent an hour finalising the details of the attack, before Carlisle gave Fury his own orders regarding his responsibility for finding any prisoners below after they had successfully boarded.

Afterwards, Fury left him to it and took a walk down to the beach, opening his shirt to let the soft breeze from the sea cool his skin. He headed south along the line of the surf, trying to absorb his surroundings; the sea, the sky, the trees, and birds of every colour imaginable singing high in the tree tops – funny, he could not remember hearing them before. He reflected on the fact that this could well be his last afternoon alive and was surprised to find he was unmoved by the thought. Death would be preferable to being exiled on this island for the rest of his life.

He turned, realising he had come further than he had

intended, and started to head back. The heat of the afternoon was starting to diminish now as early evening crept in, and by the time Fury reached camp the sun was already low over to the west. The men were all on their feet now, the shelters had been kicked flat and Carlisle was standing ready, sword buckled round his waist and pistols in his belt, looking more like a pirate than a man holding the King's commission.

'Glad you could join us, Mr Fury,' he muttered sarcastically as Fury approached, not waiting for an answer before turning to address the men. 'Lads!' he shouted. 'We will be leaving soon. Take your choice of weapon, along with a pistol for each man, but make sure they aren't loaded yet! Surprise is everything, so any man who makes a sound before my order will be flogged. There are five tins of black paint here.' He pointed to the tins on the ground. 'Pass them around and cover your faces in paint. After that, any man you see not wearing paint you are free to kill.'

That caused mirth among the men. Fury, now aware of the purpose of the paint, could see another advantage: a horde of screaming black faces coming up over the bulwark might shock the enemy into retreating for a few vital seconds, enough time for the *Amazon*s to gain a foothold on the deck.

'There is also a possibility,' Carlisle continued, 'that some of the former crew of the *Mornington* may still be held down in the hold. If the opportunity arises it will be Mr Fury's job to get below and try to release these men. If he succeeds, he will ensure that they all wrap a piece of cloth round their heads, in which case you will know they are friendly. Are there any questions?'

The men looked silently at him.

'Very well then, carry on.'

The camp broke into a bustle of activity as some men crowded round the tins of paint while others went to choose their weapons from the chest. Fury dug himself out a cutlass and a pistol and sat waiting while the paint was passed round, eventually coming to him. He dug his hand in and smeared it thickly over his face, rubbing it everywhere but taking care to avoid his eyes and mouth. That done, he went over to the stream to wash the paint off his hands while it was still wet. Sensing a figure by his side, he glanced up to see Clark.

'Beggin' yer pardon, sir, but if yer gonna try and release any prisoners on the *Mornington*, you'll need me to get yer down to the hold.'

Fury grinned.

'That's right, Clark. You are to stand by me when we board and look out for my signal to go below.'

'Aye aye, sir,' Clark replied, grinning himself now and turning to pick out his weapons.

Here was another man in shirt and breeches next to him now, Fury guessing it must be Carlisle – his face was black so Fury could not be sure. The voice was familiar enough, though.

'Are we all ready, Mr Fury?'

'Aye aye, sir. I've taken the liberty of ordering Clark to stay with me when we board, so he can lead the way below if we get the chance.'

'Very well, muster the men.'

'Aye aye, sir.'

The men fell in once more, all their faces now blacked up, carrying an assortment of cutlasses, pikes and tomahawks, with pistols stuck in belts and waistbands. Fury conducted a quick head count – thirty-six men in total, including himself and Carlisle, with another two up at the lookout.

'All present, sir,' he reported.

Carlisle nodded in acknowledgement and turned to the men.

'Remember, lads – not a sound from now on. Now follow me!' and with that he moved off towards the stream, Fury and the rest of the men following close behind.

It took a little over half an hour to cover the distance to the far side of the clearing, by which time the sun was beginning to set. With any luck, Fury thought, they should meet Cooke and Thomas on their way down from the lookout, as ordered, without having too long to wait. Fury was glad he had remembered to bring along one of the paint pots with which to blacken the lookouts' faces when they arrived.

Carlisle turned and ordered a short rest for the men so that they had a chance to refill the flasks which some of them were carrying. Fury knelt down to throw some water on his face before realising that it was covered in paint, now long dry and making the skin feel unnaturally tight. No doubt the paint was cracking under his facial expressions; he could see the same on every man around him.

He caught a movement out of the corner of his eye and turned to his right to see two men appear from the trees in the distance, both stopping dead in shock as they caught sight of them, before one began to raise his musket. Thomas and Cooke! What was the fool thinking? Even if he had mistaken them for the enemy, this was far too long a range for a musket shot.

The musket was up to the man's chin now, Thomas it looked like, his head cocked to one side as he adjusted the sights. Fury waited with sinking heart for the sound of the shot which would serve to warn the enemy of their presence. It never came; Cooke brought his arm up quickly, pushing down the musket barrel and pointing at something. Thomas obviously realised his mistake and lowered his musket, both men starting to advance once again.

Fury looked across to where Cooke had been pointing and saw Corporal Davis standing there with his marines. Even with blackened faces there was no mistaking the scarlet uniform of the marines, and it must have been that which Cooke had recognised. Very lucky, Fury thought, as the two men approached himself and Carlisle, looking curiously round at the men and grinning. For an instant Fury wondered how on earth they had recognised the two officers – they were both wearing only shirts and breeches – then he realised they were the only two wearing boots.

'Reporting as ordered, sir,' said Cooke, as they stopped in front of Carlisle and touched their foreheads in salute.

'Have you seen much of the *Mornington*?' Carlisle demanded tersely.

'She hasn't moved since she arrived, sir,' Cooke replied. 'It looks like the men spent most of the day working on her hull. A boatload rowed ashore this afternoon with axes and took back plenty of wood, sir.'

'Did they hoist the boats back in?' Fury interrupted, trying not to betray the tension in his voice as he awaited the reply.

Cooke frowned, obviously trying to recollect.

'I don't rightly know, sir. I can't remember her hoisting her boats in, but I can't be sure. Sorry, sir.'

'No matter,' Fury replied, 'we shall soon find out.'

'Any idea how many men she has?' continued Carlisle.

'Difficult to say, sir, but she looked well manned.'

'Very well,' Carlisle replied, apparently satisfied. 'There's a tin of paint somewhere – go and black your faces and get a drop of water. We'll be off soon.'

'Aye aye, sir,' they replied together, turning away.

'Thomas!' Fury called after him. 'I'll have my watch back now, if you please.'

He held out his hand while Thomas rummaged in his pocket, finally bringing out the watch and handing it over with a sheepish grin.

'Aye, sir, sorry, sir. I forgot.'

'No matter. Now go and get some paint.'

'Aye, sir.'

Thomas walked off, leaving Fury and Carlisle alone.

'It looks as if you were right, Mr Fury,' Carlisle said, turning towards him. 'Sounds as though she has sprung a leak. Let's hope it's not too serious, eh?'

'Aye, sir,' Fury replied absently, preoccupied by the thought of whether or not the *Mornington*'s boats were still lowered. If they had been hoisted back on board, it wouldn't much matter if the leak was serious or not.

Trying to thrust his worries to the back of his mind, he looked up to find that the sun had finally dipped below the western horizon. Would he ever see it again? He dismissed the thought immediately, looking at Carlisle. He couldn't take any more waiting.

'Shall I get the men started, sir?'

'Yes, Mr Fury. At once, if you please.'

Fury walked away towards the men, now sitting in groups quietly talking to one another. He ordered each group on its feet as he passed before rejoining Carlisle at their head as they started along the trees to the opposite corner of the clearing,

Fury hoping he could find the path through the trees which he had used the previous night.

It was another ten minutes before they all reached the trees on the far side, with the first of the stars now beginning to appear overhead. A quick scan by Fury revealed the trampled undergrowth and broken branches where they had entered the previous night. In they went, Fury now at the head of the column, leading the long line of men through the trees, the silence broken only by the crunching of undergrowth underfoot along with the occasional whispered curse as skin was scraped by the branches.

Ten minutes of careful marching brought him to within five yards of the back of the beach. He raised his hand as a signal to stop, stepping another pace forward to prevent men colliding with each other in the growing darkness. He dropped to his knees, pulling out his telescope and beckoning Carlisle behind him to do the same, before they both sank on to their stomachs, side by side as they edged towards the sand.

A nerve-racking couple of seconds passed as Fury fumbled with his telescope and scanned the cove, looking for the *Mornington*. Her image flashed through his lens and he lowered it slightly. There they were! The two boats were still moored by her side, bumping into her hull occasionally as the current tried to take them. From what Fury could see, she had not changed position at all since the previous night, and he was confident he would be able to reach her from the rocky headland stretching away to his right. He turned to Carlisle, still studying the scene through his glass.

'So far so good, sir,' he whispered.

Carlisle did not reply, merely looking sideways at him and nodding his head slowly, as if deep in thought. He had perhaps been wishing that something simpler could have presented itself to him, but, as it was, he now had to seriously consider Fury's plan.

'Your orders, sir?' Fury prompted.

Another long silence ensued before Carlisle finally spoke. 'Very well, Mr Fury. We do not have much choice. We'll wait here until it is completely dark, at which time you can make your way to the headland. I will lead the men over to the left approximately in line with the direction of the current.'

'Aye aye, sir,' Fury replied, before turning to Clark behind him.

'Pass the word back that we will wait here until it is completely dark.'

A quick nod from Clark was followed by whispering, which gradually faded away as the message reached the rear of the column and was shortly followed by rustling noises – to Fury's ears loud enough to wake the dead – as the men went to sit down in the gathering darkness.

Fury continued to study the *Mornington* through his glass to pass the time. He could faintly see one or two men wandering her deck, but both seemed to be concentrating on what they were doing, not taking any notice of the *Mornington*'s surroundings. With any luck they were just checking that everything was in order, and would not be on permanent guard duty.

He moved his glass a little lower, to where faint squares of light could be seen along her hull. Some of her gun ports were open to let a little air between decks. That would make his task even more risky, with the chance that one of the men could happen to look through an open gun port at the wrong time. It was to be hoped that they would be too busy entertaining themselves to notice what was going on outside. A sharp nudge on his arm brought his attention back to Carlisle next to him.

'Very well, Mr Fury. I think it's dark enough now – you may make a start for the headland. Better leave your cutlass and pistol with Clark. Good luck.'

'Thank you, sir,' Fury replied, his stomach starting to churn as he realised this was it.

He managed to wriggle out of the cutlass belt which had been slung over his shoulder and, taking his pistol from the belt at his waist, passed them both back to Clark. He then managed to wrestle his boots off – it would be impossible to swim in those – before passing those back to Clark as well. Finally he handed his watch over.

'Keep hold of them till I get back,' he whispered to him, turning away and moving quickly forward on his stomach.

Fury paused as his fingers reached the sand, twisting his body to the right as he left the trees. The headland was probably about two hundred yards away, sweeping away from the beach into the sea. He carried on over the sand on his belly, not wanting to risk being spotted if he stood up – his shirt and breeches would be much better camouflaged against the white sand.

He paused for breath and looked back from where he had come. He could see the rest of the men now crawling out of the trees and away to the left as Carlisle led them to the spot where he hoped the current would send the boats once Fury had released them.

He carried on, the trees on his right starting to curve to the left now as the start of the headland approached, and another five minutes of crawling saw the trees thin out considerably.

He crawled back in among the trees and stood up. Now that the trees had thinned it was possible to walk through them, making the going a lot quicker, even if he was treading gingerly due to the sharpness of the undergrowth on his bare feet.

Another five minutes of walking and the trees stopped abruptly as the ground gave way to the rocks leading out to the headland and the sea beyond. He looked across to his left where he could see no sign of the rest of the *Amazon*s. They had been swallowed up in the darkness, and that knowledge gave him sudden confidence that no one from the *Mornington* would be able to spot them on the beach either.

He carried on over the rocks slowly, careful not to slip in the darkness. He was level with the *Mornington* now, across to his left about a hundred yards off, no more than a black shadow against the darkness of the opposite headland, broken only by the shafts of light escaping through her gun ports.

He continued onwards, eager to get much further to seaward of her so he would not have too far to swim before he could rely on the current to take him down to her. If he entered the water too early, he would have to swim the entire hundred yards across the current and, although he was a fair swimmer, he knew that would be too much for him.

It wasn't much longer before the rocks began narrowing as he approached the end of the headland. He stopped and stood there, looking in towards the cove with the *Mornington* away to his left. Crouching down so that he could put his hands on the rocks, he started to make his way towards the water. He was thankful that the rock he was on sloped gently down to the black water, but he went down carefully nonetheless – one slip and splash could ruin the whole plan.

His left foot finally touched the water, momentarily with-drawing as the temperature of it shocked him. He had not realised it would be so cold. Gritting his teeth, he began to lower the rest of his body slowly into it, still holding on to the side of the rock and shuddering now as it covered more of him.

It was up to his chest by the time Fury, inevitably, slipped, his head going under and the small of his back hitting what must have been a submerged rock, sending a shooting pain up his spine. He came gasping to the surface, making an effort not to splash too much as he turned in the water to face the *Mornington*, waiting for the shout which would result in his capture or death.

His eyes were stinging sharply from the salt water as he waited for the alarm to be raised, but none came. He waited another minute, but everything remained quiet – surely they must have heard the splash? Perhaps not. Perhaps they were scanning the rocks at this very moment with their night glasses. He would have liked to have waited until he was sure he had not been seen, but the current was already beginning to drift him away from the rocks, and so he had no choice but to start swimming before he was swept past the *Mornington* altogether.

He struck out with his clumsy breaststroke, the exercise soon warming his limbs and leaving him panting for breath. His chest began to hurt with the effort of arching his back and keeping his head upright. The salt water seeping into his mouth as he swam caused him to retch on more than one occasion, fighting down the urge to vomit.

On and on he swam, trying to ignore the pain and the tiredness, until he was perhaps fifty yards from the rocks. The *Mornington* was sitting there, fifty yards away herself, and he stopped swimming, bringing his feet back underneath him to keep himself afloat. He could see ripples on the water caused by the current, drifting away from him directly towards the *Mornington* and signifying that he had reached the correct position.

His breath steadied and his heart slowed as he gradually drifted down towards the dark shape which was the *Mornington*. He was now at the point of no return, and he felt very alone, drifting down unarmed and unsupported on to an enemy ship. He reassured himself with the thought that there was nothing he could do about it now – he had no more strength to swim away from her even if he had wished to. That was something he had learnt in the navy, he reflected, as he drifted ever closer to his target. A stoic equanimity about things he could not change.

Here she was now, towering above him, closer and closer – so close he could hear laughter from her decks. Only ten yards now and he was heading straight for her starboard bow. Thud. He hit her hull and tried to hold on but the current pushed him along her side until he finally managed to grab on to one of the battens used for climbing on board, stopping himself in the water. He had been lucky, he thought. The two boats were no more than a few feet from him now, snubbing at the ropes which were tied to their bows leading up to the bulwarks.

He let go of the *Mornington*'s side and immediately started drifting down to the nearest boat, frantically grabbing at her bow as he collided. He held himself there for a moment, listening out for any sign that he had been seen, but there was none. Satisfied, he pulled himself up slightly, feeling for the thick rope which was leading up above his head. His hand found the knot, and a few desperate minutes of tugging and pulling with one hand finally unravelled it.

He dropped himself back down fully in the water, his left arm now burning with the exertion of holding him up for so long. The first boat was dragging down past the other as the current took it and started to move it aft towards the *Mornington*'s stern, before it would sweep it away to his right and on to the beach. As it passed the second boat, still tied at its bow, Fury pushed himself off and managed to grab the side.

A quick glance showed no faces looking over the bulwark, and so he pulled himself up with an effort and slid over the side into the bottom. He moved towards the bow of the boat carefully, expecting to hear a shout at any moment, but none came. With both hands now free the knot on the rope securing the boat was undone in seconds, at which point he slid down into the bottom and crawled along towards the stern sheets.

He could hear a slight scraping as it drifted down the *Mornington*'s side, with still no shouts of alarm or sound of shots ringing out. The chatter of voices followed by more laughter drifted down to him as he lay there. He looked up to see her elaborately gilded stern windows and her transom slipping away as the boat reached the *Mornington*'s stern and drifted across it.

Once free of the *Mornington* his breath began to steady as he looked up at the stars, wondering how long it had been since he had left Carlisle and the others at the trees. He was shivering again now, whether from his wetness or the realisation of what he had just done he could not tell. Any moment he expected to hear shouts of alarm from the *Mornington* as they discovered their boats gone, but there was merely silence. He was tempted to look up and see where he was in relation to the shore but he dared not. He would just have to wait until a scrape or a bump told him he had reached the beach.

Chapter Fourteen

Fury had no idea how long he lay there staring up at the sky, the blackness of the night softened by the thousands of stars scattered across the heavens. The gentle bobbing of the boat was quite relaxing, and, on more than one occasion, in spite of his excitement, he had found his eyelids begin to close involuntarily before he realised what he was doing and shook himself awake.

He really was quite cold now due to this long period of inactivity. His shirt and breeches were still wet and what little breeze reached the bottom of the boat was going right through him. He tried to forget his discomfort by seeing how many constellations he could spot in the sky, a task he broke off when the boat's movement altered slightly, accompanied by a gentle scraping sound.

Before he had a chance to raise himself up, he could hear splashing and soft grunts as the boat was pulled further up what he assumed must be the beach. A head appeared over the gunwale, a shocking, black face, revealing only the whites of the eyes and a grinning set of teeth.

'Well done, Mr Fury!'

It was Carlisle, whispering. Fury sat up, relief pouring

through him now that he was back with his shipmates at last. Gingerly getting up, he eased himself over the side into water which was knee-deep, and made his way quietly on to the beach accompanied by Carlisle. The men were all around, their black faces eager now that the prospect of action was finally real.

Fury looked across to where the other boat was, not more than ten feet away, being held by a couple of men. Here was Clark beside him now, holding out his cutlass, pistol and boots. He took them silently, slipping the cutlass scabbard over his shoulder and thrusting the pistol into his waistband. He held on to his boots for the time being – he had no wish to fight and die with sand in his boots. Carlisle was whispering to him again now.

'We'll board her at her bow. You take this boat, I'll lead the other.'

It was a sensible plan and one Carlisle had presumably already imparted to the men in Fury's absence. With the gun ports of the *Mornington* open they would almost certainly be spotted if they boarded at her side, and the bow would provide more rigging for the men to scramble up than the stern.

One last whispered word came from Carlisle to follow him in the lead boat, before Fury found himself climbing back in along with his men, waiting until he was seated in the stern sheets before putting his boots back on and taking the tiller.

It took only a moment for the men to settle and ship their oars, and a whispered 'Give way all' from Fury set them rowing, creeping like beetles out over the black sea towards the *Mornington*, with Carlisle in the second boat just out in front.

Still no response from the *Mornington*. Fury had been expecting one ever since they had gathered on the beach, although he suddenly realised that they had not been there for more than a few seconds before they had scrambled into the boats and set off again. It was to be hoped that the enemy were not waiting crouched behind bulwarks for their arrival – a couple of round shot thrown down into the boats from the upper deck would sink them like a stone.

On and on they crept, Fury surprised at the speed of their progress. Of course, rowing a boat was vastly different from rowing a makeshift raft with two rudimentary paddles. He turned to Clark, who was sitting nearby at one of the oars.

'When we reach her, the boat's crew will board, along with Mr Carlisle and his men. You and I will remain in the boat until the attack is underway. We shall then go through one of her gun ports and find any prisoners.'

'Aye, sir,' Clark whispered, nodding his understanding.

The idea had been forming in Fury's mind while he had lain in the boat drifting ashore, without him even realising it. It was a gamble he was taking, but only a small one. The presence of two extra men in the boarding party would make little difference to the outcome. But if they could get in unseen through one of the gun ports after all the crew had rushed on deck to defend the ship, and release any prisoners held below, it could prove decisive. He was assuming, of course, that the enemy would commit all of their men to the defence of the ship, leaving the way clear for Fury and Clark to get below unmolested. The only point which had been worrying him was that, if he failed, he could be accused of cowardice in hanging back from the attack. He consoled himself with the knowledge that, if he failed, he would probably be dead anyway.

Fury was surprised to find they were almost there now, Carlisle's boat still out ahead and steering a course to pass along the *Mornington*'s larboard side at a safe distance to lessen the chances of being spotted by someone peering out of one of the gun ports. On they crept, Carlisle's boat ahead suddenly turning to starboard as they came level with her bowsprit, heading for the larboard bow. Fury adjusted the tiller, thrusting it over to port to send the boat in Carlisle's wake towards the ship's bow.

The sound of carousing on board could be heard distinctly as they approached. So much the better – it would drown out any noise as they hooked on and boarded. Fury looked across to see Carlisle first up the ship's side, using the beak head and the bowsprit rigging as a ladder, his men following with cutlasses in hand. Fury's own boat's crew had already unshipped their oars, the man in the bows hooking on as the boat's momentum took it the last few feet to the ship's side. Faces turned towards Fury indicated they were waiting for him to give the order.

'Up you go, lads!' he whispered hoarsely, the men needing no further encouragement as they scrambled out of the boat and up over the ship's bow.

Fury waited for the last of the men to go up before moving to the bow of the boat, waiting for his chance. A sudden shout from overhead as the first of the boarders was discovered was followed swiftly by a pistol shot and then a scream as the first man was cut down. Somewhere in the back of Fury's mind it registered that the laughter and music had suddenly stopped between decks, and more ragged cheers and shouts from above combined with more shots told him they were attacking in earnest now. Carlisle had ordered them to make as much noise as possible once the attack had started in the hope that it would, in addition to their blackened faces, unsettle the enemy.

Somewhere in the background of all that shouting and screaming, Fury thought he could hear the thud of feet on planking as the ship's crew came suddenly to life, grabbing any weapon to hand and streaming on deck to defend their ship. Surely enough time had elapsed now for the men to clear the deck and rush above?

'Clark!' he shouted, finding a sudden relief in being able to raise his voice after all the hours of whispering and crawling. 'Take a pull on your oar!'

The current was pushing the boat away from the *Mornington*'s side, a black expanse of oily water now visible between them. Clark was sitting at one of the boat's larboard oars, and at the command he began pulling on it, Fury rushing back to put the tiller hard a-port.

Gradually the boat's stern began to swing to starboard, the expanse of water between them narrowing as her stern began turning in towards the *Mornington*'s side. At last they were bumping broadside on to her, the boat's bow pointing forward.

Fury jumped up and grabbed the bottom sill of the nearest open port, trying to hold the boat in that position. It was lucky that the *Mornington* herself was helping to block the current so that its strength could not be felt as much where they were. Lucky also that the port was no more than five feet above the surface of the sea, otherwise they would have struggled to climb in.

A quick order from Fury had Clark abandoning his oar and crossing to the other side of the boat, hauling himself up through one of the open ports. Even in the lee of the

Mornington's side the current was proving too much for Fury, and he could not hold the boat against the ship's side any longer. Her stern started to slip away, the gap widening until Fury's feet finally left the boat and dangled in the water while he tried desperately to haul himself up through the port. For the second time that night his arms were burning as he pulled himself up so that his chin was nearly level with the bottom of the port sill, but even then he knew he was going to fail, the strength seeping from his arms and his chin beginning to lower.

A rough hand suddenly grabbed the back of his shirt and hauled him up and through with such force that he landed on the deck on his front.

'Beggin' yer pardon, sir, I didn't realise you was so light,' Clark said, standing there helping him to his feet.

'No matter,' Fury replied, grinning in spite of himself.

He looked around the main deck, partially screened off aft by bulkheads where the captain's cabins were. The whole deck seemed to be deserted and so Fury turned back to Clark.

'Let's get below. You'd better go first.'

'Aye aye, sir,' Clark replied, turning to lead the way over to a hatchway which would take them below.

The shouts and the screams were still ringing out above, although no more pistol shots could be heard. After discharging their pistols in the initial attack there would be no time to reload, and so it was best to throw them away or use them as clubs. Fury thought he could hear the occasional crack of a musket shot – that would be Davis and his four marines, who had been ordered immediately to ascend the rigging into the tops and act as sharpshooters, picking off the enemy on deck.

They reached the hatchway, Fury remembering to draw his cutlass from its scabbard in case they met resistance before descending behind Clark. It was dark down below, in spite of the dim lighting provided by the occasional lantern. According to Fury's estimate they were amidships at the moment, so another deck lower should take them to the hold.

They reached another hatchway and descended quickly, reaching the bottom where Clark jerked his finger in the direction of a single light glowing dimly further along. Fury led the way now, the noises above diminished but still audible as he reached the small, open space which contained the dim lantern.

The sentry must have heard him approaching, for his pistol was already levelled as Fury came round the corner, a bang and a flash and smoke indicating he had fired before Fury was even aware of his presence. Fury looked down in astonishment to see where he had been hit – the man could not possibly have missed from that range, even with an inaccurate pistol. Nothing – there was no sign of a wound anywhere. He looked back up at the sentry who was also staring in astonishment as they both realised at the same time that the gun had misfired.

The sentry was already raising his other arm with another pistol when Fury lashed out instinctively with his cutlass, forcing a sharp gasp from the man as the cutlass sliced his arm, severing the nerves to his fingers and causing the second pistol to fall harmlessly to the deck. One final thrust from Fury – point first – and the blade went clean through the man's stomach and out through his back. Fury twisted the blade viciously and withdrew it with a grunt. The man slumped to the deck, the blood already bubbling in his throat as he clung on to life for a few moments more. The startled look on Clark's face as Fury turned round was evidence of how quickly the whole event had taken place.

'Men!' Fury walked over to the battened hatch leading down to the hold beneath their feet, the muffled yells from below audible above the din on deck. 'I am an officer from His Britannic Majesty's frigate *Amazon*. You will be released shortly!' He turned to Clark. 'Take care of that hatch, Clark.'

Clark acknowledged the order and prised off the battens with his cutlass as though they were matchwood, throwing the hatch cover aside.

A moment later the first head appeared, eyes squinting slightly in the dim light as he looked around, recoiling in shock at the sight of the two men with blackened faces, one with a dark red smear of blood down his cutlass.

'I am Midshipman Fury, of the *Amazon*,' Fury said quickly, in an attempt to put the man at ease.

The man climbed fully from the hold and came forward slowly, taking Fury's proffered hand after a pause.

'I am Grainger, formerly second lieutenant of the *Mornington*.'

'How many men have you down there?' Fury asked quickly; there was no time for small talk.

'About forty officers and men,' Grainger replied.

'Good. We need them up on deck immediately to assist us. Every man with a blackened face is an *Amazon*. Make sure your men are aware of that. You can collect weapons on the way.'

'Very well,' Grainger replied, 'but where is your ship?'

'There is no time to explain, sir, we must go now.'

Fury started to walk away, remembering at the last moment a vital detail and turning round. 'Make sure each man secures a piece of cloth round his head before going up on deck. Tear a strip from your shirts if you have to.'

Puzzled looks on the men's faces greeted this order, and Fury felt it best to explain.

'It will stop the *Amazon*s from killing you.'

Satisfied, he turned back to Clark and beckoned to him to lead the way up on deck.

It took only a moment to reach the gun deck once more, the screams and the clash of steel on steel growing steadily louder as they neared the weather deck. Fury was grateful that Grainger had led his men without any further questions and, as Fury looked around him, he could see they had all managed to tie rags of cloth around their heads. Even in the present circumstances, Fury could appreciate how comical they looked.

'If you can't find any weapons down here, you'll have to use whatever you can find up on deck – belaying pins and the like!' he shouted, the men all nodding their understanding.

Without a further word, he took his pistol out of his waistband and started to make his way towards the companion ladder leading up to the quarterdeck – it was logical to assume that was where the majority of the fighting would be taking place. His head reached the level of the deck and it took only a second to take in the scene.

Dead men littered the deck, some with blackened faces but the majority without, Fury noted with grim satisfaction; the element of surprise had obviously been effective. That the *Mornington* was well manned was obvious, because they were now beginning to push the *Amazon*s back, sheer weight of numbers taking its toll. The *Amazon*s on the quarterdeck were hemmed in aft of the wheel, their backs against the taffrail as they fought like madmen against a throng of men in front of them.

Fury was on deck in an instant, unseen by the enemy with their backs to him. He could sense Clark beside him and hoped that some of the prisoners had also followed with whatever weapons they could lay their hands on. Bang! The shot barked out abruptly as he discharged his pistol into the back of one of the men in front of him, quickly followed by another a moment later as Clark did the same, both men dropping to the deck immediately.

Their comrades were looking round now, startled by the sound and seeing Fury and his men for the first time. Several began to rush towards him waving cutlasses and shouting their defiance. The clash of steel and the now familiar arm-numbing jar as he deflected the first strike hardly registered with Fury as he swung the butt of his pistol with his other hand. He felt it smash into the side of the man's skull with a sickening crack, sending him crashing to the deck either unconscious or dead. Fury did not particularly care.

His blood was up now, the relief surging through him that the waiting was over and he could unleash all his fears, all his doubts, in one physical and emotional explosion. He could see Clark to his right struggling with another man, while to his left he was vaguely aware of men with rags round their heads swinging madly with belaying pins and cutlasses retrieved from the deck.

Another man was careering towards him now and Fury flung the spent pistol at his head, the man ducking to avoid it and losing his balance slightly as he approached, running straight on to the point of Fury's outstretched cutlass. The man dropped to his knees, Fury planting his boot on his chest and pushing down to wrench the blade free.

The rest of the *Amazon*s had now taken the chance to fight their way out of the corner in which they had been trapped and Fury could see men all around him struggling with their foes as the fight became scattered about the whole quarter-deck. A man came staggering backwards in his direction before finally collapsing on his back at Fury's feet, eyes open wide in the blackened face as he feebly raised his cutlass to try and save himself as his enemy dashed towards him, cutlass raised to deliver the killer blow.

Fury quickly leapt over the man on the deck, his own cutlass held high in a clumsy parry to deflect his opponent's downward strike. His momentum carried him forward, pushing the man back. Fury could smell the rum on the man's breath, his lips drawn back in a grimace to reveal crooked, yellow teeth. He suddenly surged towards Fury with surprising speed, grabbing the hilt of Fury's cutlass as it was raised in attempted parry. His face was so close now that Fury could see every detail of the man's face – every crease of skin, every hair, every scar. All this he noticed in a second as his enemy began to force him back, and Fury knew his own strength would not be enough.

He was surprised at his own calmness at this realisation, and equally surprised at the lightning movement of his right leg as it came up, almost without his knowledge, to thrust his knee into his assailant's groin. The man let go his hold on Fury's sword arm immediately as the sharp pain threatened to collapse him. He staggered backwards to try and give himself more room to recover but Fury was on him in a flash, sending the hilt of his sword into the side of his head. Again and again the hilt smashed into the man's head, before he finally went down in a heap, blood streaming from a large gash in his temple.

Fury paused for breath and looked around once again to see that the enemy were being slowly pushed back, unable to recover from the surprise of that second wave of boarders. He caught sight of Clark, still struggling with one of the enemy, and rushed over to him, slashing at the man's exposed side as he approached and sending him dropping to the deck with blood streaming through his clutching fingers.

'Clark, get to the signal halliards and get that flag down.' He jerked his cutlass upwards to where the flag of the Sultan of Mysore hung limply from the top of the mainmast.

Clark rushed off to see to it as Fury looked around again. A small pocket of the enemy had been trapped by a group of *Amazons* over by the larboard mizzen chains and were now attempting to surrender, one of the men's arms raised just too late to stop the tomahawk which came crashing down on to his shoulder. Another of the men went down from a crashing blow before the *Amazons* slowly came out of their fighting madness.

Fury scanned the deck for Lieutenant Carlisle but could not see him, another blue uniform coat catching his eye instead, struggling fiercely with one of the ex-*Morningtons* before finally striking him down. Fury ran across, picking up an empty pistol from the deck as he did so. He approached from the man's side and raised the pistol to his head, the clicking as he cocked it audible even over the noise all around them. The man looked at Fury, fear momentarily in his eyes as he thought Fury was about to shoot him.

'*M'sieur!*' Fury shouted, using one of the few French words he knew. 'Surrender!'

The man did nothing, only stood there, looking at the pistol. Fury took another step forward, the barrel of the pistol now almost touching the man's temple. He shouted again, more aggressively this time.

'Surrender!'

It crossed his mind that the man might not know what he was saying, but that thought vanished a moment later when he nodded slowly.

'*Oui*, I surrender.'

'Order your men to surrender. Do it!' Fury snapped, looking round to see that many of them had already done so, the rest still fighting in small groups.

The officer shouted something in what Fury could only vaguely recognise as French. The men who were still fighting slowly dropped their weapons and raised their hands as they realised they were beaten.

A moment of silence reigned as Fury snatched the sword out of the Frenchman's proffered hand. He looked up to see the flag slowly sinking down its halliard to the deck; a second later, cheering broke out among the men. He was aware of Clark next to him once again now, a huge grin lighting up his blackened face.

'Keep an eye on him,' Fury ordered curtly, pointing at the French officer and beginning to turn away.

He felt suddenly very weary and his only wish now was to congratulate Lieutenant Carlisle before he collapsed.

* * *

Fury looked up at the sky, dotted with stars and with the moon now shedding some light on the cluttered deck of the *Mornington*.

'Sir, sir!'

Fury looked round to see one of the men, Potter, hurrying towards him.

'Well, what is it?' he demanded.

'We've found the lieutenant, sir.'

Fury looked at him for a moment before asking the next question.

'Is he dead?'

'No, sir. He looks badly cut up, though. We found him lying unconscious on the fo'c'sle under a few bodies.'

Fury let out a breath, hugely relieved that Carlisle was still alive. He had been expecting the worst since the battle had ended with the lieutenant nowhere in sight. He did not wait for another word from Potter but swiftly made his way along the gangway to the fo'c'sle, where a group of men huddled in a circle told him where to look.

'Make way there,' he ordered, pushing his way through to the middle of the group, where Clark was propping Lieutenant Carlisle up slightly as he lay on the deck. 'Don't you men have anything better to do?' He glowered round at the ring of faces. 'See that the prisoners are searched for any hidden weapons. Then escort them here to the fo'c'sle and keep them covered with one of the swivel guns until the lieutenant here decides what to do with them.'

The men turned away, leaving Fury alone with Carlisle and Clark.

'It looks like he's lost a lot of blood, sir,' Clark said quietly as Fury knelt down beside Carlisle.

He looked very weak and had obviously not been conscious for very long, still looking very dazed and confused. His shirt was in tatters, with the deep red bloodstains showing where he had been wounded several times, most probably by cutlass slashes.

'Congratulations, sir,' Fury said, 'we've taken her.'

'Thank you, Mr Fury. How many did we lose?' The question was asked in little more than a whisper.

'I'm not sure yet, sir,' Fury confessed.

Only a matter of minutes had passed since the fighting had ended, a time spent in desperate search for Carlisle. Certainly Fury hadn't had time to ascertain the butcher's bill.

'It looks like I'll be out of action for a while, Mr Fury.' Carlisle paused, his breathing shallow. In fact the pause was so long that Fury was about to respond when finally Carlisle spoke. 'You will have to take command in the meantime and see that we reach Bombay safely.'

'Aye aye, sir,' Fury replied, suddenly conscious of a great weight resting on his shoulders.

Commanding a prize for two days when in the company of your own ship was one thing, but taking command of the *Mornington* on his own with sullen Frenchmen all about the deck was quite another.

'You can rely on me, sir,' he added, with a conviction he did not entirely feel.

Whatever doubts he was inwardly experiencing, it was important to act confident in front of Carlisle, especially in his present condition. He turned to Clark.

'Please have some men take Lieutenant Carlisle down to the captain's quarters and see that he is made comfortable there. Then enquire among the crew as to whether anyone has any medical experience. If so, they are to report to me immediately.'

'Aye aye, sir,' replied Clark, gently laying Carlisle back down as he slipped in and out of consciousness on the bloody deck.

Fury stood up wearily, trying to give himself time to think. A moment later Clark came back with three men, and together they gently lifted Carlisle and started aft towards the companion ladder leading down to the captain's quarters on the upper deck.

He looked over to starboard where some of his men had already manned both the swivel guns and were training them on the large group of despondent-looking prisoners who were shuffling along the gangway towards the fo'c'sle, their heads bowed. Fury was unable to count them with only the dim light from the stars illuminating the deck, but he estimated there were about fifty.

He groaned to himself as he realised the enormity of the task, of not only commanding his own men, but also guarding and feeding the prisoners while they made their way to Bombay. His pessimistic mood was interrupted by Clark, standing in front of him once more with a seaman behind him.

'Yes, Clark?' Fury asked.

'This is Sharp, sir. He was surgeon's mate on the *Mornington* before she was took. He's the only man aboard with any medical experience, sir.'

Fury looked at Sharp, a small, lean man with a thick crop of black hair and a pale face – to be expected of someone whose duty required him to spend most of his time between decks out of the sun.

'I am placing you in charge of the wounded, Sharp. Our commanding officer, Lieutenant Carlisle, has been badly wounded and is in the captain's cabin. You will see to him first, and then take care of the remaining wounded down in the sick berth. You will report to me every morning on their condition. If you require anything, then let me know.'

Sharp was looking at him now, a worried expression on his face.

'Well?' Fury snapped.

'Please, sir, I was only a mate, sir. I don't really know nothing 'bout medicine, sir.'

Fury softened his expression. The man was obviously apprehensive and Fury snapping at him would do no good; it would only confirm the man in his convictions about the cruelty of His Majesty's Navy.

'I understand that,' Fury replied softly, 'but you're the only man on board who has any experience with this kind of thing, so just do your best.'

'Aye aye, sir,' Sharp replied, brightening a little as he turned away with Clark and started to make his way below.

Fury looked at the sky once more, still as black as before with no hint of grey in the east to warn of the approach of dawn. He turned and looked at the mass of prisoners, cowering together under the menacing stare of the swivel guns. An idea had come to him while he was talking to Sharp. Funny how often he came up with solutions when he was thinking of something completely different.

Here was Grainger now, the East India Company lieutenant, demanding his attention. Would no one leave him alone?

'Lieutenant,' Fury said, 'thank you for your assistance.'

'You're most welcome,' Grainger replied, nodding. 'Perhaps it is time to transfer the prisoners over to the *Amazon* now.

My men and I can see *Mornington* safely back to Bombay.'

'Mr Grainger,' Fury began, trying to pick his words carefully. 'Our ship will be in Bombay by now.'

A look of shock spread over Grainger's face as Fury said this.

'We were a prize crew sent on board a merchantman, the *Bedford*,' Fury continued. 'We were caught in a cyclone, completely dismasted and wrecked on this island well over a week ago.'

'I see,' said Grainger slowly, digesting this information. 'Then I will be pleased to offer you and your men passage to Bombay as my guests.'

Fury's mouth dropped open slightly, momentarily wondering if he had heard him correctly. He looked at Grainger's face carefully; the firm mouth, the high, pointed nose and the small, beady eyes. He could see no sign that Grainger was joking.

'Lieutenant,' he began, eager to clear up any confusion immediately. 'The *Mornington* is now a prize of His Britannic Majesty's frigate *Amazon*, and, due to the injuries sustained by my commanding officer, Lieutenant Carlisle, is now under my command.'

'*Your* command!' Grainger blurted, raising his voice. 'But you're little more than a boy!'

'I am an officer in His Britannic Majesty's Navy,' Fury snapped, suddenly losing his temper. 'You will place yourself and your men under my orders until we reach Bombay.'

They stood glaring at one another, Fury thinking for a moment that Grainger was going to do something foolish. Perhaps he was, but the appearance of several *Amazon*s with cutlasses and tomahawks behind Fury dissuaded him.

'Very well,' he relented, finally. 'But we shall see what the authorities in Bombay say when we arrive.'

And with that he turned briskly and walked off, clutching at the white cloth which was still round his head and throwing it to the deck. Fury turned to see that several of the prisoners were watching events with interest, a little more hope showing in their eyes. Perhaps they considered that a split in the ranks might present an opportunity for them to regain the ship? The thought prompted Fury into making the decision which he had been pondering since the idea first came to him.

'Clark!' he shouted, unnecessarily as he was right behind him. He should have realised Clark would be one of the men backing him up with cutlass at the ready.

'Sir?'

Fury lowered his voice as he explained to Clark what he wanted doing.

'I am going to transfer the prisoners on to the island in the boats. See that both boats are manned. The cutter is to carry the marines and five seamen, all armed with muskets and pistols. They are to cover the pinnace's crew, who will be taking ashore fifteen prisoners at a time. You may go in the pinnace with a couple of pistols as an added deterrent. Understood?'

'Aye, sir,' Clark replied.

'Very well. See to it.'

He would have liked to explain to Clark his reasoning behind the decision, if only so that he could have a second opinion. The fact that he did not have enough men to safely guard the prisoners on the journey to Bombay, and that it would only take a week to send a properly manned ship back to pick them up once they reached there. It was out of the question, however; an officer explaining an order to a common seaman would be a serious danger to discipline, and so Fury had to bite his tongue.

He turned towards the prisoners to seek out the French lieutenant, spotting him immediately, looking sullen on the fringes of the group. Fury walked over to the men and beckoned the man aside.

'*M'sieur*, would you join me please?'

The question was more rhetorical than anything, the man having no choice but to join Fury with those guns trained on him. Once they were out of earshot of the rest of the prisoners, Fury turned to him to explain what he was going to do with the prisoners.

'*M'sieur*, I intend to transfer all the prisoners except those who are wounded over to the island immediately.'

The man's expression turned to one of shock as he slowly understood what Fury was saying, his mouth beginning to open in protest before Fury's raised hands coerced him into silence as he attempted to explain further.

'I will supply you with ample provisions, along with a sketch showing where you can find an abundance of fresh water. Once we reach Bombay I will immediately send a ship back to pick you up – it will take no more than a week.'

'Very well,' the Frenchman replied at length. 'It does not appear that I have much choice.'

Fury shook his head. 'You will inform your men and order them to offer no resistance. They will be well covered with muskets and pistols during the transfer.'

'Sir, I will not give such an order – it is our duty to try and escape if possible.'

'Very well,' Fury replied, 'you will remain here with me until all your men have been safely landed. The first sign of trouble and you will be the first to die – you understand, *m'sieur?*'

As if to lend weight to his threat, Fury slowly patted the handle of the pistol which was stuck in his belt. Any doubts the Frenchman may have had were dispelled as soon as he looked into Fury's cold eyes. There was another lengthy pause before he finally answered.

'*Oui*, I will do it.' He said it in little more than a whisper.

The orders that he rattled out loudly in French to his men a few moments later could have meant anything, but Fury had followed the man's worried glance from his pistol to his face, and was confident he would do as he had ordered.

Chapter Fifteen

The horizon slowly turned from black to a tinge of grey as dawn finally approached some hours later to light up the scene in the bay.

Luckily the boat which Carlisle had commanded during the attack had been secured to the *Mornington*'s bow, so that Fury had been able to order some men into her to retrieve the second boat, which had drifted away back on to the beach after Fury had abandoned it to struggle in through one of the *Mornington*'s open gun ports. After that, it had taken two hours to transfer all the prisoners to the beach along with the necessary provisions, Fury keeping the French lieutenant by his side the whole time. Finally the last boat was ready and he had seen him down into it, a rough sketch of the island hastily stuffed into the lieutenant's pocket.

Now the boats were heading back out to the *Mornington* for the last time as Fury peered through the telescope at the beach; the Frenchmen merely stood there, crowded along the waterline silently watching their former prize, some waving their fists in defiance. Once the boats' crews were back on board, Fury decided he would take a muster to see exactly how many men they had lost during the attack on the *Mornington*. Hard to think that it was only last night that he had come drifting down in the water in the dark, all alone, to let loose the boats. He shuddered slightly at the memory.

'Mr Fury.'

He turned round to see Lieutenant Grainger standing there.

'I took the liberty of having some men check the hull while the prisoners were being transferred. She took some shots between wind and water when the French attacked, but it looks as if they've made a good job of repairing them. We should be fit to sail as soon as the men are back and the boats are hoisted on board.'

'Excellent. Thank you, Mr Grainger.'

Fury was glad that Grainger had forgotten about their earlier disagreement, but was slightly irked that he might be trying to take too much on himself. Still, he had to concede that he had completely forgotten to check the hull repairs that the French had been making.

He turned back to the bulwark, watching as the two boats slowly approached. The sun was getting higher now and its strength was increasing steadily. It was lucky for the men that the prisoners had been transferred in the cool of the night – it looked as if it was going to be another sweltering day, when the pitch would start to soften in the deck seams and paint would begin to crack. The sooner they got out of this sheltered cove and into the fresh sea breeze the better, he thought, the cutter and pinnace finally reaching them and hooking on, the crews scrambling up the *Mornington*'s side to the deck.

He waited a few moments while the oarsmen went over to the scuttlebutt and helped themselves to water.

'Mr Grainger, would you be so kind as to take a muster of your men?'

Grainger nodded in the affirmative.

Fury called over to Clark to muster the men on the quarter-deck, *Amazon*s to starboard and *Mornington*s to larboard. It was several minutes before the men were finally all in place, enabling Fury to begin counting them. Twenty-eight *Amazon*s, including himself. He went round and counted again, just to make sure – still twenty-eight. That meant that ten of his men had been killed or injured during the attack: a heavy price. He suddenly realised he had no idea how many of those were injured and how many were dead. He had only been concerned with Carlisle's injury immediately after the battle, and the recollection of it increased his feeling of guilt.

Here was Grainger coming up to make his report.

'Thirty-five men left, Mr Fury, including myself.'

So, five of them had been killed in the fighting. That left him with a crew of sixty-three men, all prime seamen except for the marines. Plenty enough to handle the *Mornington*, he consoled himself.

'Men!' he shouted, scanning their faces as he stood there. 'Lieutenant Carlisle has placed me in command until he is well enough to return to duty. Mr Grainger here – he indicated with his hand to his left where Grainger was standing – 'will be second in command.' Fury thought he sensed an irksome glance from Grainger at this statement. He ignored it and continued. 'You will all receive your station bills shortly; in the meantime I want the boats hoisted in and the deck scrubbed clean. While you are at it, *Amazon*s can take the opportunity of washing the paint off their faces. That will be all.' He turned to Clark. 'See to it please, Clark.'

He watched as the men ran about in apparent confusion as Clark gave the orders, some men hauling on braces to bring the starboard fore yardarm aft, some laying aloft to rig the stay tackle to the main and fore tackle pendants, and others laying out on the yardarm to rig the main and fore yard tackles. Sufficient men waited down in the first boat to hook on the falls once the tackles were ready.

The pinnace was the first to be hoisted in, being the second largest boat the *Mornington* possessed after the launch, which was already sitting on the booms in the waist. The men ran away with the falls at Clark's command, the pinnace rising slowly up as the strain was taken on the yard tackles. Finally it was high enough to clear the rail, at which point the stay tackle amidships took the strain and the boat began to swing inboard, before being gradually lowered down into the waist to rest inside the launch.

Fury estimated it had taken about forty minutes to complete the task, and was satisfied enough to leave Clark alone to raise the smaller cutter; he wanted to be under way before midday and there were other matters he needed to see to. He went to make his way below, remembering at the last moment that he would need Grainger's help with his next task.

'Mr Grainger! Will you accompany me down to the captain's quarters, please?'

Grainger nodded his assent and Fury led the way down to the captain's day cabin. Once seated comfortably behind the former captain's desk, with his back to the stern windows and with Grainger sitting opposite him, Fury began.

'Mr Grainger, I will need your help to draw up a general station and watch bill for the men. Just the major drills such as setting, reefing and taking in sail, dropping and weighing anchor – enough to see us to Bombay. I do not propose to include a quarter bill, as the chances of us seeing action on the way are negligible.'

Grainger nodded and Fury drew several pieces of paper towards him, along with a pen and a bottle of ink from the captain's desk. The task took about two hours, interrupted only by the sounds of Sharp outside as he tended to Carlisle in the captain's sleeping cabin.

'Very good, Mr Grainger, I think we are done,' Fury said at last, sitting back in his chair and realising for the first time how hot it was in the cabin with the sun shining right through the stern windows on to his back. 'Please be so good as to inform the men of their new divisions.'

Grainger merely nodded, apparently reluctant to use the word 'sir'. Fury did not care – it would be a matter of days before they reached Bombay and then he would be out of his hair.

As soon as Grainger had left the cabin, Fury rose from the chair and went through to the sleeping quarters. Sharp was still there seeing to Carlisle, who lay motionless in the cot wrapped in bandages. Sharp turned round with a slight look of shock on his face before he realised who it was, Fury remembering at that moment that he had not yet had time to wash the paint off his face. Sharp motioned Fury to be quiet as he entered.

'How is he?' Fury whispered.

'Very weak, sir. He's lost a lot of blood but I've managed to bandage him all up, and, as long as his wounds heal cleanly, he should live.'

Fury nodded. 'Excellent, Sharp – well done. When you

have finished, would you be so kind as to bring me a bowl of water? I will be in the day cabin.'

'Aye aye, sir,' Sharp whispered, as Fury left the room to go back to the large day cabin spanning the whole width of the ship.

He went up to the desk and started to look through the contents of the drawers, finding what he was looking for as he pulled out a sextant and a boxed chronometer. Assuming they got under way and out of the cove by midday, he could find the island's position and so enable the French prisoners and the *Bedford*'s hidden stores to be picked up at a later date.

There was a rap at the door and Sharp poked his head round, before coming in and putting down a bowl full of water on the sideboard.

'Thank you, Sharp,' Fury said as the man left, walking over to the bowl and splashing water over his face, rubbing vigorously with his hands to try and wipe away the dried paint.

It took him some time to satisfy himself that he had removed all traces of it. He cursed himself for his lack of forethought as he straightened up slightly to dry his face, realising he had no towel and having to resort to drying round his eyes with the tails of his shirt. That done, he left to make his way back up on deck.

When he reached the quarterdeck, the men were putting the finishing touches to the ship's brass work, having already finished scrubbing the deck clean of bloodstains. Clark was there, as ever.

'Send a lookout up to the mainmast head,' Fury ordered.

'Aye aye, sir,' Clark acknowledged, walking over to where Cooke was standing and pointing upwards with his thumb.

Fury watched Cooke heave himself over the starboard bulwark by the main chains and start scurrying up the shrouds like a monkey, reaching the futtock shrouds and hanging backwards for a moment as he negotiated them, before hauling himself into the maintop and then onwards still up the topmast shrouds and higher.

He transferred his gaze to the men on deck, waiting with ill-concealed impatience while the work was finished and noting as he did so that the men had all now washed the paint off their faces. Finally the work was completed and the gear stowed away, Fury making sure the men were all ready before he shouted his next set of orders which would get the *Mornington* under way.

'Up anchor! All hands up anchor!' he bawled, sending the men to their newly allotted stations. 'Rig the capstan!'

The men on the gun deck got the capstan bars and fitted them into the holes around the top of the capstan, ready to push.

'Bring to the messenger!'

The smaller messenger cable was wrapped by the men on the gun deck round the barrel of the capstan three and a half times, leading forward round a vertical roller fixed to the deck and then back along the deck past the bitts, the two eyes at each end of the messenger cable fixed together with rope.

Being smaller than the anchor cable, it was easier to wrap the messenger cable round the capstan barrel, and also provided a better grip round the capstan when heaving. This was due to the fact that the cable was dry, unlike the anchor cable which would be wet and slimy after being submerged under water. The actual anchor cable itself, leading inboard through a hawsehole in the ship's bows, led aft, was secured round the riding bitts and was led below where it was coiled down in the hold. The 'nipper men' would now be securing the messenger cable to the anchor cable so that, when the capstan turned, the anchor cable would be hauled inboard by the messenger cable, before being coiled down in the hold as it came in by the men stationed there for that purpose. As the cable came in, the fastenings to the messenger cable would be released as they reached the hatchway leading to the hold, and the nipper men would run forward and secure a new fastening to the two cables.

Fury waited while the men on the gun deck prepared the messenger and fastened it in several places to the anchor cable, ready for the first heave, continuing once he had received a signal that all was now ready.

'Man the bars!'

The men below got into position ready to push the bars attached to the capstan at chest height. Five men per bar would be needed to provide sufficient force to release the anchor from the bottom and haul it aboard.

'Ready for heaving round!'

The men stood ready now at the capstan bars, chests and arms leaning on the bar, feet braced back ready for the push.

'Heave round!' Fury shouted, the men throwing their weight on to the bars. The capstan slowly began to turn as the men started to walk round, bringing the anchor cable in through the hawsehole as the ship was warped up to her anchor against the current.

'Up and down, sir,' Clark reported at last, peering over the starboard bow and letting Fury know that the cable was now vertical as the *Mornington* came directly over the anchor.

'Heave round, lads!' Fury shouted, trying to encourage the

men as they continued to push the capstan round, the slow clank-clank telling them they were making progress as the flukes of the anchor were finally wrenched free of the sea bed and the anchor began to rise.

At last Clark signalled that the stock of the anchor had burst through the surface of the clear blue water.

'Avast heaving!' Fury shouted, the men at the capstan ceasing their efforts with sweat dripping from them. The anchor was now hanging half in and half out of the water.

'Rig and hook the cat!'

Fury watched as the fall of the cat block was loosed and the large cat hook was guided on to the anchor ring, using lines attached to the block and back of the hook, which were tended by men on the fo'c'sle and beakhead.

'Man the cat! Haul taut!'

The men now tailed on to the falls of the cat block, taking up the slack and waiting for Fury's next order, which was not long coming.

'Walk away with the cat!'

The men hauled the anchor further out of the water until the ring was under the cathead.

'Belay!' he shouted, satisfied that the anchor was up far enough.

Now it was time to bring the flukes of the anchor up and secure them to the ship's side.

'Rig and hook the fish!' he bellowed.

The men were now fitting the davit, a length of timber projecting up and out, fitted into a socket in the ship's side in the fore channels, and with the fish tackle on the outward end, the falls of which led up the foremast, through a block and back down on deck, where the men would tail on to them to raise the flukes of the anchor. The davit was being supported from above by a line running to the foremast, and from side to side by a line running forward secured to the cathead, and a line running aft secured to the main channel. Again, the hook of the fish tackle, tended by a man on the fo'c'sle, was being guided along the shank of the anchor until it reached the flukes and was caught by them. This was the moment Fury had been waiting for to give his next order.

'Man the fish! Haul taut!' he shouted, prompting the men on the fish tackle to take the slack on the falls.

'Walk away with the fish!'

The men now hauled on the falls and the fluke of the anchor began to rise, bringing the shank back horizontal where men were waiting to secure the inner fluke to a timberhead, just forward of the fore chains.

'Unrig the fish!' he shouted finally, the men unhooking the fish tackle from the anchor and unrigging the fish davit.

The *Mornington* was now at the mercy of wind and current, making a slow stern board as the current began to take effect, pushing her towards the land. Fury hurriedly began to give the orders which would take her out of the cove and into the open sea.

'Back the fore course!' he bellowed, anxious that they should get her under control quickly lest she drift on to a hidden reef.

Fury cursed himself for leaving it far too late – he should have got her foresail aback as soon as the anchor had been released from the sea bed and she had been at the mercy of the current.

He could see the men scurrying aloft to lay out along the yard and release the sail, presently bunched up and secured along the yard with gaskets. The sail was let fall as one, once the men on the yard had undone all the gaskets, the canvas dropping down in great folds and the men on deck immediately hauling on the sheets to secure the lower corners of the sail. More men were now hauling on the braces, slowly swinging the yard round until at last the wind was on the forward side of the sail, pressing the canvas back against the mast.

'Port your helm,' he growled at the helmsman, the man immediately throwing the wheel over in response.

The sou'westerly wind, pushing the sail back against the mast, was acting to push the *Mornington*'s bow away from the wind, aided by the rudder, and Fury was stood waiting for the right moment to fill away and sail out of the cove. The wind was almost on the *Mornington*'s starboard beam, and Fury judged that now was the time.

'Brace round the fore yard! Let fall the main course!'

He was glad that he had a crew of able seamen as the men jumped to the order quickly, the men stationed on the fo'c'sle hauling on the braces once again to bring the fore yard back until it was square, and then round further still until the wind caught the after side of the sail, the canvas flapping before it finally filled, the men hauling on tacks and sheets to secure the corners.

'Meet her,' he growled to the helmsman, the man now turning the wheel back to centre the rudder as the *Mornington*'s sternway gradually diminished until she was stationary for a moment, before she began moving slowly ahead, the forward thrust of the fore course now taking effect.

The men stationed at the mainmast were busy loosing the big main course now, the yardmen keeping hold of the large folds of sail until the signal was given that all gaskets had been cast loose, before letting go to send the canvas tumbling down. Once the yardmen had scrambled off the yard, the men at the braces hauled the yard round until it was parallel with the fore yard, at which time the tacks and sheets were hauled home, the canvas now billowing taut as it trapped the wind. With both the fore and main courses set, the *Mornington* was making good headway now out of the cove.

Fury looked ahead to where he could see they would clear the eastern headland easily without having to tack the ship. He looked at the compass housed in the binnacle; they were heading just about sou'east now, with the wind on the starboard beam. This was as good a course to steer as any, Fury thought, until they knew their exact position and therefore what course to set. With that in mind, he started to pace the quarterdeck – up and down, up and down – waiting for noon to arrive, satisfied that his first test had been successfully negotiated. Whether by luck or by judgement, he was not quite sure.

It was not long before noon when *Mornington* finally swept clear of the outermost headland, the breeze stiffening as they came out of the lee of the land. Both Fury and Grainger were standing by the bulwark, sextants in hand, ready to take the noon sight which would, they hoped, fix their latitude. Clark was standing by with the half-hour sand glass, ready to turn it once Fury had signalled that the sun was at its highest point.

Fury could recall those first months when he had struggled with his navigation, most of all with getting a good sight of the sun at its highest point while standing on a heaving deck. Eventually, he had mastered it, and he now prided himself on being a good navigator. All his calculations on board the *Amazon* recently had agreed with the master's, more or less, so he felt it strange now that his confidence should have deserted him. Perhaps it was due to the fact that before, on the *Amazon*, his calculations had only been for his own practice and to compare with the master's. Here on the *Mornington* it was different; here his calculation would be relied upon to set the ship's course in order to reach Bombay safely. It was a daunting thought, and he was glad that he had Grainger with him to compare results – it would give him some degree of comfort at least.

Through the eyepiece of the sextant he could see the sun now slowly rising, and a short moment later a curt 'turn' from him to Clark prompted the turning of the half-hour sand glass, sending the sand rushing through and marking the start of the ship's day and the beginning of the afternoon watch.

'You can pipe the hands to dinner now, Clark,' Fury said, as he placed his sextant back in the box. It was the standard order given, and it didn't occur to Fury that there was no one to pipe the order in this instance. Clark merely turned and bellowed along the deck.

'All hands to dinner!'

Satisfied with the sight he had taken, Fury made his way below as the scramble of feet told of men rushing to mess tables, eager to see what their shipmates – the men Fury and Grainger had assigned as ship's cooks – had prepared. He reached the upper deck and turned aft with Grainger following him, both hurrying to the captain's day cabin.

He sank down at the desk with his back to the stern windows and with Grainger facing him over the other side of the desk, both scribbling silently as they worked out their position while the *Mornington* drove slowly along to the sou'east with the wind on her beam, throwing up small showers of spray as she plunged her bow into the oncoming waves.

It was a good hour by Clark's reckoning before Fury and Grainger appeared on deck once again, Fury walking over to the helmsman to give him the new course which would, all being well, take them to Bombay.

'East-nor'east a half north.'

'East-nor'east a half north, aye aye, sir,' the helmsman repeated, easing the spokes through his fingers as he turned the wheel to port to send the ship in the desired direction.

Fury stood there looking out over the larboard beam at the small hump of land which until lately had been their home. He had been uncertain as to whether to take the *Mornington* round to the west of the island to pick up the cargo of cotton that they had hidden before heading for Bombay, but had decided against it. It was unlikely the *Mornington* would have enough room in her hold to stow all the cotton, and he was also concerned about being ambushed by their late prisoners if they should find out that they were ashore. His anxiousness to reunite with the *Amazon* had finally swung it, and he was now content to leave the cargo for another ship to pick up once the prisoners had been safely removed from the island.

All Fury wanted now was to reach Bombay safely and rejoin his ship, and it had been a relief when Grainger's calculation of their position proved virtually identical to his own. It gave him a degree of comfort that the course he had given the helmsman was correct.

The *Mornington* was slowly bringing her stern round now towards the wind, and a moment later she finally settled down with the wind fine on her starboard quarter.

'East-nor'east a half north, sir,' reported the helmsman, confirming that the *Mornington* was now sailing on that course.

'Keep her at that,' Fury ordered, looking up at the sails to decide what she could carry.

They were currently under fore course and main course only, that having been sufficient to take them out of the cove while they could work out their position. With the wind now fine on the quarter, however, the main course was taking some of the wind out of the fore course, making his first order obvious.

'Clew up the weather main course!' he shouted, disturbing the watch on deck from their relaxations.

Halliards were hauled on, the clew lines slowly raising the lower starboard corner of the main course up to the yard above, where it was secured by the yardmen. Fury looked forward to where he could see the fore course drawing much better now that it was not blocked by part of the main course. He stood there a moment, feeling the wind on his cheeks and watching how the ship behaved, before deciding to press on with more sail.

'Loose topsails and t'gallants!' he roared, sending the men rushing to their stations once again.

Of course, with the loss of *Mornington*'s fore topgallant mast, the only t'gallants which could be set were the main and the mizzen. They were effective enough on this point of sail, but Fury made a mental note that if the wind backed round to the south he would have to take them in. With the wind abeam, the lack of the fore topgallant sail to balance out the effect of the main and mizzen would most likely cause her head to come up into the wind, thus requiring the helmsman to carry too much weather helm.

He looked up at the fore, main and mizzen masts, to see that the topmen had finished the job of throwing off the gaskets and were all off the topsail yards. The men on deck were hauling away to sheet home the topsails, before the halliards were manned to raise the yard up to the topmast cap, ready to be braced round in the desired direction. Fury watched as they worked, a shouted word from Clark or Grainger encouraging or berating as appropriate.

Once the topsails were set and drawing well, the men set to work loosing the topgallants high above the deck, completing the task without a hitch. Fury could feel the difference already, the *Mornington*'s speed picking up as she surged forward under her new press of canvas, occasionally slicing the top off a wave and sending the spray flying over the fo'c'sle. Her deck was now canting a little more steeply as the lofty sail resulted in a greater heel, Fury having to grab on to the bulwark for a moment until he got used to the new motion – he had still not fully regained his sea legs after their time on the island.

The ship's bell rang out. Six bells – three o'clock in the afternoon. With any luck they should reach Bombay in three days, he reflected, feeling suddenly light-hearted at the thought of finally rejoining the *Amazon*, and trying to picture his uncle's face when he came gliding into Bombay harbour in the *Mornington* rather than the *Bedford*. There had been times in the past three weeks when it had looked as if they were never going to make it, and he was relieved now that the worst was over.

* * *

262

For the rest of the first day and all the next the *Mornington* thrashed along under all the sail she could carry, driven forward by the fresh sou'westerly wind under the searing heat of the sun and the relentless blue of the sky.

Now, as dawn approached on the second full day away from the island, Fury could see through the stern windows that it was going to be another hot day. The six men stationed around the deck as lookouts during the night would be waiting to be relieved by the lookout scampering aloft to the mainmast head, as the visible horizon gradually expanded.

Fury moved over to the wash basin set on the sideboard, the water in it now tepid and stale. Nevertheless it was refreshing to plunge his face into it, rising to look into the mirror sat beside it. He could hardly recognise the face that he saw. The brown mop of hair was now hanging raggedly forward over his forehead and was a little too long for comfort, while his deep-set blue eyes looked back at him with detachment from his deeply tanned face, so that it felt as if he was looking at a stranger. The scar on his chin from that splinter wound taken on the *Amazon* was still pink and would likely be permanent. His attention now drawn to his chin, he ran his hand over it; no, he would not have to bother shaving again just yet.

He stood there, reflecting on their progress since leaving the island. The men's spirits had been steadily rising the closer they got to Bombay, the reel of the log line showing they were making a steady nine knots. With any luck they should reach Bombay by lunchtime tomorrow, if the wind kept fair.

Fury had thought it best to keep the men busy during the previous day, scrubbing and polishing everything during the morning watch, with the afternoon spent checking every inch of rigging for signs of chafe. His relationship with

Grainger had improved too. Whether he had earned the man's grudging respect by the way he had handled the *Mornington*, or whether Grainger had merely had time to calm down and reflect, Fury neither knew nor cared.

A clatter next door brought him sharply back to the present – that would be Sharp seeing to Lieutenant Carlisle's wounds. He had done a good job of keeping the wounds clean so that no infection had set in yet. Now all that Carlisle needed was plenty of rest until he had recovered his strength enough to get back on his feet.

It crossed Fury's mind to pop in and see him as he left the captain's large day cabin, but decided against it. He wanted to go up on deck first and check everything was as it should be. It would be, of course; if any changes had been necessary to course or sails, he would have been called by the officer of the watch, but it was as well to make sure now. He would have plenty of time later to sit with Carlisle.

He passed through the dining cabin and out on to the upper deck, the two rows of black nine-pounders stretching away on either side of him. Striding forward and still fastening his shirt as he went, he approached the companion ladder and made his way up, reaching the quarterdeck in a moment. It was surprising how quickly the sun rose, he reflected, as he walked over to the binnacle, silently acknowledging the salute of the helmsman and Clark, who was officer of the watch, as he did so.

East-nor'east a half north. They had not needed to deviate once from that course during the past two days. He sensed the wind had changed slightly and he looked aloft to see the yards braced up more sharply than the previous night, confirming his suspicions. The wind must have backed a trifle during the night, and Fury felt proud that the mere feel of it on his cheek had been enough to tell him. It was probably now at sou'west by south; still more than fair to keep them on their desired course.

He looked across at the horizon to the east, stretching away for a mile or more now that the sun had appeared from below the curvature of the earth. Very soon it would be uncomfortable to stand here under the glare of that sun, Fury mused, beginning to pace up and down the starboard side of the quarterdeck. Clark made no attempt to talk to him as he paced and Fury was glad – he was not the greatest of company first thing in the morning. Once this brisk pacing had woken him up fully, he would go down and do his duty – making small talk with a very weak Carlisle. Until then, he would enjoy this sense of freedom while he could, he decided.

Chapter Sixteen

'Sail ho!'

The shout from the masthead lookout drifted down and reached Fury as he was leaving Lieutenant Carlisle's cabin after spending almost an hour with him. Abandoning his plans to return to his own cabin, he rushed forward towards the companion ladder, hearing Grainger's bellowed reply of 'Where away?' as he went. There was a pause – enough time for Fury to bound up the ladder and on to the quarterdeck – before the lookout replied.

'Fine on the starboard bow, sir! She's reaching northwards!'

Grainger was looking at him as he approached, but he said nothing, instead turning his face skyward to the masthead.

'What do you make of her?'

Another pause as the lookout studied the strange sail through his glass, before the reply came.

'Hard to tell, sir. I can only see her topgallants, but she's ship rigged for sure!'

Fury started pacing as if the movement of his legs would get his brain working. Should they alter course to the south until the strange sail was out of sight? On their present course they would already pass well astern of her, but there was a

266

chance they would be seen. On the other hand, only one hundred miles or so away from Bombay, it would be unlikely that she was hostile, and her course suggested she was heading towards the Indian port.

In the end his desire to reach Bombay as soon as possible asserted itself, and he decided to carry on their present course. Having made his decision, he turned round towards Grainger, opening his mouth to begin his order – an order which died on his lips as a faint noise reached his ears, like clapping thunder far away in the distance. He looked questioningly at Grainger.

'Gunfire?'

Grainger nodded slowly.

'It sounds like it.'

Damn it! What should he do now? There were only a limited number of reasons why a ship would be firing her broadside. Either a merchant ship was being attacked by a privateer or pirate, or a ship of war was attacking a privateer or pirate. In either case it was his duty to investigate further and assist if necessary.

'We will continue on our present course, Mr Grainger. Have the ship cleared for action, but don't send the men to quarters yet.' He realised as he said it that they had not drawn up a quarter bill for the crew; he had not thought it necessary for the three days it would take to reach safety. He turned to Clark. 'Have Lieutenant Carlisle moved to the cockpit.'

'Aye aye, sir,' Clark acknowledged.

There was no question of Carlisle remaining in the captain's quarters. When the ship cleared for action the bulkheads making up the captain's cabins would be struck down in the hold, leaving the whole of the upper deck clear from bow to stern.

Fury turned back to Grainger, who was bellowing for all hands and giving the orders which would prepare the *Mornington* for battle.

'I am going aloft, Mr Grainger,' he said, striding over to the starboard main chains without waiting for an answer. He swung himself out into the channels and started the long climb up the shrouds.

Up and up he went, hand over hand, the shrouds narrowing as he reached higher and the ratlines sinking under his weight. He reached the bottom of the futtock shrouds and swung himself out backwards to climb up and over the main top. On and on, his breath shortening due to the exertion, until at last he reached the man perched at the masthead.

The deck below seemed tiny, the gentle pitch and roll of the ship as she made her way north-east exaggerated up here, so that one moment they were over the deck, the next moment they were hanging with nothing but the blue of the sea beneath them. The sweat was pouring over him now, his shirt clinging to his body and his hair plastered to his forehead.

Cooper, the lookout sitting next to him at the masthead, was grinning in excitement as he handed Fury the telescope and pointed out ahead with one finger. Fury looped his arm around the rigging, wiped his forehead with his sleeve, and balanced the telescope as he scanned the horizon. It took him some moments to find the strange sail, still hull down over the horizon as she was. They must be gaining on them; he could see her topsails and topgallants now, and she was dead ahead, crossing their bow as the *Mornington* reached to the north-east.

Now that Fury was still again and his heartbeat had slowed, he could clearly hear intermittent claps of gunfire. Obviously they were still engaged. He cleared his throat before bellowing to the deck below.

'Mr Grainger! Alter course one point to larboard!'

Grainger shouted his acknowledgement and turned to the helmsman to give the necessary order, irrespective of the fact that the helmsman had heard Fury's order perfectly well himself.

Fury scanned through the telescope again, although it took some minutes before the *Mornington*'s slight alteration of course had any effect, her bow gradually swinging to bring the strange sail to starboard once more. Fury estimated that on this course they would pass well within sight of her from the deck as they crossed her wake.

He sat there in silence looking through the telescope, as gradually the sporadic gunfire grew more distinct and he could make out not only her topmasts and topgallants, but her lower masts as well. Very soon her hull would be visible, giving Fury a better idea of what she was, although the fact that she had reduced down to topsails only suggested she might well be a man o' war.

So intent was he on catching the first glimpse of her hull, it took him some moments to realise more masts were visible beyond her – another ship, obviously the vessel she was engaged with. Ah! Now her hull was appearing above the crest of the horizon. Fury studied it intently, struggling to keep the image in his lens as the mast swayed to and fro with the movement of the ship. She looked like a frigate but it was difficult to be sure from this distance. He could see faint wreaths of smoke from her hidden, starboard side, as she fired off her broadsides at the opponent beyond. He passed the telescope back to Cooper.

'What do you make of her, Cooper?'

Cooper put the telescope to his eye and studied her for a few moments.

'She looks like a frigate to me, sir, an' quite a heavy one. She certainly don't look like the *Amazon*, sir.'

That was the whole point, Fury thought; there had not been enough time for the commodore commanding these waters, Cornwallis, to have sent a frigate round from Madras. So if she was not the *Amazon*, there was only one other possibility Fury could think of – *Magicienne*.

'Report the minute you can make out anything more,' he ordered, trying to keep his voice matter-of-fact as the implications sank in.

'Aye aye, sir,' Cooper replied, continuing to study the sail through the telescope.

Fury grabbed the backstay and started to descend, hand over hand, being careful to avoid sliding. He had made that mistake shortly after joining the navy in his excitement to get to the deck, resulting in severe friction burns which had not only torn the skin from his hands and kept him on light duties for a week, but had also incensed the captain enough to order one of the bosun's mates to give him a caning.

He reached the deck, to be accosted immediately by Grainger, eager for news.

'She's a frigate – and not one of ours by the look of her. The other vessel is not yet in sight.'

Grainger took a second or two to digest this information, before proceeding with his report.

'Ship cleared for action, Mr Fury, but I haven't ordered the decks to be sanded yet.'

Fury nodded in agreement. Before every engagement the decks were wetted and sprinkled with sand to provide the crew with better grip on the planking. It would be a while yet before they were even within long gunshot range, and by that time the decks would be well dried again.

'Clark!' he shouted, Clark appearing as if from nowhere in front of him.

'Sir?'

'Do we still have that damn Sultan of Mysore flag?' Fury asked.

'Yes, sir,' Clark replied.

'Then hoist it right away, but make sure we have our flag bent on ready to hoist as soon as we need it.'

'Aye aye, sir!'

Clark hurried off to the flag locker while Fury turned back to Grainger.

'I will take a look around the ship.'

The time would pass more quickly if he kept himself busy, and it would also give him time to think before giving his next order – he was acutely conscious that the *Mornington* was not committed to anything yet. A word from him could change her course and send her well away from the danger ahead.

A quick glance round the quarterdeck and fo'c'sle was enough. He could see the hammocks stowed in the nettings on top of the bulwarks to protect the men on deck from small arms fire, and the splinter netting had been rigged over the deck to provide protection from flying splinters and falling spars.

He reached the upper deck where the bulkheads forming the captain's quarters were no longer there, providing a clear view all along the deck, the guns still secured and port lids closed. He went along each side, noting all the equipment which had been laid out between the guns – wads, buckets of water, lengths of slow match, sponges, rammers and hand-spikes, along with the balls stored about the deck in the shot garlands. The pikes were all stowed in racks around the three masts, while cutlasses were hanging from the ship's side between each gun, Fury checking several as he went round to make sure they had a sharp edge. Satisfied, he made his way back on deck, realising uncomfortably that he had still not made his mind up about what to do.

'Deck there!'

That was Cooper, hailing them from the mainmast head.

'Deck here!' Fury bellowed back. 'What is it?'

'I can see the other ship now, sir!' A small pause, as if to build up the tension on the deck, before he continued. 'She looks like the *Amazon* to me, sir!'

Fury stood there as the implications of that last report slowly sank in. He was surprised to discover he felt strangely relieved, the indecision of the past hour now disappearing; his decision about what to do next had been taken out of his hands – his only concern now was how to tackle the situation.

The *Amazon* was only a thirty-two, carrying twelve-pounders on her main deck. She would be heavily outgunned if the other ship was in fact the *Magicienne* with those long eighteen-pounders on her main deck. It was highly likely *Amazon* was in a bad way already if they had been exchanging broadsides at close range, so it was up to him to get there as quickly as possible and relieve the pressure. He swung round to find Clark beside him.

'Muster the men please, Clark.'

'Aye aye, sir,' Clark replied, hurrying away.

Fury looked up to where the courses, topsails and top-gallants were all drawing well. He could not see the flag streaming out at the masthead, but knew it would be the same flag as the *Magicienne* was flying. That ought to give them a few vital moments to get into position before they hauled down the flag and raised their own prior to firing.

'Men assembled, sir.'

That was Clark, interrupting his thoughts. Fury followed him to the quarterdeck rail, looking down to where the men were grouped in the waist.

'Men!' he shouted. 'The *Amazon* is over there along with what looks like the *Magicienne*. As we come up to them I intend to rake *Magicienne* as we cross her stern, so look alive for my orders. After that it will be a case of firing as our guns bear. I will have you all assigned to quarters shortly. That will be all.'

As if to emphasise the urgency of the situation, the dull clap of another broadside drifted across the water, Fury looking up to see if there was any way he could get them within range sooner. A quick glance told him it would not be wise to clap on any more sail at this point, so all he could do was to make sure the course they were heading would take them to within as close a range as possible of the *Magicienne*. He took a tele-scope from the drawer in the binnacle box and trained it forward, catching sight of *Magicienne* in the distance, probably about two miles ahead now on the larboard bow.

'Come up two more points to larboard,' he growled at the helmsman, telescope still to his eye.

The helmsman acknowledged, and gradually the *Mornington* began to swing until the *Magicienne* was fine on the starboard bow once again. Fury turned to Grainger, standing beside him.

'Mr Grainger, would you please be so kind as to allocate the crew to their quarters?'

Grainger's face was looking confused now.

'But—'

'I know, I know,' Fury interrupted testily. 'We did not draw up a quarter bill. But they are all able seamen. Once we are in range, I will want all hands to shorten sail down to topsails only. After that I will want twenty men to remain on deck to handle the sails – the rest can be used as gun crews. Have the guns on both sides loaded with grape on top of round shot, and run out. You will be in command of the upper deck. After that you will have to distribute the crews among the guns as you see fit.'

'Aye aye, sir,' Grainger replied, Fury not noticing that it was the first time that he had called him 'sir' since they had met.

'Mr Grainger!' he called after him, suddenly realising he had missed something very important. 'You will have to station some men to bring up fresh cartridges from the magazine. Make sure the magazine is sealed off with a damp fearnought screen and the men take all the necessary precautions.'

Grainger nodded his understanding as he left to assign the crew to their stations. The sight of Corporal Davis standing on the quarterdeck, resplendent in scarlet tunic and white cross belt, reminded Fury of something else he had forgotten. He made his way over to him, wondering as he approached how on earth the man could stand the heat in his uniform.

'Mr Davis. You will station your men in the fighting tops – two in the maintop and two in the foretop. From there they will keep up a constant fire on the enemy's deck with the swivel guns and with muskets. I will leave your own position to your discretion.'

Davis saluted rigidly.

'Oh, and Davis. Have all your men stripped of their jackets. And that includes you.'

If someone on board the *Magicienne* were to spot the scarlet of the marines' uniforms as they approached, their advantage of surprise would be ruined.

'Yes, sah!' Davis said, saluting once again before leaving to order his men up into the tops.

Standing there alone now, Fury could think of nothing else that needed doing for the time being, and so he settled down to wait while the *Mornington* drove along on a course which would intersect the *Magicienne*'s path. He had learned from the start that life in the navy was a life of extremes – long periods of waiting followed by bursts of intense activity. Pretty soon they would be plunged into one of their most intense activities yet.

He grabbed the telescope once again from the binnacle and moved to the larboard side to look forward. Only a mile and a half to go now to the *Magicienne*, and he could see *Amazon* beyond her, perhaps only a cable separating the two ships as they headed slowly northwards under topsails alone, their sides erupting into flame and smoke as they fired into one another. The sound of gunfire was almost continual as the crews reloaded and fired at their own pace, and Fury, watching the flashes, was sure the *Amazon*'s rate of fire was slightly faster than her opponent, but only slightly. The French ship obviously had a well-trained crew then, because they were usually far slower than their British counterparts. Here was Grainger again, ready to report.

'I have told off the men for the gun crews, sir, and all guns on both sides have been loaded with grape and round shot.'

'Very good, Mr Grainger,' Fury replied. 'As soon as we are down to topsails only, wash down and sand the decks, then have the men go to their guns and run out both sides ready for my orders.'

'Aye aye, sir,' Grainger acknowledged, leaving him alone once more by the bulwark.

This was it. His first command of a ship going into action. Fury could almost feel the weight of the responsibility bearing down on him. It was much more than leading a mere boarding party; now his very skill as a seaman, in handling the ship, would determine their success or failure, life or death. It would do no good to dwell on the subject, he thought, raising the telescope once more to try and take his mind away from it.

He trained the lens on *Magicienne* first, but it was impossible to estimate the damage she was receiving because her engaged side was facing away from the *Mornington*. He caught sight of the lavish name emblazoned across her stern – *Magicienne* – and felt a little relief that his guess had proved correct. He moved the lens across and studied *Amazon* closely, unable to see any real sign of damage to her hull. Understandable perhaps; the French had a habit of firing high at the enemy's rigging, in order to disable them.

Fury was hoping that the sight of the *Mornington*, which the French captain would believe was his ally, would persuade him to try and board *Amazon* earlier than he would otherwise have attempted. That would give Fury a chance to lay the *Mornington* alongside and board; the shock of seeing sixty screaming men coming at them when they had expected reinforcements might prove crucial. His one big fear was that he would reveal his hand too early to the French captain, giving him time to sheer off from the *Amazon* and increase the range, shooting the both of them to pieces – those eighteen-pounders were much more accurate than his own nine-pounders or the *Amazon*'s twelve-pounders.

He lowered the telescope to see how far they had to go – it was easier to judge the distance with the naked eye. A little less than a mile away now, perhaps? Something caught his eye and he whipped the telescope back up. Yes, there it was! *Amazon*'s main topgallant mast was sagging forward towards the foremast, held up only by its rigging. A shot had probably parted one of the stays supporting it, causing it to snap just above the topmast cap.

Fury was anxious to keep watching as the sounds grew gradually louder and louder, but he was conscious that the distance was closing quite rapidly now and he still had preparations to make. He turned back to the wheel, picking up a speaking trumpet from its becket – it was amazing how that gunfire carried – and started shouting his orders.

'All hands! All hands! Stand by to shorten sail!'

The men were all on deck in their usual stations for altering sail and were waiting quietly for his orders.

'Man topgallant clew lines and buntlines! Stand by topgallant halliards and sheets!'

The men on deck were all in position now.

'Let go topgallant sheets and halliards! Clew down!'

The men at the sheets slackened them off to spill the wind from the sail while the men stationed at the halliards took up the strain, before slowly letting go the halliards to bring the topgallant yard down to the topmast caps, with the sails now billowing out in front of the yards.

'Topmen lay out!'

The topmen stationed in the rigging spilled out on to the

topgallant yards, edging along using the footropes until they were in position.

'Clew up!'

The men on deck hauled on the buntlines and clew lines, bringing the foot and lower corners of the sails up towards the yards where the men were ready to grasp them and secure the folds to the yards using the gaskets.

Fury stole a moment to look forward once more while the men were securing the canvas to the yards. Even without his telescope, he was surprised at how close *Magicienne* and *Amazon* were, still wreathed in fire and smoke about half a mile ahead. *Amazon*'s main topgallant mast was still sagging forward and her topsails were littered with shot holes. The two protagonists were just passing *Mornington*'s bow, so that with any luck they should be able to pass close astern of them.

It was difficult to say how close *Magicienne* and *Amazon* were to each other, but the fact that Fury could see part of *Magicienne*'s starboard quarter suggested she had changed course slightly to converge slowly with the *Amazon*. He had been right! It looked as though the French captain, on sighting *Mornington*, had decided to try and board. It was now up to them to time their approach right so that *Magicienne* would have no chance of sheering off once she realised that the *Mornington* had been recaptured.

He dragged his attention away from the fight ahead and back to his own ship, where the men had now finished furling the topgallant sails and were waiting for his next orders.

'Stand by to take in the courses!' he shouted, raising the speaking trumpet to his lips once again. 'Man clew garnets, buntlines and leech lines!'

The men on deck were ready.

'Haul taut!'

The men ran away with the lines, the big fore and main courses rising up towards the yards by the lines attached to their corners, sides and foot.

'Lay aloft! Furl courses!'

The topmen scampered up the shrouds and out along the lower yards, grabbing the great folds of sail and fisting them into shape before securing them to the yards with the gaskets. Fury waited in silence while the men made their way back to the deck, the *Mornington* now sailing along under her topsails alone.

'Hands to quarters!' he bellowed, the men immediately rushing to their newly allotted stations, Fury hoping they would remember them.

A couple of minutes later the deck was empty save for about twenty men, those Grainger had assigned to sail handling. Fury made his way to the quarterdeck rail, looking down to where he could see the ports had already been opened on the upper deck and men were now straining to run the guns out. They did not have enough men to serve all the guns on one side even, but that did not matter as she would only be engaged on one side at a time. Once the first broadsides had been fired, they would have to engage with only eight out of the ten guns a side available, there being only around forty men to man the guns. Hopefully they would be able to board *Magicienne* before their lack of men at the guns became too much of a problem.

He could hear Grainger shouting down below, even over the continuous sounds of gunfire echoing across the water. A moment later he could see water swilling about the deck from the head pumps that had been rigged, followed by men with buckets of sand, scattering it all around to give the men a better foothold on the deck while running out the guns. Satisfied that they would be ready down below, Fury turned his attention back to the weather deck. *Mornington*'s speed had slowed perceptibly since she had reduced sail, but she was now only a quarter of a mile – two cables – away from the *Magicienne*, and Fury knew that those last moments would pass rapidly.

'Clark!'

'Aye, sir?'

'When I give the signal I want that flag' – he pointed upwards to the masthead – 'hauled down and our own colours run up. Understood?'

'Yes, sir.'

Fury turned to the helmsman to order a slight alteration of course to larboard to ensure they passed close enough for their grapeshot to have effect when they crossed the stern of the *Magicienne*. He rushed back to the quarterdeck rail and shouted down to Grainger.

'Mr Grainger! We will be passing astern of *Magicienne* soon. Have the larboard side guns manned and ready – you are to fire as each gun bears!'

'Aye aye, sir!' came the shouted reply from Grainger.

Fury turned to the men stationed on deck now.

'Men! Take your stations at the braces. I want the ship handled like lightning when the time comes!'

He saw nods of acknowledgement in response to his order, and felt suddenly satisfied that everything was ready. There was nothing left to do but wait, as the *Mornington* drove into each successive wave with a short pitch and roll, each one taking her closer and closer to the French frigate.

Chapter Seventeen

Fury had no idea how long he stood there watching and waiting, occasionally giving an order to the helmsman to alter course slightly to larboard so that they could keep up with the two frigates. They were about thirty yards off *Magicienne*'s larboard quarter now, the *Amazon* beyond her partly hidden by the clouds of choking smoke thrown up by the guns.

A sudden clearing of the smoke as it was whipped away by the sou'westerly wind presented a clear view of the *Amazon*, her rigging now in tatters and her hull badly scarred from shot. As *Magicienne* had closed on her she had obviously started aiming at the hull, and Fury could see now that the two ships were only ten yards or so apart, with the *Magicienne* slowly converging on *Amazon*. Fury realised that by either luck or judgement – probably the former – his manoeuvre was going to be perfectly timed. By the time the French realised that the *Mornington* was back in British hands, it would be too late for them to avoid running on board the *Amazon*.

He snatched a telescope up and trained it forward. Smoke had hidden the *Amazon*'s deck once again but he could see *Magicienne*'s quite clearly. There were only twenty yards to go now before their jib boom would be scraping over *Magicienne*'s quarter; it was time to show their hand. Telescope still trained on the Frenchman's quarterdeck, he bellowed his orders.

'Helmsman! Hard a-port!'

The man at the wheel ran the spokes through his hands clockwise, sending the tiller down below over to the larboard side. The *Mornington*'s bow started to swing round so that Fury continually had to train the telescope round to the left to keep it focused on the French frigate's quarterdeck as they began to cut across her stern.

'Clark! Run up the colours!'

Clark had been waiting for that order and the false flag they had been sailing under came sliding down in no time, quickly followed by the hoisting of their own ensign.

The wind was almost on the starboard quarter now, the helmsman beginning to straighten the rudder and the men on deck bracing the yards up a little on their new course in response to a sharp order from Fury.

He still had his telescope trained on the French quarter-deck, where he could see a short, stubby man with a lofty, arrogant face in a resplendent uniform – probably the captain – looking over at them with a smile on his face. He even started to wave, a motion which was cut off halfway through as he caught sight of the *Mornington*'s colours being run up, his face turning to near panic as he stared, realising that any minute now he would be raked. He half turned to shout some orders to the men around him but it was too late – they were almost on board the *Amazon*, and the *Mornington*'s bow was passing her stern now; they had nowhere to go.

The first gun went off forward, Fury able to feel the hull heave slightly under his feet as the gun recoiled, followed slowly by each gun in succession along the larboard side as they passed the *Magicienne*, her lavish stern gallery windows and gilt decoration obliterated as the barrage of fire came smashing along the whole length of her deck.

Looking through the telescope still, Fury could see splinters being thrown up on her quarterdeck as musket balls slammed into her planking – that would be Davis and his marines in the fighting tops with the swivel guns. He saw one of the uniformed men standing near the captain go down, his arm below the elbow almost hanging off after being shattered by several musket balls. Other seamen on the quarterdeck went down writhing and screaming, blood flowing from their wounds as the deadly hail of musket balls swept across the deck.

Even over the gunfire Fury thought he could hear screams coming from the French ship as he looked across, but he could not be sure, and the smoke drifting up from their own guns on the main deck was now interrupting his view.

He realised with a start that the last of their guns had fired; they were past the *Magicienne* now and approaching the *Amazon*, which was still firing raggedly. The speed of it all had taken him by surprise and he swung round quickly to bellow his next orders, knowing every inch they made on this course was taking them further and further down to leeward, which would mean extra delay in beating back to help the *Amazon* as she tried to fend off the horde of boarders massing along the Frenchman's bulwarks.

The easiest course of action would be to lay the *Mornington* alongside the *Amazon* on her disengaged side – which he could do now as he passed along her stern – but he was afraid that Barber might not have seen *Mornington* hoist their own colours. If the *Amazon*'s crew attacked, thinking they were being boarded on both sides, it would be a disaster. All these considerations flashed through his mind in an instant before he decided to tack ship and lay her alongside the Frenchman; the delay in beating back up against the wind was outweighed by the advantage of attacking the *Magicienne* from both sides. Besides, the crew of the *Amazon* could hold them off, even if they were outnumbered. Fury had seen enough evidence in the past month not to underestimate the ordinary British seaman. He turned to the helmsman at the wheel.

'Hard a-port! Bring her round into the wind!'

'Aye aye, sir,' the man replied flatly, spinning the spokes of the wheel through his fingers once again.

Fury looked back over the larboard quarter to where they had just passed the *Amazon*, and could see that the *Magicienne* had already run on board her, the sound of the great guns crashing out as they fired into each other at point-blank range. Their spars had been lashed together to keep the two ships side by side as men poured screaming on to the *Magicienne*'s bulwarks, trying to board the *Amazon* and being repelled by a combination of musket fire and boarding pike.

He turned away as the *Mornington* began slowly to swing round to starboard in response to the helmsman, trying to put out of his mind the plight of the *Amazon* and his shipmates. He would need to concentrate all his efforts on manoeuvring the *Mornington* to get alongside the *Magicienne* as quickly as possible.

He strode closer to the binnacle in front of the wheel and peered down at the compass card housed within. The *Mornington* had turned through a quarter of a circle now and was currently heading south. Her yards had not been touched yet and as a result were now pointing into the eye of the wind, the leeches of the sails flapping as the wind caught them.

'Stand by the mizzen braces!' he yelled, waiting while the *Mornington* continued her swing to a more sou'westerly heading, carried on by her momentum. 'Back the mizzen topsail!'

The men at the braces hauled the yard slowly back to square, and then sharp up on the other side until the wind caught the forward side of the sail, pushing the canvas back against the mast. The *Mornington*'s way was now diminishing rapidly as the backed mizzen topsail slowed her down. Fury waited until she had come to a stop before turning to the helmsman once more.

'Helm a-starboard!'

Slowly the *Mornington* gathered sternway as the pressure of the mizzen topsail against the mast pushed her back, the rudder now helping to swing her bow into the wind. Fury was studying the compass card, waiting until she reached a heading where she could fill and beat back up to the *Magicienne*.

A square-rigged ship such as the *Mornington* could not sail any closer than about six points to the wind, so with the wind from the sou'west their best heading would be west-nor'west. Slowly – painfully slowly, it seemed to Fury – the needle on the compass card moved round as the *Mornington*'s bow passed the eye of the wind while she continued her stern board. He could hear the topsails flapping as she swung – west by south, west, west by north, until finally the needle reached west-nor'west.

'Brace the fore and main yards round!'

The men at the fore and main braces hauled away, swinging the yards round until all were now parallel with each other, the sails flapping once again before slowly filling as the wind caught them.

'Meet her! Full and bye!'

The helmsman immediately swung the wheel back to right the rudder as the forward pressure on the sails gradually slowed and then stopped her sternway, before pressing her forward.

Fury looked at the compass once more – nor'west by west now, on the larboard tack. He watched the helmsman looking up at the luff of the sails as the *Mornington* gathered more way on her. It was not necessary to tell the man what course to lay – all his experience would help him in keeping the *Mornington* as close to the wind as possible. A slight flutter along the weather leech of the sails would tell him he was pointing too close to the wind, and he would throw her head off a fraction.

Fury strode over to the starboard side of the quarterdeck, satisfied that the *Mornington* was now sailing as close to the wind as she could, and stole a glance at the *Magicienne* and the *Amazon*, still locked together in a fierce struggle about a cable away on the starboard bow. From what Fury could see, both ships had ceased firing into each other; probably every man was needed on deck with pistol and cutlass. He passed back over to the quarterdeck rail, leaning over to peer down into the waist.

'Mr Grainger!'

'Aye, sir?' Grainger replied.

'Stand by starboard side guns. We will be passing *Magicienne* again shortly, so fire as each gun bears. After that, I want the guns secured and every man on deck with cutlass, pike or tomahawk, and pistols. I will lay her alongside and we will then be boarding. Inform all the non-*Amazon*s that they are to keep shouting "Amazon" as they board in order that they are recognised as friends.'

Grainger acknowledged his understanding, Fury uncertain as to whether he could detect a hint of surprise in the man's voice at the knowledge that they would shortly be boarding a thirty-six-gun frigate. He crossed back to the bulwark to watch as they slowly beat back up to where the two ships lay, tangled together. He was sweating profusely under his shirt as he suddenly became conscious of how hot it was under that clear sky and glaring sun. Strange how all surroundings seemed to disappear during action, until a moment's inactivity brought everything back to consciousness.

He looked up towards the main top, shielding his eyes from the glare of the sun as he sought out the marine corporal stationed there.

'Mr Davis! You and your men will remain up there and keep up small arms fire on the enemy's deck when we board!'

'Yes, sah!' Davis acknowledged, in his distinctive parade-ground voice.

Fury turned back to watch their progress. Now, what had he forgotten? There must be something. He forced himself to think through the next events – broadside, lay her alongside, board . . . that was it! Once he laid the *Mornington* alongside the *Magicienne* he would need to secure them together, else with her topsails set they would easily separate.

He looked around for Clark, finally seeing him hurrying up the ladder and on to the quarterdeck, cutlass and pistols in his hands.

'I brought you these, sir,' he said, handing Fury the weapons.

Fury slung the cutlass scabbard over his shoulder and thrust the pistols into his waistband, guiltily realising that in all probability he would have leapt on to the enemy's deck before remembering he had no weapons.

'Thank you, Clark. We'll be up to them in no time, so I want five men stationed along the starboard side, ready with grapnels to secure us when we get alongside.'

'Aye aye, sir,' Clark replied, knuckling his forehead and bellowing names out as he walked forward.

Fury turned back to the bulwark where they were now approaching *Amazon*'s starboard quarter. Even from here he could see the fierce fighting on her quarterdeck as Captain Barber and his men struggled to repel the boarders. There was no fighting on the *Magicienne*'s deck, but there were still at least fifty men stationed there, Fury estimated.

Their jib boom was approaching the *Magicienne* now, all too slowly it seemed to Fury. Grainger would have to train his guns round to fire forward, as they were coming up at an angle on the two ships' sterns so as to make Fury's task of laying her alongside the *Magicienne* easier. On and on they went, *Mornington*'s bowsprit reaching forward now until it looked level with the Frenchman's stern.

Fury was startled by the crash of the first gun going off forward, just as the *Amazon*'s stern galleries were passing him on the quarterdeck. Slowly, each gun crashed out as they bore in turn. Fury leaned out over the bulwark and looked forward along the starboard side – they were clearing *Magicienne*'s larboard quarter by little more than a couple of feet. An amazing piece of good fortune.

He sprang back suddenly as a piece of bulwark five inches away from him kicked up splinters. It took him a moment to realise that the men in the *Magicienne*'s fighting tops were firing down on to *Mornington*'s deck, and by leaning out over the bulwark he had made himself a prime target. Forcing himself to move slowly and deliberately, he started pacing up and down.

He swallowed hard, surprised at how dry his mouth felt. This was not like facing a broadside – that was pure chance whether one lived or died. This was much more difficult to face, knowing that his life depended on the skills, or lack of them, of men firing muskets.

The planking around the quarterdeck was starting to kick up splinters in several places now, and Fury saw one seaman go down screaming with a musket ball in his upper thigh, the blood spouting on to the deck as he fell. He was conscious that their own guns were no longer firing and he saw the first of the crews coming up the ladder to the quarterdeck, armed with a combination of cutlasses, pikes and tomahawks, with pistols stuffed into belts, ready to board when he gave the order. He stopped pacing and looked over to where they were just about to pass *Magicienne*'s larboard quarter.

'Helmsman!' he snapped, anxious lest he had left it too late. 'Port your helm!'

The wheel spun quickly clockwise as the helmsman pushed the spokes through his hands, a moment later *Mornington*'s bow swinging further northward away from the wind. All thoughts of sharpshooters had left him now as his concentration was fully focused on putting her close alongside the enemy. He could see there would be a small gap between the two ships once they were parallel with each other, and he muttered a quick order to the helmsman to keep the helm hard over.

The *Mornington* swung slowly through the compass points until at last she was heading somewhere east of north, and

Fury could see that her bows were now pointing in towards the hull of the *Magicienne*. He felt a sudden panic as he remembered the men with the grapnels, the panic turning to relief as he saw them stationed there, five all along the starboard side, each one gently swinging the grapnel and line in his hand as he waited to throw it.

He looked forward to where the men were massed along the starboard side, weapons in hand, with Grainger up on the fo'c'sle. Fury felt a twinge of envy as he realised that Grainger would get to board first, once the bows had touched. His envy evaporated as a loud splintering crash from forward told that they had hit, and he could see at least two grapnels flying across to the enemy's bulwark.

'Starboard your helm!' he shouted to the helmsman, trying to make himself heard above the din now as the men on the fo'c'sle went up over the bulwark and on to the *Magicienne*'s fo'c'sle, screaming like madmen and waving cutlasses and tomahawks as the men on *Magicienne*'s deck rushed forward to try to repel them.

Fury drew his cutlass and took one of the pistols from his waistband, making sure it was fully cocked before pushing his way through the mass of men to the bulwark, grasping one of the mizzen shrouds and hauling himself up until he was standing on top of the rail. An agonisingly slow wait ensued as the *Mornington*'s stern gradually swung in towards the *Magicienne*, helped along by the rudder and the men heaving on the grapnel lines.

Smaller and smaller the gap became, until at last it was only a couple of feet, Fury preparing to jump before becoming aware of men rushing towards them on the *Magicienne*'s quarterdeck. They had thought they were safe because of the gap between the two ships, and were only now realising their mistake.

He fired his pistol at the first man in the crowd, who went down clutching his bloody face, his scream piercing the air even above the din of the fighting. Fury flung the now useless weapon into the crowd of men as he pulled the remaining pistol from his waistband, cocked it and jumped across with a scream of 'At 'em, lads!'

He landed on the deck of *Magicienne*, staggering forward, his body bent over nearly double as he struggled to stay on his feet. He was up to the first man in a flash, the man's cutlass going over his head as Fury plunged into him, his arm outstretched – more to keep his balance than anything – to find that his cutlass point had gone right through the man's stomach, a look of shock lining his face as he looked down at the blade half hidden within his torso, which Fury was now beginning to withdraw with a twist. Another man to Fury's right lunged at him before he could get the cutlass free, but his assailant did not see the second pistol still in Fury's other hand. There was a momentary look of terror on his face as Fury instinctively raised and fired the pistol, sending him crashing to the deck. He could sense his men around him now, cutting and slashing at the enemy before them, the constant sounds of shot reaching his ears above the din, whether from men in the fighting tops or from the seamen on deck, Fury neither knew nor cared.

More men were in front of him now, demanding his attention, his cutlass seemingly with a mind of its own as it parried blades to the left or right, and then a moment later raised high to protect his head from a down-swinging sword. Cut, slash, stab – trying to keep moving slowly forward all the while to keep the enemy on the back foot.

A sharp burning pain shot through his left arm as he was caught by a cutlass blade, the arm of his shirt turning red as he snatched a glance at it. He was struggling to keep his feet now as he moved slowly forward with his men, picking his way over the bodies strewn on the deck and trying not to slip on the blood which was seeping slowly across the planking.

He became aware that he was not as hemmed in as moments earlier, and he looked around to see that the fighting had become more piecemeal as men attacked in smaller groups about the deck. A movement out of the corner of his eye caused him to swing round, only just raising his cutlass in time to block the man's swing, the force of it sending Fury back off balance, stepping on bodies as he went. He finally lost his footing in a pool of blood, his feet slipping out from under him and sending him crashing on his back to the deck, cracking his head and flinging his cutlass across the planking, out of reach.

Fury lay dazed for a second before he became aware of the man coming forward and standing over him, his eyes lit up and his face contorted into a fierce demonic grin as he raised his cutlass to finish the job. Fury waited for the inevitable. But now his assailant's face no longer looked fierce, but almost relaxed, and Fury began to try and slide back out of reach as the man stood there momentarily, before pitching forward and landing on top of him. Fury put his arms round him to fling him off, his fingers coming away warm and sticky as they closed over what must have been a hole in his back from a musket ball. He had a vague impression of a man waving to him from the *Mornington*'s maintop as he staggered to his feet and retrieved his cutlass, shaking his head vigorously to clear his mind.

He took a quick look forward to where Grainger had obviously secured the fo'c'sle with his men, Fury catching his eye and pointing over to the *Amazon*, receiving a nod of acknowledgement in response. Fury hurried over to the *Magicienne*'s starboard side bulwark, slashing at a man crossing his path as he went and realising just how utterably tired he felt. He noticed his left arm was beginning to ache as he reached the bulwark and turned back to his men.

'Follow me, lads – over to the *Amazon*!'

The men cheered raggedly and surged towards him, Fury forgetting the exhaustion and the pain as another wave of fighting madness swept over him. One foot up and he was on to the top of the bulwark, looking down at the mass of men hacking away at each other. Without a pause he jumped across and landed on the *Amazon*'s deck, a strange feeling of security coming over him as he did so, as if he had finally made it back home.

He pressed forward with his men, all shouting 'Amazon' to identify themselves while swinging away at the bodies in front of them. The *Magicienne*'s boarders turned suddenly, surprised at this sudden attack from their rear. Fury lunged at the first man, catching him before he had time to defend himself, his cutlass going straight through the man's stomach. He made sure that this time his cutlass was withdrawn in an instant and was ready to parry a lunge from a second man in front of him, Fury stepping slightly to the side as he made the parry and so sending his opponent forward, off balance. One small swing and he had sliced the man's side open, sending him gasping on to his face to the deck.

Another face was now in front of him, the features blurred by Fury's fighting madness as he swung down with all the strength left in him, the man's raised cutlass parrying the blow but sending him reeling back against the mizzen mast. Fury swung again as he moved forward in pursuit, but again the man's blade was there in parry. He was breathing heavily now, using the last few reserves of his energy. He raised his cutlass one more time, his opponent's blade going up automatically in defence. Realising he was losing his strength, Fury lurched forward and grabbed the man's cutlass arm by the wrist, pressing his weight against him and bringing his knee up squarely to the man's groin, backing off as the man instinctively doubled over, his cutlass arm now lowering to protect his groin and leaving an open path to his head. Fury's cutlass caught his unprotected head on the right-hand side, slipping off and on to the base of the neck and shoulder. The man fell forward against Fury's legs, forcing him to step back as he looked down at the blood smeared over his breeches.

Swallowing the feeling of nausea which the sight evoked, he turned quickly to be ready for the next attack, only to see men beginning to surrender about the deck. Coming across a swarthy-looking man with bloodied shirt, Fury immediately raised his cutlass to strike him, stopping just in time as the man dropped his sword and raised his hands in the air.

'I surrender!' The words were said with a thick French accent.

Fury ignored him, striding past; now that he was back on board *Amazon*, he realised just how much strain the responsibility of the past few weeks had placed on him, and he was glad he could now leave the man's surrender to another. A movement towards him to his left made him swing round, cutlass ready once again despite the strain he was now feeling in his arm. He lowered it slowly as he recognised Mr Douglas, the *Amazon's* first lieutenant.

'Well, Mr Fury, this is a surprise!'

'Yes, sir,' Fury replied.

'You arrived just in time. For a moment there I thought we were done for.'

Fury did not know what to say to that, so he stood in silence, Douglas looking him up and down.

'My word, Mr Fury, you do look a sight! Do you require the surgeon?'

Fury looked down at himself, at his blood-stained breeches and his blood-soaked left sleeve, the sight of it reminding him of the gash he had received in the arm.

'No, sir,' he replied, weakly – why was his head spinning so much? He bit down on his tongue to get a grip on himself. 'Is the captain about, sir?'

Douglas pointed forward to the quarterdeck rail.

'Over there, accepting the sword of one of the French officers. Perhaps you had better report to him.'

'Aye aye, sir,' Fury said slowly, saluting and walking forward to where Captain Barber was standing, a look of surprise spreading over his face as he caught sight of his nephew.

'Good God! How on earth did you get here, Mr Fury?'

'I am in temporary command of the *Mornington* there, sir.' He pointed wearily to the *Mornington*, still lying alongside the *Magicienne*. 'We were on our way to Bombay when we spotted you, sir.'

'And what of Lieutenant Carlisle and the *Bedford*?' Captain Barber asked incredulously.

'Lieutenant Carlisle is down below in the *Mornington*, sir.

He was badly injured when we cut her out. We lost the *Bedford* on a reef after the cyclone, sir.'

There was a small pause while Captain Barber digested this.

'Very well. You can give me a full report later. I shall look forward to reading that. In the meantime, you can set yourself to securing the prisoners and –' He stopped short as he saw Fury swaying slightly on his feet. 'Are you well, Mr Fury?'

The captain's voice seemed to be coming from far away now. Fury opened his mouth to reply but nothing came out. Instead he was vaguely aware of the deck coming up to meet him, and then everything turned to black . . .

Chapter Eighteen

His Britannic Majesty's thirty-two-gun frigate *Amazon* limped into the wide harbour at Bombay under a sky dotted with high, white clouds. She was followed close astern by what was formerly the French National frigate *Magicienne*, of thirty-six guns, and lastly by the former East India Company flagship, *Mornington*, of twenty-four guns.

The entire harbour was watching them by now, having seen the strange ships come up over the horizon just after dawn. Doubtless they had also seen, when within range, the British ensign flying over another, unfamiliar, flag, in the last two ships. The sight had sent wild gossip and speculation flying about the shore.

Fury, standing on the quarterdeck of the *Amazon*, jumped slightly as the first gun of *Amazon*'s salute went off forward. He smiled to himself as he thought of the gunner, pacing about down on the upper deck behind the guns, muttering away to himself using the age-old method of ensuring the salute was correctly timed: 'Fire one. If I wasn't a gunner, I wouldn't be here – fire two. If I wasn't a gunner . . .' A short time later another, more distant boom signalled the beginning of the return salute from the fort overlooking the bay, across to larboard.

All the while, Fury could hear the constant creak of the yards, the squeal of the blocks as ropes rendered through them, and the occasional flapping of a sail as the wind dropped temporarily – all the sounds expected in a ship under sail. Over these sounds he could also hear the constant rushing of water, betraying the fact that the *Amazon* had recently been in action and had suffered severe hull damage, enough to ensure the pumps were at work for three out of every four hours, trying to keep up with the water rushing in through numerous shot holes.

'And a half less eight!'

That was the leadsman standing in the main chains, reporting slowly as he heaved the lead and reported the water's depth. Captain Barber was standing over by the quartermaster, directing the *Amazon* to her anchorage, glad no doubt to have finally made it.

It was lucky the engagement with *Magicienne* had been within one and a half days' sailing of Bombay; any further and they might not have made it. They had barely enough men to sail the three ships, never mind the crews that were needed to work the pumps in the *Amazon* and the *Magicienne*, and the men needed to guard the hundred and fifty or so French prisoners that were currently secured down below in the *Amazon*'s hold.

Barber was shouting out his orders now, the quartermaster spinning the wheel to bring the *Amazon*'s bow into the wind. A moment later she came to a momentary standstill as her way was lost by the backward pressure of the wind on the topsails. Another shouted order and the men on the fo'c'sle by the starboard cathead let go the bower anchor, which dropped into the sea with a tremendous splash. The cable, ranged on the main deck, veered out rapidly through the hawsehole as the anchor sank, eventually hitting the bottom of the bay.

The *Amazon* was drifting slowly back now, the cable paying out steadily until enough had been veered to allow the anchor to sit horizontally on the sea bed, at which time it was secured around the riding bitts, and deck stoppers were attached to keep the cable held. Barber was giving the final order now which sent the topmen scampering aloft to furl the topsails.

Fury looked aft to where *Magicienne* was following in their wake to take up anchorage over to starboard under the temporary command of the *Amazon*'s first lieutenant, Mr Douglas. Fury would not be surprised if Douglas was promoted after this action. After a successful single-ship action it was usual to promote the first lieutenant to commander, although with the navy reduced to peacetime establishment he would find it nearly impossible to get a ship. Better to stay with the *Amazon* as her first lieutenant, Fury thought.

He turned his attention to the *Mornington*, bringing up the rear under the temporary command of her former captain, Sowell, who had been found immured down below on board the *Magicienne*, along with many other of the East India Company's seamen.

The captain had received Fury's report, as well as that of Lieutenant Carlisle, verbally, while they were both still in the sick bay, and had grudgingly admitted that there was little they could have done to save the *Bedford*. The *Amazon* herself had been badly thrown about by the cyclone, as had the *Otter* under Lieutenant Douglas.

Both had managed to reach Bombay soon after it had subsided, Captain Barber waiting a few days for the arrival of the *Bedford*, which never came. He had therefore decided to recall his officers and crew from the *Otter*, and had set sail to look for them. It was on their way back to Bombay, after failing to sight them, that the *Amazon* had fallen in with the *Magicienne*, at which point the *Mornington* had arrived on the scene. Fury had since learnt that the French captain, Dubriec, had been killed during the boarding.

With both Fury and Carlisle in the sick bay, Barber had been severely short of officers to command the prizes for the short journey back. Still, there was nothing Fury could do about that. He was suffering from exhaustion and loss of blood due to the deep gash he had received in his left arm, Pike had said. Even now, two days later, he still felt slightly weak, and he could still hardly move his arm, even without the bandaging.

Still, looking at the *Mornington* coming in now, he wasn't too disappointed not to be in command. It would be a daunting task bringing her safely to anchor under the eyes of the entire city, including the Governor most likely. Sowell was handling her well enough, short-handed though he was. She came gracefully in under topsails and swung round into the wind, veering out a scope of cable as she anchored to bring her in line with the *Amazon*.

Fury was interested to know what would happen with regard to the *Mornington*. Technically she was a British prize, and Captain Barber was therefore well within his rights to claim his share of any prize money, as well as pressing as many of her former crew into the navy as he wished. She was, however, formerly the flagship of the East India Company, and it would be an unwise captain who voluntarily crossed swords with them, especially a captain with little or no influence, like Barber.

He looked round, his thoughts disturbed by the noise of activity. The men were busy hoisting out the captain's barge from the booms held over the waist. Fury could see members of the barge's crew waiting to make their way down into it once it was lowered and secured, and he looked round for the captain, but he was no longer there. No doubt he was down below in his cabin, gathering his reports to make his call ashore to the Governor, a fact which was confirmed some minutes later when he came hurrying back on deck, already sweating profusely under his full dress uniform, carrying a presentation sword, a bundle of papers under his arm. A quick glance round the deck, a quiet word with the master, Mr Hoggarth, and then he was gone; down over the side into his barge where his crew were waiting to ferry him to the jetty.

Almost immediately Hoggarth spun round and was shouting the orders which would bring the French prisoners up from below and have them taken ashore, where some hot and airless prison awaited.

Fury stood by one of the larboard six-pounder guns stationed on the *Amazon's* quarterdeck, with his right foot resting on the gun carriage, his body almost wilting under the harsh glare of the sun. The last of the provisions had been hoisted on board and he could hear Lieutenant Carlisle shouting orders to the men which would see the provisions stowed below down in the hold. The men on deck unrigged the tackles from the fore and mainmast pendants, along with the yardarm tackles which had been used to haul the stores on board.

The captain had recently returned from visiting the Governor ashore – probably to say his farewells – and everybody in the ship was expecting the *Amazon* to weigh anchor and head for home shortly.

It had been several weeks since they had finally arrived in Bombay, their captures following astern like obedient dogs behind their master. Over the last few weeks the crew of the *Amazon*, including Fury, had been kept extremely busy effecting repairs. After the battle with the *Magicienne*, the *Amazon* had been in no fit state to sail back round the Cape of Good Hope to England. The injured among the crew had been transferred to the hospital ashore, and the *Amazon* had been warped to the Naval Dockyard situated on the north side of Bombay harbour. There she was lightened of all her stores and guns, which were placed in storage within the dockyard and kept under guard. She was careened in the dry dock, while her hull was repaired by the *Amazon*'s men under the guidance of the ship's carpenter and his mates. Captain Barber did not trust the staff at the dockyard to complete the work to his satisfaction, and using his own men meant he had some control over the timescale of the repairs.

Once the hull had been repaired, new coppering was placed over the bottom to protect it from rot, a job which had taken some time. After that had been completed, she had been refloated, and the men had set to work repairing the rigging and sails, helped by the fact that the dockyard had a ropewalk to supply them with all the rope they needed.

Finally, once all necessary repairs had been complete, the stores were put back in – taking great care that her trim was not altered – along with the new provisions they would need during the five or so months it would take them to reach Portsmouth once more.

During the time *Amazon* had been in dry dock having her

hull repaired, the officers, including Fury, had taken the opportunity to explore the city, unable as they were to contribute
much to the ship's refitting until the work on the hull was complete. Walking through the many bazaars and markets was a
new experience for Fury, where the heady aroma of spices
invaded the senses. The heat within the city walls was oppressive, the fresh wind blowing into the harbour having no chance
of penetrating the many buildings bordering the anchorage. Even so, Fury found it pleasant to get away from the
routine of shipboard life, if only for a few days. Perhaps it was
the only way he could attempt to forget about some of the
terrible things he had seen over the past couple of months.

A pity, Fury thought, that those times had flown by so
quickly. Once the hull was finished and she was refloated, the
work for the officers began in earnest, so that opportunities
for any leisure time were limited. In fact, the only time since
then that he could remember doing anything other than
sleeping or working was on one occasion when Captain Barber
was invited to a ball at Government House with the Governor
and other local dignitaries, and, having the opportunity of
inviting some of his officers, selected Fury among them.

No doubt Barber thought the chance to mix with these
people would provide Fury with good experience of behaviour and manners; it was true that, after so many months at
sea, Fury had few of the social graces that gentlemen would
require. Nevertheless he found the evening a strain. Having
to put on his best uniform, even in the relative cool of the
early evening, was uncomfortable, and the heat in the room
in which the ball was held was extremely oppressive, no
doubt increased by the many candles that had been lit around
the room. Fury had found the guests overbearing and

pompous. The men were obviously mostly rich merchants, whose only topics of conversation were money and trade, while the women – almost all middle-aged English women with one or two daughters present – would talk about nothing but the latest fashions.

He had found himself sitting opposite one such lady in her middle forties at the dinner table, and, although he could not be certain, he was sure she had caressed his foot beneath the table. The look she gave him as he glanced at her in shock was enough to suggest to Fury that it had been her, and he had been glad that a polite question from one of his neighbours about life in the Royal Navy had given him the chance to dive deep into conversation with the man, his feet by that time both firmly withdrawn out of her reach under his chair.

After the meal, he grew quickly bored with watching the seemingly endless dancing along with the other 'young gentlemen' from the *Amazon*, none of whom danced once, all preferring to sit watching while tossing back far more glasses of wine than was truly good for them. They were all agreed that the only enjoyable part of the evening had been the food served, some of which dishes Fury could not even recognise; possibly local specialities, and all delicious. Infinitely better than the salt beef or pork that was served to them on board one of His Majesty's ships, along with the biscuit – alive with weevils – which was hard enough to break one's teeth on, all washed down with water sitting stagnant in casks for months, alive with algae and other green bits.

He stared over at *Mornington*, sitting in the anchorage about a cable's length from the *Amazon*. Once minor repairs had been made to her, she had been sent out to collect the prisoners and stores they had left behind on the island, arriving back safely a week later. Captain Barber had agreed to let her remain in the service of the East India Company, being the only ship of force that they now possessed out here, and had therefore surfeited his prize money in order to avoid offending the authorities.

'Passing the word for Mr Fury!'

He was brought out of his reverie by the sound of the marine sentry stationed on the upper deck outside the captain's quarters shouting his name. They were about to get under way shortly, so what the captain wanted with him now Fury was at a loss to know.

He looked down at his clothes which consisted only of breeches and shirt, the latter now plastered to his back with the sweat which was pouring off him. The officers on the *Amazon* were all lucky that they had a captain who did not insist on formal dress while engaged in daily shipboard routine. In fact, apart from the Governor's ball, Fury could not remember the last time he had worn his uniform jacket, so long had they been in this climate. Nevertheless, as he walked forward to the ladder leading down from the quarterdeck to the upper deck, he wished he had enough time to dash below and change his shirt before going in to see the captain. It was out of the question, however; no midshipman would be wise to make his captain wait for him, especially when the captain was a stickler for promptness.

He had arrived outside the captain's quarters now, passing the marine sentry who came to attention and reported his arrival in a voice which would have beaten Fury's best quarterdeck bellow. Captain Barber was sitting behind his desk busy with paperwork when Fury entered, looking up just momentarily to wave Fury to a chair opposite, before carrying on writing. Fury sank down gratefully into the chair.

He took the opportunity to look round the cabin as he waited for the captain's attention. The sparse furnishings gave an indication of the captain's wealth, or lack of it, Fury thought bitterly. The desk which the captain worked at, along with a sideboard and a few chairs dotted about, were all that he could see, except for the stubby black breeches of the twelve-pounder cannon which were secured by their tackles on either side of the cabin. Nevertheless, it was luxury compared to the midshipman's berth, and Fury's mind began to wander to a time when he might command such a ship.

He brought his mind back to reality with an effort, reflecting on the fact that the navy's peacetime establishment was small, with very little chance for promotion unless you were brilliant, very lucky or just well connected. Fury could not in all honesty count himself in any of those categories. Still, other opportunities might present themselves, Fury thought. For months before leaving England there had been growing unrest at events across the Channel, and rumours had been flying about the village where he had lived that war was inevitable.

Many people in England had been sympathetic at the storming of the Bastille in 1789, but that had been dampened considerably by the subsequent pillaging and murdering of anyone remotely resembling the nobility by the general popu-lace, along with their pompous declarations of liberty and equality for all. It seemed certain that their own King, George III, would have no choice but to act at the first sign of the French trying to spread their disaffection across the Channel.

Even so, Fury was still not selfish enough to welcome a war with France merely to help his own naval career.

The sound of shuffling papers cleared the rest of his thoughts and he looked up to see Barber placing them in his desk drawer, before sitting back in his chair and looking at Fury for a moment.

'How are things with you, John? All well, I trust?' he asked.

'Aye, sir, very well, thank you,' Fury replied, realising by the use of his first name that this was an informal chat.

'We shall be setting sail for England within a couple of hours. I shan't miss this damned heat, I can tell you.'

Fury said nothing; this was one of those occasions when it was best to let the captain ramble on until he finally got to the point.

'You've done well, John, in the past couple of months. A touch of luck here and there, but on the whole it's been through your own hard work and attention to duty.'

Fury was beginning to wonder where this was leading. Barber suddenly sat forward in his chair, as if his rambling was over and it was time to get down to business.

'As you know, after our recent exploits I am short of several officers.'

It was true; Lieutenant Scott had been killed in action at his guns during the fight with the *Bedford* and the *Otter*, while a couple of midshipmen had also been killed since then. Fury was beginning to get nervous now.

'It is with this in mind that I have decided to make you acting lieutenant, to replace Scott.'

Fury's mind was racing.

'Sir, I –' It was true – he did not know what to say.

'Oh, don't thank me,' Barber interrupted testily. 'You've

earned it. By the time we reach England, you should be approaching your three years' service as midshipman . . .'

He left Fury to draw his own conclusions at that. Midshipmen needed at least six years at sea, including three years in their current rank, before they could take the examination for lieutenant. Although Fury had not even been at sea for a year and a half, he had been on the ship's books for much longer than that, having been signed on by Captain Barber when he was eleven in order for him to get his 'sea time' in. It was a common trick, apparently, and one to which the navy turned a blind eye. It was not as if the captains were doing it for financial gain, because midshipmen received no pay for their services. His elation turned suddenly to disappointment as he realised that the captain was obviously forgetting an important point.

'But, sir – my age . . . ?'

To pass for lieutenant, the candidate had to be at least nineteen years old. Assuming Fury took his examination in six months, he would still be only just seventeen.

'Never mind about that!' Barber replied indignantly. 'The regulations merely state that the candidate appears to be nineteen. All the board is interested in is your seamanship and navigation. Convince them that you can claw your way off a lee shore in a gale of wind and that you can calculate your position accurately in a heavy sea and they will be satisfied.'

'Yes, sir, I understand.'

'You are being given an excellent chance here, Mr Fury, so make the best of it. If you fail the examination, you will revert to midshipman and will have to wait months before you can retake it. Even one year's seniority is significant.' He looked at Fury sternly, presumably satisfying himself that the point had sunk in, before continuing. 'Very well then, you are dismissed.'

'Aye aye, sir,' Fury replied, standing and nearly hitting his head on the deck beams in his excitement.

He walked out with his head in a whirl. Acting lieutenant! If he managed to pass his examination, his seniority would start from today, making him one of the youngest lieutenants in the service. Not only that, but he would now get his own cabin – albeit a tiny one – and would be eligible to mess in the wardroom with the other senior officers.

He started to make his way below to let his current messmates know the news. The thought of leaving them was a sobering one. He counted every one of them as a close friend, especially after going through battle together. It was enough to take the edge off the excitement he was feeling and make him curse his own stupid emotions. There would be no more socialising with them, and no more childish pranks with each other. They were now separated by the invisible barrier of discipline, and, as he reached the bottom of the companion ladder on the gun deck, the realisation of it saddened him a little.

HMS Expedient

Peter Smalley

1786: Captain William Rennie and Lieutenant James Hayter are on the beach and on half pay when they are given a prime commission: *HMS Expedient* is a 36 gun frigate which is to be sent to the South Seas on a scientific expedition.

But there is something odd and disturbing about the nature of their task. They sense that they are not being told the whole truth about the forthcoming expedition? Why is their voyage through the Atlantic dogged by sabotage and why are they followed by a mysterious man of war? And what are the secret orders which may only be opened once they round the Cape of Good Horn?

The answers lies on a beautiful uncharted island, in the remotest corner of the Pacific immensity, to which the storm-battered Expedient limps for desperately needed repairs. Soon the dangers of the voyage will pale in comparison with what the crew discover there, across the limpid waters of the lagoon.

'Smalley has written a real page-turner, engrossing and enthralling, stuffed with memorable characters. Highly recommended.' *Daily Express*

'Following in the wake of Hornblower and Patrick O Brian . . . there is enough to satisfy the most belligerent armchair warrior: cutlasses, cannibals, as well as a hunt for buried treasure. All this plus good taut writing gets Peter Smalley's series off to a flying start' *Sunday Telegraph*

arrow books

Colours Aloft!

Alexander Kent

SEPTEMBER 1803

Vice-Admiral Sir Richard Bolitho finds himself the new master of the *Argonaute*, a French flagship taken in battle. With the Peace of Armiens in ruins, he must leave the safety of Falmouth.

What lies ahead is the grim reality of war at close quarters - where Bolitho who will be called upon to anticipate the overall intention of the French fleet. But the battle has also become a personal vendetta between himself and the French admiral who formerly sailed the *Argonaute*.

Bolitho and his men are driven to a final rendezvous where no quarter is asked or given.

arrow books

Form Line of Battle

Alexander Kent

June 1793, Gibraltar

The gathering might of revolutionary France prepares to engulf Europe in another bloody war. As in the past, Britain will stand or fall by the fighting power of her fleet.

For Richard Bolitho, the renewal of hostilities means a fresh command and the chance of action after long months of inactivity. However, his mission to support Lord Hood in the monarchist-inspired occupation of Toulon has gone awry. Bolitho and the crew of the *Hyperion* are trapped by the French near a dry Mediterranean island. The great ship-of-the-line's battered hull begins to groan as her sails snap in the hot wind.

'One of our foremost writers of naval fiction'
Sunday Times

arrow books

The Only Victor

Alexander Kent

FEBRUARY 1806

The frigate carrying Vice-Admiral Sir Richard Bolitho drops anchor off the shores of southern Africa. It is only four months since the resounding victory over the combined Franco-Spanish fleet at Trafalgar, and the death of England's greatest naval hero.

Bolitho's instructions are to assist in hastening the campaign in Africa, where an expeditionary force is attempting to recapture Cape Town from the Dutch. Outside Europe few have yet heard of the battle of Trafalgar, and Bolitho's news is met with both optimism and disappointment as he reminds the senior officers that, despite the victory, Napolean's defeat is by no means assured. The men who follow Bolitho's flag into battle are to discover, not for the first time, that death is the only victor.

arrow books